W9-DAJ-609

WHITMAN'S TOMB

Stories from the Pines

WHITMAN'S TOMB

Stories from the Pines

Robert Bateman

Plexus Publishing, Inc.

Published by:
Plexus Publishing, Inc.
143 Old Marlton Pike
Medford, NJ 08055

Manufactured in the United States of America

ISBN 0-937548-32-4

Cover Photo: Thomas H. Hogan, IV
Cover Design: Bette Tumasz
Book design and composition: Sandra Hickling
Publisher: Thomas H. Hogan

to
Coral Lansbury

Contents

Whalebones

By February, my memories of Christmas morning and hastily opened presents had subsided, leaving behind a jumble of past holiday impressions mixed with a yearning for paralyzing snowfalls, which rarely came, and summer pleasures, that seemed too far off to be real. My weekdays were spent in parochial school, where I was introduced to the knowledge thought appropriate by the Church for a gangling, twelve-year-old boy who was easily distracted. My devotion to my studies frequently wavered as I thought about my friends, many of whom attended public school, and what I would do with them during the hoped-for snowy weekends or during the coming summer days, when I would be free from nuns and priests and catechism. Somehow most of my friends had escaped the drills and ear-pulling and the weekly visits to the confessional and were allowed to concentrate on what I thought, at the time, were more important things like sports and school dances. The rigor of their classes seemed to be adjusted to fit these other activities, and I envied them. But my parents felt it best that I miss the freedoms others enjoyed. Of course at my young age, I didn't understand their insistence that I be educated by the Church. But I grudgingly respected their idea that

I would be better off away from the distractions of the ordinary secular world.

As I tried to follow the lessons presented to my class by Sister Katherine, an unattractive woman who had recently returned from a mission in Central America, I imagined myself and my rough friends leaving the winter months and the greyness which these months had created to run the narrow, unpaved carriage lanes that laced my town. We traipsed the alleyways in a pack of five or six past garages, kitchen windows, and trash cans, shouting to each other in the descending summer night, confident that our boldness and the late hour were indications of our maturity, but still interested in the irresponsible pranks of children. With whispered notice, we kneeled in dense head-high shrubbery and planned assaults on Manzonni's sprawling garden, paying particular attention to his grapes, which hung like clusters of small dark pearls in their trellised rows. Once inside his fenced yard, we would gorge ourselves until we had had enough or until Manzonni heard our quiet talk and low laughter and charged us with his hoe from the cover of the tool shed, which was attached to the rear of his house. His curses would reverberate along the string of clapboard homes, reminding me in an odd way of the Sunday incantations uttered in Latin by Father Corso, the oldest of our parish's priests. Our usually successful escape from Manzonni and other self-imposed predicaments only bolstered our celebrity with each other and strengthened our desire to reinvade forbidden territory on other evenings when the moon remained hidden and the dripping light which ran from the windows of close-by houses was negligible.

My best friend, Stevie DeBolt, lived next to us then and his sister, Rose, still lives in the family house. But Stevie and his parents are long gone, moving to Florida in the seventies, trying to escape the damp winters and whatever unpleasant memories they had of their former lives at the edge of the Pines. Rose is happily married now and has three children. And since I live not far from town and visit my parents often, I see her as she and her children pile in or out of the family van or when she's working outside, trying to keep pace with nature and what her children always leave in their wakes. We wave and exchange a few brief words, nothing more than civil formalities. We never discuss our childhood, except to say how much things have changed around town and how close suburbia is with its shopping malls and traffic jams and how the Pines have risen in popularity since we graduated from high school and went to college. But when I was twelve and she fifteen, Rose DeBolt was much more important to me.

Back then Rose rarely joined my male friends in play and most of the time she was very removed from any of our activities, her attention gravitating toward cheerleading and older boys who had cars and money to spend on her. In my eyes her distance only bolstered her allure. Her aloofness permitted my imagination to heap upon her a mysterious complexity which I realized, as I grew a little older, didn't exist. But back in the late fifties I would catch glimpses of her, just as I do as an adult, and those early, fleeting looks, which were mostly surreptitious, provided me with a sense of wonder about the powers of her presence over me.

Being the oldest child of four offered me several advantages. I was the first boy to receive new clothing and as I outgrew it my younger brother was handed the worn article to wear, which by then was two years out of fashion and always mended or patched. I was held up as an example for my brother and two sisters. Act more like your brother, Jimmy, and less like babies, my mother said repeatedly to my misbehaving siblings. I even escaped several chores as my younger brother and two sisters grew old enough to take over an assortment of daily jobs. And with my seniority came the opportunity to live on the third floor of our house, a sanctuary that was a place of undiscovered treasures, which remained packed in boxes across the hall, and a place of privacy, too. When part of the attic was turned into my bedroom, I was afforded a distance, if I chose to remain secluded, from many of the everyday activities of my family. On the third floor my thoughts were allowed to grow and develop without the constant interruption caused by the bickering of younger children.

During the evenings I would escape there, taking my homework and a snack with me, sometimes not emerging, except to use the second floor bathroom, until the next morning. From my vantage point I could see the yards of several houses. Their neatness varied from the well-tended order of the Gorman family plot, where every blade of grass apparently had a place and the toys were lined neatly in a row that followed the contours of the foundation, to the casual disorganization of the DeBolt yard, where patches of grass had been turned into dirt by the hard play of my friends and the disinterest of Stevie's father, who drove his own delivery truck and worked long hours. Mr. DeBolt had lost part of one hand and his best friend at Omaha Beach and was somewhat of a hero with my gang. At the rear of Stevie's yard Mr. DeBolt had dumped used parts from his truck, and they were allowed to rust in a tangled brown heap among the garbage cans and old bicycles that bordered the lane behind our houses. Closer to the back door Mrs. DeBolt kept two large potted gardenias, which she moved inside when the weather was too harsh, but left outside during spring and summer when they would burst into bloom and fill the surrounding yards with a heavy incense, overcoming the musty odors of buttonwoods and ruptured brick walkways and smoldering mounds of cut grass and leaves. At night, when my bedroom windows were open, the fragrance reached me as I scanned the darkness, but the scent didn't remind me of gardenias or their guardian, Mrs. DeBolt—only of Rose.

The best part of my third floor bedroom was the look it offered me of Rose's bedroom, which was on the second floor of the DeBolt home, just across the two parallel driveways that separated our houses, a short distance I could measure in feet rather than yards. From the safety of my room I watched her comings and goings, if her shades weren't drawn or her lights turned off. I learned her schedule: when she woke in the morning, what time she dressed for school and undressed for bed, when she did her homework, what time she bathed. Whenever possible I waited for her appearance, squinting until my eyes ached, hoping to see Rose naked, or at least in some revealing pose that would prove to be memorable. After months of impatient waiting and of never discovering an open shade at the crucial moment when my desire would be rewarded, I received an old pair of binoculars from my father, who explained to me as I charged upstairs clutching the case that he had bought them at a yard sale in Vincentown and that I should take care of them because they were worth more than he had paid. But rather than bringing Rose closer, the binoculars only permitted a more detailed view of her unevenly drawn shades with their lighted edges or of her darkened room, where I might catch a glimpse of an unidentifiable limb.

I watched Stevie's sister with my newly acquired binoculars for the better part of that school year. She brushed her hair, read, did her homework, pulled the shades, danced to the music on her radio, straightened her room, but never offered me what I was seeking. When her boyfriend would appear, his car squeaking in the driveway like old bed springs, Rose rushed downstairs to meet him, and I grew disillusioned and angry because of her unbridled enthusiasm toward him, thinking that he had what I wanted and that, at twelve with my voice trying to find its lower range and my skin covered with red blemishes, I was no competition for him.

I was convinced that Rose would never think of me as anything other than Stevie's friend, or little Stevie's friend, as she liked to call her unamused brother in front of our buddies. I became certain that Rose was lost to me and my private ardor. Then one morning when the temperature was well below freezing and I was late for school, my resignation was stayed and for a brief time I permitted myself to consider other, more promising possibilities. That morning, as I passed the DeBolt's front porch, I heard the door open and close behind me. I slowed my pace without looking back, thinking it might be Rose, and waiting to hear her footsteps behind me.

"Morning Jimmy," Rose said as she reached my side.

For some unknown reason I couldn't manage any more than a hello, even though I finally had her to myself, at least for a few blocks. Rose's hair was braided that morning; its black coil curved over one shoulder. Her striped scarf was wrapped around her neck and brushed the front of her chin. She wore her boyfriend's red and grey school jacket and I quickly concluded that she had to be cold, even though I could see a wool sweater beneath it.

"Nice day," she said, apparently ignoring the weather, looking at a passing car and clasping her books against her covered chest.

"Yeah," I replied, trying to extend the conversation, but thinking of nothing worth saying.

We trudged closer to the intersection where she would turn away and toward the high school. It became painfully evident to me that I hadn't had the chance to speak to Rose alone, without her brother eavesdropping or without being part of a larger family conversation, for what seemed like a year. I had to say something.

"Pete was supposed to give me a ride this morning, but he's sick," Rose offered.

"Too bad," I said. "Would you like me to carry your books then?" I asked, not realizing that I wanted to do it until I had spoken.

Rose laughed lightly and then I was sure that I had said something foolish. Did boys her age carry books for their girls? I asked myself. But she handed me her things without comment and slipped her bare hands into her boyfriend's jacket pockets.

After a minute passed and the corner loomed ahead of us, its cracked concrete visible from where we walked, she said, "I know you watch me."

My stomach exploded. I could taste its bile as it rose to my green face. I wanted to escape, to drop her books and make my way to school. How did she know? I imagined that she had seen me and told her boyfriend, Pete, and that he was going to kill me in front of my friends, who would find my fascination with Rose hilarious.

"I don't mind," she finally said. "I like it, sort of."

I didn't know how to respond. I tried to force my mouth to move, tried to find the air needed to speak; my tongue was stranded somewhere between my teeth and throat.

"Have you heard about the whale?" she said, changing the subject before I had a chance to respond to what she had just revealed.

"No," I mumbled.

"My father brought an advertisement home last night. He picked it up on one of his routes. Somebody has a whale, which the advertisement says is over a hundred feet long. And they've put it on a barge and they're towing it up the Egg Harbor River from the bay. They have its mouth propped open with boards or something and you can go inside and walk around. Somebody took out its guts."

"Its viscera," I added, trying to sound knowledgeable.

"Yeah, whatever. And you can have your picture taken for three dollars and even buy a piece of whalebone if you want. They have a little talk at each show—ten o'clock in the morning and at two in the afternoon and at four o'clock. And they play ocean music on a record player."

"Are you going?"

"Can't. It's tomorrow. I have school and my father says it's all nonsense and not worth the time. I don't think he's right, but—"

"It must smell."

"That's what Stevie said. But my father says it's too cold for it to stink much. Been below freezing for sixteen days. He says the river is still open and the tow boat just pushes through the porridge with no sweat, but the whale is probably as hard as a block of ice."

Then we reached the fateful corner and stopped. When Rose asked for her books, I resisted.

"I'll walk you all the way," I said firmly. With her earlier pronouncement, I felt as if I had some kind of foothold with her and didn't want to relinquish my position yet.

"Aren't you late for school?"

"That's all right," I responded with an equal amount of confidence.

Rose shrugged as she turned the corner and I followed her.

"I'd really like to see it. It's probably really neat," she continued, still thinking about the stranded animal. "I'd do anything to get a picture of it. I'd even hang it in my bedroom," she said softly, glancing at me with what I thought was a look that carried with it hidden meaning.

"What about Pete?"

"He has the flu. He wouldn't be interested anyway," she said dejectedly. "He'd have to be in a really good mood, too."

At that moment I thought I knew how to impress her. "I'll go," I pronounced. "Tomorrow."

"But what about school?"

"My parents let me take a day off occasionally," I lied. "Do you think I could catch a ride with your dad if he's going that way?"

"I guess, but you'd have to ask him to make sure."

We walked in silence for a minute. Rose waved to a car that passed. "That's Rita Tighe and her boyfriend Perry. It's a cool car, isn't it? Pete's thinking about buying one just like it."

"And I'll bring back a picture for you and a piece of whalebone if you want—as souvenirs," I continued, trying to reestablish my interest in the whale and satisfy Rose.

"I'd like that," she said, craning her neck to follow Perry's car as it turned down a side street.

We traveled another block before reaching her school. I hesitantly handed her her books, which carried with them the scent of her perfume and were the only things of Rose's I could remember ever holding. I recalled how I had slipped furtively into her room when I was visiting Stevie and she was out and

8

Stevie was downstairs or in the bathroom. But these rare occasions only provided the illusion of contact with her things.

"I'll be over to ask him tonight," I said, dreaming of what this simple act would mean between us. And Rose, although I didn't think I would take the place of Pete next week, might eventually see that I was what she needed and even more. Women live longer than men anyway, I added to my equation, sure that our age difference was not important now because she had given me what I considered to be a sign.

As I walked toward my school, certain that Sister Katherine already had a reprimand waiting, I conceived a course of action. First, I would have to speak with Stevie so that he didn't upset my plan. That evening I would tell Mr. DeBolt that I wanted to ride with him in the morning, if possible, and in the afternoon I would hitchhike back to town. My parents wouldn't uncover my activities until it was too late. I knew that eventually there would be a punishment to endure, but at that instant I thought Rose was worth anything they could come up with. Even if I was banished to my room for a month because of my mendacity, I thought that Rose would be in her room across the drives and, convinced of my interest in her by my willingness to risk punishment, would leave her light on and her shades undrawn. Hours of punishment would be transformed into nights of something quite different from what my parents had imagined.

That evening I revealed my plan to Stevie, who responded first by saying he wished he could come along, then by saying how my parents were going to kill me when they found out. I didn't mention his sister. Stevie had no knowledge of my attraction to Rose, and if I had told him that she was the reason for my going I was certain he would have laughed, saying that Rose was only his sister and not that pretty, not pretty enough in Stevie's eyes to risk what I was willing to face.

Mr. DeBolt arrived home late that evening. I managed to hang around the house with Stevie until he appeared. I waited for him to finish his dinner, which Mrs. DeBolt had slid into the oven and started to reheat when she heard his truck enter the alley. Then as he started to climb the stairs for bed, I caught him on the landing.

"Mr. DeBolt," I said as I followed Stevie downstairs from his room. "I was wondering if you could give me a ride tomorrow?"

Mr. DeBolt was startled. He looked at me through a few disheveled strands of black hair. He needed a shave. Obviously Rose hadn't said anything to him. I thought for a moment that she had forgotten, then reasoned that she was upstairs in her room, listening to her radio, and that she would have spoken to him in a few minutes.

"To see the whale," I said.

"Oh," he replied, not showing that he knew what I was talking about.

"On the river. The one in the advertisement you brought home."

"I remember." He slipped his hand inside his unbuttoned shirt and scratched. "The blue."

"Are you going that way?"

"Six o'clock," he said. "Be waiting in my truck back in the alley. Don't be late because time is money," he added as he trudged past me, sliding his disfigured hand along the banister.

When I reached the back porch, I was ecstatic. Mr. DeBolt hadn't questioned my interest, hadn't even asked about school or my parents. I quickly counted the hours until morning.

"Maybe he thinks you already asked your mom and dad," Stevie said.

"Fine," I replied. "Just don't let him call my house if you can help it. At least not until tomorrow when he comes home from work. Or your mom. Okay?"

"What about the ride back? That's a long way to hitch."

"I'll worry about that after I see it," I answered. "After the whale."

That night I didn't sleep for more than two hours in anticipation of my trip the next morning. Before I went to my bedroom, I told my mother that I had to go to school early. Something to do with a class project and a meeting of group leaders, I said nonchalantly. She didn't question me, and when I thought I was safe from any further scrutiny, I hurried to my bedroom. I spent the early part of the night watching Rose's windows, thinking when she pulled her shades that she knowingly gazed up at my blackened window just as she had looked at me early that morning on the way to school. But when her hand fell away from the last pull, my view was just as blocked as before, something that I assured myself would be permanently reversed with my successful return the next day.

In the morning I moved silently around my bedroom, avoiding the looser floorboards and walking along the edge of the steps as I descended to the second floor, past the closed bedroom doors of the others, and then to the first floor. As I sat at the kitchen table eating breakfast, I glanced at the DeBolt house, waiting to see lights and Mr. DeBolt moving around the kitchen, but he didn't appear.

When I finished I left the house fifteen minutes early, carrying what I normally did on school days through the cold, dark yard. I hid my books under a discarded pile of newspapers in our garage, but kept my brown lunch bag with me. I slipped my hand into my pocket, feeling the money I had managed to save—bills I had originally planned to use for my mother's birthday gift in April. Then I hopped the low wire fence between the yards and entered Mr. DeBolt's truck, finding the bench seat littered with discarded food wrappers and soda bottles and white, yellow, and blue invoice sheets. An empty bottle rolled to the floor then to the bottom of the open door, banging the hollow metal with a loud, clanking pop. For a second I was worried that one of my parents had heard the sound, but after quietly closing the truck door and a moment of crouching on the seat, I raised my head and looked at my house. No lights had appeared so I sat, thinking I was safe and sensing as I scanned the house that it wasn't quite as cold as previous mornings had been.

It wasn't until six-thirty that Mr. DeBolt emerged from the rear door of his house, letting the door slam with a ferocity which suggested he was angry about something.

"Damn alarm clock," he said as he bounded into his truck, carrying a cup of coffee in one hand and his keys in the other. "Now let's hope this heap starts."

I didn't respond. I knew that Mr. DeBolt wasn't in the mood to discuss the time of day with me and my fears that he had forgotten me and that in fifteen minutes my parents would be awake and moving around our kitchen. I closed my eyes and prayed that the engine would start.

"I have a few stops to make first," he said, cranking the ignition twice without success. He swore under his breath and twisted the key one more time. The engine turned slowly, dragging with each revolution. "Come on," he coaxed. Then it started, backfiring once and filling the yard with smoke in the process. "Peterson's and the warehouse," he said as he put the transmission in gear and we rolled down the lane toward the street. "Then we'll head on down there. Should be there about nine or so." Mr. DeBolt glanced at me, his eyebrows arching. "Your mom okayed this, right?"

"Yeah," I heard myself say. "There's no problem."

"How're you going to get back? I could swing back by there around four, if you want."

"That's all right," I said, not wanting to return that late because of my parents. I quickly calculated that if I waited for Mr. DeBolt it would be past five o'clock when we pulled into town. "I already have a lift," I said, not wanting to tell him that I would be hitchhiking.

At nine o'clock, we were nowhere near the river. Mr. DeBolt had to wait for a pickup to be loaded at the warehouse; then his truck developed a number of problems, each one of which Mr. DeBolt diagnosed with precision and managed to fix or delay until, he explained, he had the time and money to have his truck properly repaired.

By noon, with his truck jerking erratically because of what he said was a bad fuel pump, we approached the river. My previous plan to see the whale at ten and hitchhike back to town where I would arrive before the end of the school day had been abandoned. Now I would have to wait until two o'clock and try to return before dinner. I fabricated a story about the same group that was supposed to meet in the morning before school getting together after school as well. I would claim that I was the group leader and couldn't leave the others without my input. My mother would be suspicious, but I had no choice.

"Put your hand outside the window," Mr. DeBolt said as we entered the town where the barge and its cargo were already docked.

I looked at him.

"Go ahead," he urged. "Feel the air."

I unrolled my window and stuck my hand outside.

"Notice anything?"

"What?" I said, still not knowing what he was getting at. "It feels like wind to me."

"It's warm. The sun's out," he announced. "Looks like spring."

"It does," I agreed, still not knowing what he was trying to tell me.

"Must be forty, forty-five degrees out there."

"You think?"

"Could be close to fifty."

"Maybe," I said.

"It's about time." He slapped the steering wheel with his good hand. "It wasn't supposed to warm up until Sunday."

"I guess it won't snow."

"That's a dirty word in my business," Mr. DeBolt responded. "Damn dirty. Nothing but trouble."

"Is there a store around?" I asked, wanting to leave a subject that most adults seemed to dislike. "I've never been down here before."

Stevie's father pointed through the windshield at a two-story building that stood on the corner. "It's only a block to the river," he said as he swung his truck to the side of the street and stopped. "You're sure you don't want to wait for me to give you a ride back?" he said to me as I opened the door and climbed down. "Wouldn't be a problem."

13

"No thanks." I wondered how long I might have to wait for him and his undependable truck. "It's taken care of, but thanks for the ride here."

He reached for his wallet. "Buy Rose a souvenir. She said she wanted something when she saw the circular, so—"

"I will. But I have plenty of money, really. Anyway, you gave me the ride. I owe you," I concluded, remembering the line from a television show.

I watched Mr. Debolt's truck disappear around the corner, and heard his gearbox grinding loudly as he double clutched and tried to overcome what he had said earlier was a shit of a transmission.

I entered the store and bought a soda. Then I returned to the covered porch and sat on one of the benches that framed the store's front door. I had expected a crowd in the small town but speculated anyone interested in seeing the whale must be at the river. The weather had turned warm, just as Mr. DeBolt had claimed, and as I opened my lunch bag I gleefully thought that the whale wouldn't survive the temperature and that this could be the last opportunity to see the dead animal. The freezing weather might not return for a week. And if the whale did disappear, its importance would only be magnified with Rose.

Several copies of the advertisement that Rose had seen were stapled to the posts which supported the overhang in front of the store. There was a photograph of the behemoth atop the barge, its mouth open and a man and a woman standing next to the animal with their hands extended toward the gaping cavity. Lights and streamers had been strung from poles around the perimeter of the gigantic barge, creating a series of swooping arches that suggested a festive mood rather than the morbid spectacle enclosed by them.

As I finished my lunch I thought about Rose again and how close I was to impressing her. I decided to walk to where the whale was moored. If I'm lucky, I thought, maybe someone will let me in early. I didn't need to hear the lecture or whatever it was. I didn't need to listen to a recording of the ocean. I only

wanted a picture of the beached carcass and a piece of whalebone so that I could hand them to Rose.

When I reached the river, first seeing the broad sweep of its
iron water and the far bank lined with knife-tipped cedar trees
and the drawbridge that spanned it, my heartbeat increased and
I broke a sweat under the clothing made for temperatures much
colder than it was. I still had my school blazer on under my coat
and decided to remove the jacket, carefully turning it inside out
and folding it as my mother had taught me. Before I turned
toward the dock, I watched a bird circle over the opening created by the river, riding invisible currents.

Then I descended a gravel and sand bank and walked
between two sweet gums that were surrounded by sedge and
briers. I could hear an occasional car crossing the nearby bridge,
its tires drumming on the steel grate that marked the section of
the flat span that rose to allow boats to pass in the channel. The
ground where I walked was covered with discarded handbills
that announced the arrival of the whale, most of them soiled
with wet, muddy footprints.

Once I was clear of the bank and its trees, the bulkhead stood
before me, its timbers filling the air with the smell of old cedar
and creosote and partially absorbed river water. But the dock
was empty; the barge holding the whale wasn't there. For a
moment I thought I was in the wrong place, that there was
another dock on the far side of the bridge, and that other customers had made the same mistake. But as I stared at an advertisement on the ground, I was convinced that I hadn't made an
error. I glanced along the shoreline, which was quickly over-
taken by trees and underbrush. A few pilings stood in the tealike
water, forming a rough rectangle that jutted into the river for
twenty feet and was being worn away, splinter by splinter, by
the tide. I saw someone walking along the bank just where the
forest obliterated the shoreline, and I called to him as he
methodically paced the strip of sand, moving in my direction.

"Where's the whale?" I said after catching his attention.

"Gone," he answered as he stuck circulars with a stick and put them in a canvas bag hooked to his belt. "And they left one hell of a mess for me to clean up. Must have been two hundred people here this morning."

"Gone?"

"Too hot. By ten this morning the law told them to shove off. The thing was smelling up the place. Someone said it was a health hazard."

"But—"

"If you look down toward the bay," he turned, pointing down river, "you can still see it." His arm moved for a moment, sweeping through the air, then stopped. "There. Across the river, way down near the meadows."

I followed his finger, searching for the barge, straining to see what I had come for.

"See it?"

"That tiny speck?"

"Yep. Was a lot bigger than that an hour ago. Bigger than a house when it was here. A regular leviathan. That's what the man they called the professor said."

"Are they stopping any place? Did they say anything?"

"Nope. Nothing."

"Did they leave any souvenirs behind? Pictures? Anything?"

"Nope. They had some key chains. Said they were made from bone. Looked like plastic to me though. Just like something you'd win down at Wildwood. And they weren't giving anything to anyone."

I turned away from him, thinking that my efforts to see the whale and impress Rose were lost to the weather.

"You're sure they won't be back?" I asked, knowing the answer.

"Not with that whale. It was sagging and everything—on top of the stink. And the phonograph didn't even work. I imagine they'll dump the carcass in the ocean, where it belonged in the first place."

I walked back to the corner store and bought another soda and a pack of Tastycakes. The clerk, who wasn't the same one who was in the store earlier, smiled and wanted to talk about the whale, but suddenly I wasn't interested. He said he had taken his girlfriend to see it. But his girlfriend wouldn't go inside because it smelled so bad. He showed me a small, grainy, black-and-white photograph of a man and woman standing in front of a large grey mass which he said was the whale. I gazed at it for a minute, trying to ascertain what I had missed and what my adventure would cost me. I thanked him for the look and turned away from the counter.

I traced the rows of canned goods, cereals, and fishing tackle until I found a selection of postcards. I turned the wire rack, thumbing through the colored pictures of Batsto and cranberry bogs and the Carranza Memorial and blueberry fields; then I removed one. It didn't matter which one, but I remember it was a picture of the river, free of boats and barges. At the time I only wanted to prove to Rose that I had been there, that I had ignored everything I had known to please her. But as I left the store with the postcard wedged in my shirt pocket and stuck out my thumb, I realized that my vain attempt to prove my worthiness would probably end with burning disappointment for Rose and my parents, who were certain to discover what I had done. And this disappointment, which had already started to grow and find its way back to those I cared for, had touched me as well.

Reading Obituaries

After dinner they abandoned the cluttered table, leaving their plates and glasses and silverware in disarray, and walked single file into what Uncle Tig called his sun room. Brian ducked as he stepped beneath a low, exposed beam just before the open doorway, the first time he had managed to avoid the obstacle since he had started visiting Lucy's great uncle several months before.

"Did you see in the paper that Tommy Minnock has died?" Tig asked as his guests sat on the musty sofa that faced a row of windows and a sliding glass door. "This past weekend," Tig sadly added as he fell into his sagging club chair with what sounded like a metallic sigh.

With this, Brian turned away from Tig and toward the marsh beyond the windows. His attention was held there only for a moment, suspended between what Tig was saying and what the marsh suggested, but it was long enough for Brian to decide what he wanted to do. He looked sideways at the profile of his still-curious fiancée. Oh God, he thought, knowing that his hard, prolonged glance, which was intended as a signal that it was already time to change the subject and avert what would inevitably follow, had had no effect on her. Lucy hadn't blinked, even though she knew what always came on the fleeting heels of a dinner with Uncle Tig, especially after retiring to what Brian had renamed the fun room. First came the story of someone's death, a supposed friend or acquaintance of the Clifton family or more often than not of Lucy's uncle, which would be quickly followed by a round of questions from Tig about death or about what Brian thought, the usually unknown and quite dead stranger floating just beneath the surface of the conversation, listening, waiting with an eternal grin for Brian to be trapped.

"Tommy Minnock," Uncle Tig said again, relishing the sound of the man's name with a snap of his tongue and lips. "Tommy Minnock! Dead! Can you believe it?"

Lucy shook her head, her unruly wisps of blond hair translucent in the natural light of a spent afternoon. She blindly reached for Brian's hand across the cat-frayed gold fabric of the sofa, still unaware that Brian was waiting for her to acknowledge his not too subtle hint. "Another one of our friends?" Lucy asked, suddenly bereaved by the news of the stranger's demise.

"Yes," her uncle replied. "Another one gone. And with it, one less friend, one less member of the Clifton camp."

"They must all be dead by now," Brian calculated sarcastically, thinking his tone would catch Lucy's attention. He squeezed her hand to emphasize his desire to end what he thought might be the last of a series of visits to Tig's home, the seat of the Clifton family and the place from which the official approval of his engagement to Lucy would be issued.

"There will never be another like Tommy Minnock. Not in my lifetime. But then ninety-one years is a long time to live. Right, Lucy?" Tig straightened one leg, his knee cracking with the movement. "I suspect it sounds like forever when you're twenty-five, doesn't it?"

Brian rolled his eyes, then closed the lids. His head dropped back on the sofa with a soft thump. "Here we go," he mumbled, realizing that Uncle Tig was a little hard of hearing, but saying it loud enough for Lucy to hear, hoping to succeed where he had apparently already failed. Within his own darkness, Brian counted the visits to the house not too far outside of Tuckahoe, a house surrounded by salt marsh and the weblike veins of tidal creeks. There was the first trip, Brian recalled. The let's-get-to-know-one-another visit. Nothing much said during that one, he thought. Sized me up. Tried to see how he could get at me—where my weaknesses were. Asked about the bank and if I had voted for the cowboy actor or the man from Massachusetts. Made that comment about Dante and moneylenders and how fat times were for those who already had made it. Then the second visit and his dear dead friend Fitzroy or Fitzpatrick or Fitzwhatever. And the third. Somebody had just died, a second cousin. Struck by lightning. Twice. All over one weekend. Lived through the first; didn't make it through the second. Then the fourth and fifth, each filled with some crazy shit about corpses and politics and money and books. Yeah, always a book or two thrown in. I can't believe you haven't read that, Tig always said. What did you do at that college you went to? And Lucy, Brian had concluded, was part of it, part of the family ritual—going along with the old bastard, hanging on every word as if he had something important to say, even after he had begged her to short circuit Tig when he started.

"Tommy could endure the most excruciating pain," Uncle Tig pronounced. "He even beat cancer once."

Lucy, despite the sharp pressure being exerted on her hand, despite what her intended wanted her to avoid, innocently asked, "Where was Mr. Minnock from?"

"Damn," Brian whispered.

"The last few years he lived over in Ocean County in one of those retirement communities. I think he was from somewhere up near New York City, originally. Of course, none of that is significant, truly significant."

On with it, Brian thought. Let's go. Let's get it over with. Just spit it out. Spare us the biography. Spare us.

Tig lifted his meaty hand, allowing his chapped elbow to remain firmly grounded on the chair. "Like I said, pain was nothing to him. Nothing," he repeated, cutting the air with his open

21

hand to punctuate the word before he let it return to the chair. "And now—"

"Gone," Brian interrupted.

"Exactly," Tig said, his pitch falling slightly. "Finished."

Outside, the wind disturbed the slender plumed reeds and salt hay that surrounded the house; the touching foliage responded gracefully, sounding like slowly poured gravel as the bladelike leaves struck each other. Then the musky scent of low tide crept through the lower rooms of the house, smelling to Brian like a fouled septic system, but like life to Tig and his niece and all the Cliftons, living and dead, who had harvested the salt hay on their land until northeasters had slowly eroded and destroyed the natural banks of the meadows. Brian had innocently commented on the odor during his initial visit. How can you stand that smell? he had asked, committing the first of his many mistakes before Uncle Tig and the occasional stray Clifton who usually appeared just before one of Brian's naive blunders.

"Minnock was an entertainer up until the Depression. Vaudeville. Working people used to line up and pay good money to see him, to see just how much he could take. And he never disappointed them. Never said that he couldn't take it, that it was too much. Night after night, week after week, he was up there onstage. The Human Horse, they called him. The Human Horse. Then, for some reason, folks stopped coming, stopped just as fast as they had started. Maybe it was the Crash, maybe not. Even Tommy wasn't sure. But when the Depression hit, no one would book him, no one who was willing to pay anything. And after that, he became a salesman."

"Fitting," Brian concluded, his eyes still closed, purposely suggesting that he wasn't interested and that he hoped Lucy's uncle would stop.

Tig gazed at Brian's reclined form: his legs stretched across the floor, his arms folded across his chest, his head resting on the material of the sofa. "Maybe," Tig said, withdrawing from his story for a second as he considered for the hundredth time his niece's selection of a husband. Then, thinking that his niece deserved his perseverance, he said, "When I saw him in Trenton it was 1922. I was there on business with my father, and after meeting with people all day we decided to take in a variety show at the Third Street Theatre. Something to do. Didn't know what to expect, although we had heard a little about Tommy. I don't remember where.

"When the lights came down after the other entertainers had performed, dancing and joking and singing," Tig said, "the crowd got very quiet. Even the rowdies, who were out in full force that night up in the balcony seats, didn't make any cracks—not a peep. It was about as near to complete silence as possible with that many people in one room. It was as if the darkness prevented anyone from speaking. A spotlight followed two men in tuxes as they wheeled a box with a black curtain around it onto the stage. It was about eight or nine feet high—ten at the most—and almost that wide, and solid, too—no squeaking, no shaking, like it didn't have wheels. Then one of the men, the taller of the two I think, disappeared behind the contraption for a minute before returning with a red toolbox—the old upright kind. As he knelt, the other man pulled a cord and the dark cover slowly parted. The crowd gasped when they saw Tommy Minnock standing there against a white wheel, naked except for a pair of shorts, a wide leather belt strapped around his waist. His feet rested on two blocks of wood and his arms were stretched out. Each arm and leg was fastened in place by straps and steel buckles." Tig stopped and fumbled with one of the arm covers of his chair, waiting for a reaction, preferably from Brian, but only silence filled his pause.

"He wasn't too much older than you," Lucy finally offered, sensing her uncle wanted some kind of acknowledgment. "In 1922 you would have been twenty-one."

Brilliant, Brian thought, wishing that Tig's pause would be the end of it but knowing that any comment, regardless of its origin, would cause him to continue on the same course. Lucy appeared to be ignoring everything they had discussed.

"That's right," Uncle Tig said, but then reconsidered. "Although he was what they call an old soul, I think." He glanced at Brian, still determined to hear his reaction. "They talk much about old souls around the bank, son?"

"What?" Brian asked, his eyes still closed. "Old what?"

"Old souls?"

"No, never."

"I'm not surprised."

"I never could get that," Brian said, his recalcitrance weakening. "Don't you have to believe in reincarnation to believe that? You know, today a person, tomorrow a fly? Don't kill it because it could be your old uncle—"

"It's only an expression," Lucy snapped, suddenly annoyed by Brian's continuing sarcasm. "People who don't can use it. Right, Uncle Tig?"

"Unless you work in a bank, I suppose," Tig responded. "Old accounts, maybe, but nothing much about souls around a bank."

Brian smiled and opened his eyes, imagining that Tig would be waiting for another reply, a continuation of what had occurred during other visits when he had forced Brian to comment. But when Brian found him, Tig was gazing at the marsh.

"I'll never forget it," Tig remembered, not taking his eyes away from the glass and the scene beyond. "Tommy never acknowledged the men next to him. He seemed to focus on the crowd, not on any one person, although wherever you were sitting you felt like he knew you were there. I'm sure he couldn't actually see anyone because of the lights. But inside you felt like he was looking at you and knew everything about you. Everything. And still no one spoke a word. Absolute quiet.

"Then, as the man with the toolbox removed a hammer and a handful of nails, Tommy Minnock started. 'After the ball is over,' he sang. His voice was clear and filled with spirit despite what was happening. 'After the break of morn.' By the time he hit the last word of the second line, the man with the hammer started to drive nails through his feet, never breaking the rhythm of the tune that Tommy was performing. 'After the dancers' leav-

ing,' he continued. The other fellow, the one without the hammer, turned the wheel as the man drove nails through Tommy's
hands; all the while Tommy was upside down and still singing.
'After the stars are gone.'"

"God!" Brian said abruptly, squeezing Lucy's hand one more
time but not feeling any response until she drew it away and
placed it across her lap. "Do we have to listen to this?"

"You can imagine what some people in the audience were
doing." Tig hesitated, waiting for Brian to regain his composure.
"A few shouts of disgust, a few sighs; someone fainted in the
next row. Then, after the nails were in place, they spun him.
Around and around, his fresh blood creating swirling lines along
the edge of the flat white wheel. He finished and started his
song again. And the men continued to spin him, Tommy's blood
finding its way across the wheel, even running under his body
and out the other side. As he finished the song for a third time,
the big curtain closed across the stage, its heavy bottom dragging slightly, a hiss coming from its wires and pulleys. The bolt
of light vanished.

"A few minutes of uneven silence passed. Occasionally someone whispered something. It was still dark in the theatre because
the houselights hadn't come up. The woman next to me was crying into her handkerchief. Then that single spot snapped back
on, the green curtain parted, and Tommy Minnock reappeared.
His hands were wrapped in bandages, his legs from his knees
down were lost to the footlights. His wheel and assistants had
vanished. Then the house broke into a roar. People went insane.
Their applause was like nothing I had ever heard. And Tommy
Minnock smiled, his face kind of serene as he waved to his audience, waved as if he had not been part of anything unusual and
had just performed a song-and-dance routine. The crowd
belonged to him. They loved him, if that's the right word. People
threw money onto the stage and jewelry, too—whatever they
had. They stamped their feet so hard that the floor shook. Then
Minnock stepped back, away from the lights and his admirers,
and the curtain closed. The show was over."

25

"No more freaks?" Brian said, lifting his head lazily and glancing at Lucy's uncle.

Tig held back, then weighed, "How could anyone follow that?"

"Weren't there laws against that sort of thing then? There must be nowadays," Brian returned with a tender jab to Lucy's side. "Civilized people don't do those sorts of things, don't enjoy that sort of stuff."

"Don't they?" Uncle Tig asked, his voice clear, his eyes falling like lead on Brian.

"Damn," Brian said under his breath, knowing that Tig had him exactly where he wanted him. He closed his eyes again, seeing the entire plan laid out before him. Each visit, each discussion more unusual and morbid than the one before. And Brian caught in a defensive position, trying to hold his own against Tig's memories and the dead and now Tommy Minnock.

"Well?" Lucy said, impatiently. "Uncle Tig has a point. Think about it."

"I don't know what they're called."

"What exactly are you talking about?" Lucy faced Brian, who motioned toward the door with his head and realized before his head stopped moving that his only choice was to answer her.

"Freak show laws, maybe," he stumbled. "Geek codes. I don't know. It's nothing I know about. The only thing I do know is that real people don't enjoy things like that. It's sick. Twisted."

"Hmm," Tig said. "Tommy Minnock was a real person, a good man, an honest man. Not too many of those around. Not everyone in that theatre could be called sick, could they, Brian? I mean that would be one hell of a generalization."

Brian took a deep breath, wanting to break Tig's tempo. He felt like they were in the midst of the final movement of a symphony and Tig was its conductor. "Just how did you come to know him?" Brian wondered, trying to reverse his position. Maybe, he reasoned, he could find a way out of explaining himself. "When you first saw him you didn't know him."

"Not for years after that night. He had started working at Staples' big department store in Vineland, sometime in the thirties. I went in tnere one day and there he was, scars and all. It had been nearly twenty-five years, but how could anyone forget his face after seeing him onstage? I bought him lunch. And every time I was up there after that, I stopped to say hello and talk, maybe have lunch if it was that time of the day. But I always checked to see if he was working. Always."

"Did you ever ask him why he did it?" the younger man pressed. "That would be the question for me. Why would anyone do that to himself? Why would this Minnock guy put himself through that?"

"I never asked, but he told me, anyway."

Brian waited, thinking that Tig would offer what he had heard without prompting, but Lucy's uncle was quiet. He could hear Tig's cats chasing something in a faraway room, their paws striking wood and carpet. Finally Brian said, "Okay, why? Why did he do it? I want to know."

Uncle Tig smiled. "So you're interested, or at least curious, and of course civilized as well?"

Lucy drummed the fingers of her right hand on the sofa, wanting Brian to explain himself. He knew that he would have plenty of explaining to do if he said much more. And for an instant he thought she was enjoying his discomfort, but quickly convinced himself that that was his imagination and nothing more. "Yes, I'm interested, just for the sake of conversation," he said to Tig. "But remember it's your story. I'm the guest. I'm just listening."

"Tommy said he did it for money. He had obligations. A family. He was uneducated. But he did have this abnormal tolerance and he decided to work with it."

"Money!" Brian exclaimed. "He let somebody drive nails into him for money?"

"Yes," Uncle Tig replied. "Is that so strange?"

Brian thought for a second. "Yes. I mean—well, anything's possible." He ran his hand through his hair, the short, stiff bristles resisting his palm. "It's a screwy world." He looked at Tig, then Lucy, and then back at Tig. "Really screwy."

"Yes or no?"

"I guess it could happen," Brian admitted.

"I thought you might say that."

"People do a lot of stuff to get money," Brian added. "Pretty amazing stuff."

"They do," Tig agreed. "Such as?" he said, trailing off and waiting for Brian to fill in his blank.

"Steal, murder, sell drugs, sell each other, sell all types of things, work occasionally, if they're not on welfare, that is. You name it."

"They even visit great uncles," Tig speculated.

Brian shrugged, preferring not to answer. Sweat ran down the back of his neck, slipping beneath his collar and saturating his undershirt. Brian had promised himself and sworn to Lucy that Tig wouldn't put him in this position again, but he was there and as angry about it as the first time it had occurred. His eyes wandered around the glass-enclosed room, unsure of what Tig would say next, but convinced he wouldn't like it.

"But what do you think Tommy Minnock was selling?" Tig asked, ignoring Brian's nervous reticence. "A lot of people paid hard-earned money to see him, people who could have spent the money elsewhere. What did he have that they wanted?"

Brian could feel the eyes of Lucy and her uncle on his perspiring face. "Beats me," he ruled, his voice sharper than before. "From what you said, people seemed to be in awe of what he was doing to himself. How should I know? What do you think I am, a damn psychic?"

"That's a good question." Tig's words were charged with smugness. "A fine question."

"Thrills," Brian suddenly blurted. "All of those people got a chance to experience something strange, something perverted without having to touch it themselves. Like witnessing an execution. God! Why do I—"

"Hope," Tig said flatly. "He was selling them hope."

"What?"

"Hope, I said."

"How do you explain that?"

"The opposite of despair, I suspect. Tommy Minnock sold hope. What better thing could he offer anyone?"

"I don't get it." Brian rose from the sofa. But Lucy ignored him and stared at her uncle, nodding at his last comment. "How could you believe that?"

"Despair," Lucy said as she turned away from Tig. "Despair. It's easy, Brian. Think about it."

"It's a bunch of bullshit," Brian stammered, realizing that his reaction was predictable. "What's the point, anyway?" he exclaimed, leaving them in the sun room as he awkwardly slipped outside through the sliding door that effortlessly rolled open then closed behind him despite his clumsiness. For a moment Brian thought Lucy had stood behind him and with her short, deliberate strides was following him, matching his pace, resolved to support his hasty exit from her uncle's house. But that wasn't the case.

Outside, he leaned against his car and smoked a cigarette, filling his nostrils with the smell of tobacco, trying to camouflage the persistent scent of the marsh. "I won't go back in there," he said to himself. "Ever."

So he waited for Lucy to appear, shifting his weight from foot to foot, the white shells of the driveway cracking under his soles. Twenty minutes passed. The tide was coming in, gradually creeping back into the estuaries from the ocean and bay, slowly shrinking the steel-grey mud flats until only water, reeds, and sky were visible. Lucy isn't coming, he thought as lights suddenly illuminated parts of Uncle Tig's house, but then she appeared, her face locked in a frown, her step straight and quick.

As Brian drove down the access road that sliced through head-high reeds and rare stands of spartina, he was relieved to leave Uncle Tig and his endless questions behind. He tried to talk to Lucy, but she ignored him, preferring to gaze outside at the green-brown wall of sedge as it blurred past them. He tried putting his hand on her thigh, but she resisted, crossing her legs and turning her round knees away. And then, just as dusk started to surround them, Brian said that he was sorry and that he hadn't meant to be rude.

"It doesn't matter," Lucy said without emotion.

"I don't believe you," he replied. "I know you better than that. I know how much you admire him."

"Really, it doesn't," she repeated, deciding, at least for the time being, not to mention what her great uncle had said to her during Brian's sudden absence.

"You're sure?"

"Yes," Lucy concluded, her eyes still following whatever was left to see in the decreasing light just outside the car.

Saraband

Matlaw waits for his daughter in the lee of the dilapidated garage with its peeling white paint and streaked windows. Cool rain, hardly more than mist, clings to the gutterless lip of the roof and the hair of Matlaw's bare right arm. He is angry and impatient, but he doesn't move and can't be seen from the dark road less than ten feet away. He squirms his damp, sockless feet inside his enormous, unlaced wing tips, noticing that the blister which appeared yesterday, and seemed to be gone this morning, has returned and hurts. He unconsciously caresses the finger holes of the English recorder in his pocket and silently recalls a melody written by Bach, or was it Purcell? At this moment, he can't remember.

Inside the garage sits his silver Olds Delta 98 with its 455-cubic-inch engine, slumberous but lethal. He can see its dull outline through the small window next to his head. He loves the terrific power of its engine. He rides behind its steering wheel as if he controls the planet from the driver's seat. Everyone in town knows Matlaw's car. He has killed three unchained dogs and a loose pot-bellied pig, someone's errant pet, without remorse. He has sideswiped a dairy cow and almost killed a small child as well. He receives angry phone calls, police warnings, and speeding tickets, but he can't slow down, can't stop urging his four-barrel carburetor to slam open and inhale gas and air into its gaping chambers. When he and his car careen recklessly along the uneven country roads which reach out for miles around his wife Edna's house, Matlaw feels alive, even near the edge. Edna refuses to ride with him, she refuses to sleep with him, she refuses to give him his own bedroom in the house. He sleeps naked in a garage room over his drowsy steel beast, which in a perverse way appeals to him. Edna likes it that way.

Jackie, who is a senior in high school, is out with her latest boyfriend Jason, also known as Jay. Matlaw doesn't know his last name and his age remains a mystery. He suspects that Jason is in his late thirties because of Jackie's references to his bad times in Nam. But Matlaw thinks Jason can pass for twenty-five, especially when he shaves. When questioned by her father about her boyfriend's birth date, Jackie has proclaimed that age is not relevant, adding that Matlaw, of all people, shouldn't disparage someone because of his age. She makes allusions to Matlaw's past whenever she needs to illustrate a disputed point. She refuses to let Matlaw shake his personal history. Jackie is a smart girl. She knows too much about Matlaw for him to set an example when it comes to conduct. But he persists, thinking that his wife will not intervene. In her fading middle age, Edna has become somewhat of a libertine, which she attributes entirely to Matlaw's influence. He has decided to argue with Jackie about dating Jason and her other irresponsible activities until she understands and accepts her father's wisdom. Tonight will not be different, except that he will confront his daughter's companion.

In his covert attempt to discover the facts about Jason, Matlaw didn't discover much. Jason is new to the Jersey Pines, doesn't seem to work, and has no relatives in the area. He lives alone in a converted migrant shack on the edge of a cranberry bog reservoir. He has no visible source for his income but isn't on the unemployment dole. One night, after Matlaw reprimanded Jackie about her late hours and Jason's background, she screamed that Jay had a trust fund and was partially disabled from being in Nam. Matlaw doesn't believe her, and suspects that drugs have something to do with Jason's apparent independence. Jason frequents a bar just outside of town called the Barrelhouse, which is a known hangout for local troublemakers and other miscreants, as Matlaw has labeled them. And for Matlaw, this is a sign of Jason's deviance.

Matlaw glances at his wife's house, looming behind him in its chipping languor. Edna's bedroom light is on. He can't see inside the room from where he stands and imagines she is asleep, unaware that the book she has been reading has fallen to the carpeted floor. A slight gurgle escapes from her parted lips with each relaxed breath. Her pink arm has slipped from the side of the mattress. Matlaw misses being with her at night but knows that he willingly sacrificed their companionship years ago. Edna will not accept him as anything more than a man who should be pitied and perhaps even protected, and never again as a man who deserves her unconditional love.

After Matlaw announced with a dramatist's flair that he was leaving Edna for a blond-haired coed in one of his history classes, she fled Maine with their daughter. Edna found a job teaching at an elementary school in the Pines, near her hometown and the few remaining members of her family. At the time, Matlaw felt rejuvenated, hoping that the deadness which seemed to be engulfing his private and professional life would vanish. New blood would make him a healthier person and a better scholar. And it did for a little more than two years, the time it took for Tiffany, his new love, to discover that Dr. Matlaw was not what she had thought, not someone with whom to spend a lifetime, not someone to see grow old and die. Once his young protégée graduated, she wanted to attend graduate school in Wisconsin, a decision Matlaw had supported before their relationship was consummated, but now regretted. The deadness returned. He would have to stay in Maine because he had tenure and couldn't give it up. He knew that even with the promise of summer and marriage his lover would leave him. Matlaw sensed that he was no longer fashionable, that she would find new intellects to be impressed by, that Tiffany's parents didn't approve of him, that his persistent trepidation was strangling their love.

Once at graduate school, it didn't take Tiffany more than a semester to find someone. Matlaw's once blithe romance, something that was supposed to bring him lifelong happiness, ended abruptly. His nerves felt like hot, unspliced wires. In an attempt to resurrect his spirit, he taught himself to play the recorder and appreciate good vodka. He decided to go on sabbatical and started smoking again. But his complex research plans, work which would have filled more than two sabbaticals, remained untouched during his free year. His bid for spiritual and professional renewal resulted in loneliness. He lost all interest in teaching. And although a few colleagues had had affairs with students in the past, and one or two had even married students, Matlaw felt his failed relationship was atypical. After his relationship's unpoetic demise and the wasted sabbatical, he became paranoid and felt that he was the butt of his associates' jokes. He was the aging, uncoordinated hulk who shuffled awkwardly around campus, brushing cigarette ashes from his lapels and sniffing after coeds. Matlaw had violated an unwritten rule and allowed a student to get the upper hand.

When he returned from his sabbatical and admitted that his great plans for research were never realized, his confession was met with silence. He taught and drank for one more year; then he resigned. Matlaw waited for his colleagues' objections, but beyond a polite passing remark or two, the protestations never came. This bolstered his suspicions that his colleagues were truly glad to see him go. He became certain of his unpopular status on campus. Even his closest friends never offered anything beyond their best wishes. Once out of teaching, he spent a long period of frenzied time practicing the recorder and idly dreaming about returning to an accepting Edna, a wish much like his other plans because it was only partially realized.

A bead of rainwater drips from his nose. He tries to see the dial of his luminescent watch, moving it near his weak eyes. He thinks it says 2:10, but isn't sure. Moisture has found its way inside the watch's waterproof seal. The wind blows for a second, sending rain over the dark lip of the roof and near his raw face. Matlaw listens intently, thinking Jason's Bronco is approaching, but nothing comes. He will wait until dawn if necessary. Jason will not elude him, as Matlaw feels he has done in the past. And Jackie, his only child, will finally see how her boyfriend wilts under his wise but tough interrogation. He still hears a melody, although now it is slightly atonal, inverted, running, as it swirls somewhere inside his head.

On the previous Saturday, he spied on his daughter. She left the house in the morning, making a vague reference to shopping as she carried a half-eaten piece of toast outside. He could see the pink bathing suit she tried to hide beneath her clothing. It was warm, the type of day when most people think about swimming. She took Edna's compact car and Matlaw followed her at a safe distance in his Olds. He knew she was going to Jason's house and that they would swim in the small cedar-ringed reservoir near the closed spillway. When Jackie turned on the sand road that led to the bogs, Matlaw parked. With his spyglass bouncing on his chest, he walked through a large section of laurel which eventually gave way to a stand of blackjacks and scrub. When Matlaw reached the reservoir, he crouched in a gum and pepperbush thicket.

Jason's house was about a hundred yards away, just on the other side of the tannin-stained water. Cedar trees arched and twisted above Matlaw. He watched the house through his spyglass. He could hear music coming from inside, but it was unrecognizable. For a moment he thought it was Tony Bennett, but somehow convinced himself that it was a metal band doing a bizarre, swinging spoof. The shack had a new deck attached to its rear and within a minute his daughter appeared, wearing only her pink bikini. She reclined in one of the chairs that were placed around the deck. Matlaw chortled over his own intuition. Jackie wasn't a match for him yet, he thought. She fanned herself with her hands, then took a drink from what Matlaw suspected was a can of beer. Jason passed through the rear door onto the deck, his kinky red hair electric in the sunlight, his body freckled. Matlaw readjusted his spyglass. He couldn't believe that his first glimpse of Jason's naked body was real, but after refocusing the glass saw that it was. Jackie clapped her hands, smiling at her boyfriend as he danced in a ballroom style to the music; then she opened her arms and Jason entered her embrace. Matlaw couldn't watch. He shouted something unintelligible, not considering what the result of his outburst would be. The couple looked in his direction; then he remembered they couldn't see him. Jason cursed as they hesitated then entered the house, slamming the screen door behind them. Matlaw waited for a few minutes, still crouching in the thicket and swatting gnats from his face, but Jackie didn't reappear. The sweet scent of the blooming pepperbush sickened him.

He returned to his car and smoked a cigarette, uncertain of what he should do. His first impulse was to drive his Olds into the very house where his daughter was probably making love. Wood would shatter, dishes would crash. Jackie would think the world was coming to an end. And Jason would be prostrate under his steel-belted radials. But Matlaw decided against it. He would discuss the incident with Edna. This was a family matter, he surmised, and they would decide together on the most appropriate action.

When he reached the house, Edna was weeding in the vegetable garden. Her kneeling, hunched form seemed so small. From a distance a person other than Matlaw or Jackie might mistake her for a child. His unlaced shoes filled with dirt as he approached her. He tried not to step on any seedlings or other important areas, but he didn't succeed. His size and gait defied the garden's organization. He couldn't distinguish between the natural and the cultivated.

"Do you know where I've come from?"

"No," Edna said without looking up. A straw hat brim covered her shoulders, and Matlaw couldn't see her face.

"Just a few minutes ago?"

"No, I said." She moved her weed bucket.

"That character's house. What's his name?"

"Jay."

"Jason."

"One and the same," she sang.

"Do you know that your daughter is over there with him drinking beer, and on top of that, he's naked?"

"No, but I'm not surprised." Edna didn't break her rhythm, her hands moving from the weeds to the bucket. "It's normal."

"But—"

"One beer never hurt anyone Grant, and besides she's on the pill."

"That doesn't mean she has to be screwing the son of a bitch on his porch in the middle of the day where the whole god-damned world can see her."

"Grant. Don't concern yourself with Jackie's personal life. You don't make a very good judge of character. You never did. And spying on your daughter, well." Edna's voice trailed off as she stood and walked away unceremoniously. She removed her soiled work gloves and disappeared into the garden shed.

"And that's all you have to say?" Matlaw yelled, but Edna didn't answer.

The rain stops. The pine trees across the road look less like a single black mass and gain definition. He hears another engine. This time he knows it is Jackie and Jason. Matlaw steps away from the garage just as Jason's rusty Bronco screeches to a stop in front of the building. Jackie jumps out, startled to see her indignant father waiting at the edge of the cracked paving. Matlaw's hand leaves his recorder and reaches with its twin to grab Jackie's tan arms.

"I want to talk to you and him," Matlaw says to his daughter, but Jason speeds away before the words leave Matlaw's mouth.

"What?"

"I want to talk to you and Jason or Jay or whatever you're calling him this week."

Jackie looks over her shoulder and says calmly, "You're too late. He's gone." She breaks free of him and starts toward the house. "Tomorrow maybe."

Matlaw grimaces. "We'll see about that." His blister burns but he manages to trot into the garage through an unlocked side door.

"Hey!"

"We'll see if the bastard has anything to say." Matlaw gets into his Olds and cranks the engine. The garage shakes when it starts. Jackie follows and bangs on the locked passenger door until he lets her in. She tries to grab the ignition and he pushes her hand away. "Don't!" he says. Matlaw won't be swayed.

"Can't we do this tomorrow?"

"No way," he whispers as the electric door opens and the car springs from the garage.

Matlaw presses the pedal to the floor as his daughter protests. He doesn't listen. As the car's speed increases, Matlaw's adrenaline saturates his mood. The engine's power seems to transcend its shell and the car's chassis, finding a way into his body. In a minute the indistinct glow of Jason's taillights appear. When it reaches ninety, Matlaw levels the Olds off. The car still has forty or fifty miles an hour left, but he doesn't need the speed. Jason is losing ground, his taillights growing larger by the second. Jackie starts to speak, but stops. Now the complete truck is visible. Matlaw can read the license plate. Then they meet, but only for a second, their bumpers touching with a thud. Jason slows then accelerates, pushing his green Bronco near its limit. Matlaw follows him, and his engine has enough power to allow him to pull the Olds beside the other man. Jason's eyes shoot to Matlaw's snickering face; he is surprised to see Jackie in the passenger seat. She raises her hands and mouths the word "stop," not trying to be heard over the hurtling steel.

Matlaw opens his window and yells, "Pull over you bastard," bumping the side of his Olds into the Bronco for emphasis.

Jason applies his brakes and stops on the wet shoulder, sand and gravel peppering the undercarriage. Matlaw follows him. His headlights illuminate the younger man as he emerges from his freshly dented four-wheel. Matlaw isn't impressed and wonders what his daughter sees in Jason. Even Edna seems to like him. Matlaw is outnumbered, but this only fortifies his resolve.

"Don't do anything else stupid," Jackie says nervously to her father.

Matlaw looks at her, winks for no reason, and leaves the driver's seat, lumbering onto his feet. His soles scrape across the gravel, rolling over the smaller stones and pushing the larger ones aside. Blood drips quietly from his blistered heel, but he doesn't notice.

The men face each other between their vehicles. Jackie doesn't watch from her seat. By the time they meet, she is standing next to them. Her father is a head taller and a hundred pounds heavier than Jason.

"I've been wanting to talk to you," Matlaw says, his left hand slipping inside his pants to check on his recorder. Jason thinks Matlaw is reaching for a weapon, or at least Matlaw hopes this is the case. The thought leaves Matlaw with a short-lived surge of pleasure. He really wants to hurt Jason, not talk with him. Matlaw suspects that violence and not words will be the only thing Jason understands.

"Couldn't it wait?" Jason snaps through the tangle of hair on his face. "I mean you're acting like a—"

"Not another minute."

"Now why don't we all go home and sleep on this?" Jackie offers, wanting to check her father's unpredictable temper.

"You mean over there on loverboy's deck? That's where you like to sleep, isn't it? Or do you just like to dance there?" Matlaw wiggles his hips. His lips pucker; then his mouth drops to a snarl. Matlaw would like Jason to make a move so he'll have an excuse to pummel him, so he'll be able to tell Edna that Jackie's boyfriend fired first. But Matlaw can't contain his anger.

"Hey man."

"Why you—on Saturday—was that you we heard?" His daughter interrupts, crossing her arms. She is convinced of her father's guilt.

"I don't know what you're talking about," Matlaw answers, not looking away from Jason, but sensing his daughter's dismay. "This is between Jason here and me. Go back to the car," Matlaw says firmly with what he thinks is a parental voice, but Jackie ignores him. He will deal with her later.

"Have you been sneaking around my place?"

Matlaw doesn't like Jason's tone so he pushes him and says, "What are you going to do about it if I have? Talk to your druggie friends over at the old Barrelhouse?"

Jason falls against the tailgate of his truck, not knowing what will come next but ready to defend himself.

"Cut this shit out, Dad! Somebody's going to get hurt." Jackie emphasizes her last word as she tries to force herself between the men.

"I want you to leave my daughter alone." Matlaw bends forward, placing his nose near Jason's face. "Do you hear me?" Matlaw is startled by the smoothness of Jason's skin. For an instant his focus wavers. He remembers the feel of Tiffany's flesh under his monstrous hands, of Edna's skin years before, of Jackie's during her infancy. A sour ache flashes in his stomach and reaches his chest, then disappears.

"I'm eighteen Dad and I'll see—"

Matlaw glances at his daughter for a second, squinting as if he can't see her pale face which hovers in the light just above a shadowy body.

"Fuck you, man, and fuck your car, too. It's a big fucking hog," Jason hisses at Matlaw. "Just like you. Why don't you leave Jackie and her mom alone? They don't need your crap."

Matlaw grabs Jason by the neck as Jackie futilely tries to separate them, but they are trapped in the incandesence of the headlights. Matlaw feels Jason's throat wrinkle under his tightening grip, and he knows that he could kill him. Jason gasps for air, trying to escape by sliding to the left and right. Realizing that

Matlaw is too strong and heavy to avoid, Jason slams his knee into Matlaw's crotch. Suddenly, Matlaw releases him and falls against the Olds, his left side bending on the hood and grill. There is a snapping sound not made by bone or steel. Matlaw hears it and wants to do something, but the motion of his hand is arrested as he groans and drops to one knee. When the initial pain passes, he reaches into his left pocket and removes his splintered English recorder. This is not what is supposed to happen, he thinks. In disbelief, his eyes follow the break; his fingertips feel the sharp edges of the newly exposed wood.

"You little asshole," he shouts as he regains his balance.

Now, Jackie steps between the men and when Matlaw moves toward Jason, she slaps her father. Matlaw looks at her determined face in the frozen glare of the headlights. His recorder drops to the ground and tears well in his eyes.

Gather at the River

It's funny how families grow apart and the years sneak by, until the only things left to bring folks together are weddings, if you can find a way to get off work and don't live a million miles away and have the money to go where you have to go, and funerals, which usually have the power to draw families together for a few agonizing days regardless of each person's daily routine. Even bosses react different to a body's final act in this world, granting a day or two of leave, without pay of course, away from the drudgery of business to allow for another kind of burden.

I suspect that of the two, funerals hold the most power, a kind of mysterious force that grabs at people's windpipes and makes them realize, but maybe not admit, that one day the rectangular box, upholstered with material only the dead could appreciate, will hold them. Their loved ones will be staring down at them, thinking about their own gruesome ends or trying to deny death by thinking of a new car or truck or the odds of hitting a blue-light special on panty hose at Kmart or winning the lottery even. Anything to brush the mortal truth away.

Weddings offer new promise for the future, companionship which will keep loneliness away, the furthering of the family line,

43

and practically everything else associated with happiness. But these things only provide couples with a make-believe future, one which they plan on having; that dreamed up future doesn't offer any kind of certainty because it isn't real. There's a good chance divorce will put a stop to their bliss before their fourth or fifth anniversary—mine didn't even last that long—and snap the happily married twosome and all of their unfulfilled longings back to reality, where they will dream again of finding the ideal man or woman somewhere along the cracked and resurfaced roads we all travel.

But funerals bring finality to families—the end, at least as we know it. That much is as clear as glass. Death doesn't offer any hope for the future; no promises are made, although we hear a lot about the next world and Jesus and the rest, especially when someone has died. Some folks who belong to families that have fallen apart and gone their separate ways say it's a shame that it takes funerals to bring families all together, that it would be nice to share time with each other when someone hasn't dropped stone-cold dead. And even though those thoughts are sincere at the moment and everyone agrees that it should be done, it isn't. Once people get in their cars and start down the highway, their thoughts return to other things like bills and jobs and what they're going to do Saturday night.

I made a promise to myself when I turned onto the Garden State Parkway and headed south that death would simply be death, that thoughts of family reunions and Fourth of July picnics and anniversaries and all the rest wouldn't win my momentary okay. This funeral wouldn't hold the key to a renewed family spirit. I wouldn't agree to get together next week or next month or even to write or phone. Why prolong the fantasy that death is meant to renew things when it is a definite end to everything we know? I would let death stand, as a sign to the living, that it is there and waiting for each of us. I didn't want to be guilty of cheating death of its rightful place.

My twin sister, Patsy, had died four days before. She was only thirty, although it was a hardened, joyless thirty. She was killed crossing a dreary highway in Baltimore, a four-lane road lined with bars and liquor stores and gas stations and decrepit motels. How she got there will take some serious explaining. Her body had been carried back to New Gretna in the back of a van customized for such important tasks. On off days it was probably used to transport kids to ball games and fast food places, a strange mingling of life with other possibilities. Near there we would bury her, the members of my disrupted and somewhat extended family. My stepfather, the Reverend Preston Hardwick of the Tabernacle of Worship Church, a church he founded, would supply the eulogy, which is ironic because the Reverend Hardwick had a great deal to do with Patsy being in Baltimore in the first place.

My real dad's name was Jimmy Rodgers Sawyer and for years we lived near Bass River, south of Chatsworth. Way back would be a good description of where we stayed in those days. And being way back in the Pines was an admirable place to be. My dad, who had left the Army while stationed at Fort Dix, was from down near the Delaware Bay and after the service worked odd jobs, fixed cars, and did some seasonal work in the cranberry bogs and blueberry fields and cedar swamps. At times when we were younger and life seemed so much simpler, we would gather sphagnum and cones or go clamming in a leaky garvey for extra money, my mom and dad and my two brothers and my sister and me. All six of us. One big happy Piney family working toward one common goal, or two—food and Dad's beer. Food, of course, was a necessity, but for my dad so was beer; even the cheap stuff that came out of Pennsylvania would do. During the fat times, he liked to move up to stuff like Michelob. But usually times were anything but fat, so whatever was the cheapest had to do.

Outside of beer, my dad's other passion was country music. C & W is what he called it in those days. His brand of country was quite different from what we hear over the radio and on TV today. His favorite performers didn't sell tacos or eyeglasses or roasted chicken or soda. His favorites came from poverty and heartbreak—hard times is what they were about. They didn't use lasers or dry ice smoke on stage; they just sang, sang about their pain and what it was like to be alone and broken, not because that would sell records but because they had experienced it first hand and knew that others had, too. My dad wouldn't think much of country videos or all the award shows on TV these days. He wouldn't find much, if any, of the new country sound entertaining, and I suspect that he might hate most of it, despise it as much as his soft heart would let him. I'm sure he would think that he had died at the right time, just before country lost its rhinestones and hay rides and big luxury cars. He never made it past the seventies so he was spared most of the new country phenomenon. And that suits me and probably him, if there still is a him, just fine.

His love of C & W led him to place upon each of his children a name that in his book carried with it legendary qualities. The only name that was off limits for us Sawyers was Hank Williams, a singer whose name my dad thought should be retired forever and a day, like they do numbers on jerseys. But in my dad's mind Hank Williams' number was the equal of all the numbers in an entire sport or maybe even all sports; he couldn't be beat. Period.

My twin sister Patsy's full name was Patsy Cline Sawyer and my name is Kitty Wells Sawyer. And my brothers, who are two and three years younger than me, are named Marty Robbins Sawyer and Buddy Holly Sawyer. My brother Buddy Holly suffered brain damage before he was born which ruined any chance he had of moving beyond five or six years old. Of course Buddy Holly wasn't really a country performer but my dad thought a lot of him, and my brother's beginning was just as tragic as the real Buddy Holly's end. My sister and me wanted to name him Elvis, but Dad hated Elvis, which he said had to do with the king going Hollywood.

Now all of this probably sounds cute and a little stupid, but parents pick names for their kids based on the sound of the name itself or because someone already has the name, whether it is a relative, a movie star, a character in a book, or whatever. My dad was an only child who loved his music and idolized certain musicians. It's all pretty logical if you look at it that way. His naming was based on the same principle everyone uses and he thought a musician's name had worked just fine for him, so why not for his kids.

To promote his brand of country, which in his mind was the best but still needed promoting, he ran a bootleg radio station over boosted CB channels. He didn't have a regular operating schedule and obviously no license. He knew he was skirting the law but he would say that it was worth it, adding that we should never do anything wrong unless we were willing to pay the price. And he said he was ready to if he had to. Just about every evening, almost always by ten o'clock, he'd be out in his studio, a converted coop in the back yard, broadcasting C & W hits to anyone in the area who was interested and knew where to look.

"This is Piney Power radio, coming to you from somewhere in the heart of the Pines, USA," he would say as his gas generator chugged along outside. He insisted that it was cheaper to generate the power he needed rather than run a line from the house. Plus the electric company couldn't turn the coop off like it sometimes did the house. "And this is—well I'll leave my name out it folks, for legal reasons and what not," he would add. "We've had a request ladies and gents. Eddy Arnold's yep, yep, yahoo, "Cattle Call." So here it is. Hope you enjoy it as much as I do."

After a couple of hours he would pass out, a little drunk and a little tired, but happy. The generator would run until it was out of gas, unless he came to before it ran out of fuel. More often than not he put the record player on automatic and a song like "Cattle Call" would drift out on the air waves again and again. Through the years he wore out twenty-two copies of that particular song, which has to be a record of some kind and probably should be in a book.

My mom put up with this for about fifteen years. Of course the way she saw all of this was different from the rest of us. I saw my father as a gentle if somewhat drunk man, a romantic, who loved the the C & W legends and their sad tales. As I grew older he embarrassed me in front of my friends a few times, that is until I stopped bringing them around the house. And I could live with that. But my mom decided at some point that she had had enough. You see, my mom wanted something more. She wanted a man who responded to her needs. She wanted a nicer house. Although she was only thirty-three, she wondered what exactly would become of her when she got old. She was dead set against being put in a nursing home for the poor and doing hula dances for fun. But my dad wasn't one for making plans for the future. He lived in the present and in the past, too. The future was only as far away as tomorrow for him. Like my dad, my mom hadn't graduated from high school and knew that a job, one that would bring enough money in to get what she wanted, wouldn't be easy to come by. And a good man, the type of man my mom thought she needed and even deserved, was harder to come by than a good job. My dad was ten years older than her, had no prospects, and didn't want any. His life was fine, as he saw it.

And then my mom found religion and started attending the Reverend Hardwick's Tabernacle. I think she prayed for an answer, from what I can recall, every day and night for months on end, until her prayers were answered, that is answered in the form of Reverend Hardwick. You see, I don't think she really wanted to leave my dad, but he had to change, had to meet her halfway, but he wouldn't or couldn't. She even wanted to stay in the Pines, even though a lot of people were drifting off to bigger towns and better jobs. Dad wasn't going to become what he called middle-class respectable for a few extra dollars a month or even his wife.

My mother was a good-looking woman with a full head of beautiful red hair and I can see how a man, even a man of the cloth who was widowed and had two children of his own, would be attracted to her. So after leaving Dad and getting a job at Agway and living apart with us kids in a two-bedroom house outside Hammonton for over a year, she got her divorce. Patsy and me worked part-time jobs to help out. But even with three of us working there wasn't much money and the worries she wanted to leave behind so bad didn't want to go away. The reverend had his own problems, problems of a different sort which my mother wasn't aware of until after they were married and all of us were living in the reverend's big house over near New Gretna. By that time my sister and me were seventeen and my brothers were fifteen and fourteen. The reverend's children, Mary and Preston, Jr. were thirteen and eleven. That made eight of us. And it wasn't long before my mom's attempt to improve her lot caused big problems for everyone.

On the day after my mom's wedding, my real dad was electrocuted as he fooled with his generator. It was around one in the morning and it was an accident, something that could have happened at any time. Later that morning, one of his friends found him in his dirty khaki pants and his sleeveless undershirt, slumped over the stalled generator. But because it happened the day after my mom's marriage, it was of greater importance to her. The reverend offered to bury my dad physically—he already had in other ways—and my mother quietly accepted. My sister and me, along with my brothers, thought it pretty weird but there was little choice and our questions were met with silence. My dad's family didn't have any money. The Army would pay for some of the costs, him being a vet, but my mom's new station in life and her guilt over what had taken place prevented her from letting my dad be buried without all the trappings of a proper funeral.

Looking back at this incident, I can see that this one act might have been the last kindness the reverend ever showed my mom, giving her exactly what she wanted for her first husband's burial. After the funeral it seemed that the reverend's temperament changed from what we had known—for a preacher he was pretty relaxed—to something quite different. Maybe it had to do with my mom not having any family and nowhere to turn, or with her last kindness toward her first love. But the reverend started to get nasty, not only to my mom but to all of us Sawyers.

Within a month of my dad's death, the reverend started asking my mom questions about where she went and who she talked to. He said that the Hardwicks had an image to maintain. He never accused her of cheating on him with those words. Slipping out, is what he called it, which was his way of saying it without saying it. He never actually said my mom would even consider being with another man. But you could tell that he thought there was one. The sweetness between them went away, drop by drop, until nothing was left except for cold, hard communication. They functioned as husband and wife, publicly and around their children. The reverend had too much to lose to make a visible change. A divorce coming on the heels of marrying a recently divorced woman who was a relatively new member of the church would be hard to explain away, especially to a growing, concerned congregation. I began to suspect that his first wife had to die to get away from him, even if she had to abandon her children in death, not because she was sick or mean, but because the reverend proved to be meaner, and as sticky as a fly strip, when it came to separating.

"Delores," he would say when he thought his children weren't listening. "What do you imagine a man thinks about a woman who drifts from bed to bed? Do you think that that man respects the woman or does he consider her a whore, someone who provides a service like pumping gas or ringing up groceries?" Then his voice would get even more sarcastic after glancing at Mary and Preston, Jr. if they were across the room. "And if it's merely a service to the man, what about the woman? Would the memories be more important than the reputation that's sure to follow? I mean, is the grass greener on the other side, or is it just nice to walk on?"

My mother would stare at him, but wouldn't answer. I'm not sure what she was thinking at the time, or if she was trying to block it out. For a while Patsy and me thought she would leave him and take all of us with her. But then I think Mom realized that maybe she didn't need the reverend himself, only what he provided. Patsy and me had our own rooms in the reverend's house and there was an extra car, things we would surely lose if Mom left him.

So my mother stayed on and is still with the reverend today, despite everything that has happened between them. As far as I know, this still goes on, but not nearly as much. With Dad she would speak her mind and Dad wouldn't say much back. He'd just walk out to his coop. With the reverend, she's never made much noise. Maybe she's afraid he wouldn't take it. The reverend, being a reverend, isn't the type to keep his mouth shut about anything, especially if he can make a person feel small. Whatever she thought or thinks about the man, she keeps to herself. Not that I see her more than once a year. When I finished high school, I got out of there as fast as my legs would go. And that was almost a year after Patsy quit school and took a job in a supermarket down near Pomona, and got married to a man who got her pregnant, and then walked.

The next thing that happened around the Hardwick house, only a couple of months after the wedding, was the reverend accusing Marty of trying to screw his daughter, Mary. The first time the reverend did it was one morning after breakfast. Mary whispered something to her father, who was standing near the icebox, all the while looking at Marty, and the next thing I knew the reverend and Marty were going at it.

"You filthy little heathen," the reverend swore as he crossed the kitchen.

At first Marty didn't know that he was being cornered or that the reverend was talking to him. He continued to sit at the table and read the back of his cereal box.

"Did you hear me, boy?"

"What are you talking about?" Marty said, startled by the sound of his stepfather's voice and glancing once at the reverend, then at Mary, then returning to his box of Coco Puffs.

The reverend reached for a paring knife that was on the table next to a cut peach and said, "You son of a bitch!" With that the reverend knocked the open Coco Puffs from the table; tiny hardened pebbles of chocolate-flavored sugar flew from the box and bounced on the floor.

"Are you crazy?" Marty shouted, leaping from his seat, knowing that he was in deep water.

"If you ever want to use that thing between your legs, you'd better keep it where it is when you're around my daughter. Do you hear me, wild man?"

Preston, Jr., who was sitting at the table across from Marty, didn't know what to think for a second. Buddy Holly started to cry. Then Preston, Jr. started to giggle, suddenly realizing what his daddy was talking about. But Mom only stared, trying to blink away what was in front of her. After hesitating, she finally took a step toward Marty, looking like she might do something, but the action was too fast for her.

"You're the only one who's wild around here, you bastard," Marty said.

"Mary told me what you've been up to, about your dirty tricks. She's a virgin and until she's married boy, she's going to stay that way."

"Well she's a goddamned liar, too."

That remark was too much for the reverend. Once the words dropped from my brother's tongue, and the reverend heard Marty use the Lord's name in vain, he tried to cut him with the knife, although I'm not sure that the reverend would have done it. But Marty wasn't waiting to see if the man was bluffing. He headed for the screen door, sliding his back against the knotty pine paneling of the kitchen, before the knife could make a second pass.

The reverend turned to my mother and said, "I don't want him sleeping in this house another night."

"But Preston," my mother protested, "where's he going to—"

"In the van," he snapped before she could complete her thought. "It's summer and there's a cot in the back. And the thing's up on blocks, so the delinquent can't steal it. He can use the bathroom and eat in here, but that's it." The reverend threw the knife on the table and left.

So that night Marty slept in the van. Being summer, it gave everyone a few months to think about what had happened before it turned cold. Oddly enough it provided Marty with a more private place than his old bedroom, which he had shared with Buddy, to play around with the reverend's daughter.

It was from Marty that my sister and me learned about the reverend and his past and his daughter, who would always be known to us as the Virgin Mary from that moment on. Mary had been turned down by Marty, who didn't have any plans to sleep with her, at least at the point when the reverend tried to attack him. Mary was almost fourteen, which for Marty seemed to be the true moral age of consent, but she wasn't a virgin, not by a mile. Once Marty started crashing in the old orange van, Mary visited him on a regular basis. Marty figured that he was going to be found guilty eventually so until that time he would take advantage of the situation as much as possible, even though the Virgin Mary's birthday wasn't for a few more weeks.

During that same summer, the reverend started what I could only describe as making eyes at my sister and me. At first, I thought I was imagining it. I ignored him. When I caught him looking my way, I looked a different way, avoiding his leer like a pile of dog shit. But then Patsy told me that he had grabbed her, his version of the laying on of hands, and suggested that he could heal any fears she might have about love, and that he was gentle and all that bull crap. Patsy didn't know what to do. She was always higher strung than me. I know she didn't want Mom to find out. At the time, I didn't know why but now I'm convinced that there was a little more grabbing than Patsy let on.

Then I saw that what I wanted to call unreal was more than real. It was at about the time that Marty told us what Mary had told him about her father and mother's feeble marriage, and that the good reverend had a reputation for preying on the most attractive members of his flock. I wasn't surprised when I heard it, after hearing Patsy tell her story, and knowing that people who claim to be sinless and pure and all of that are usually the first to fall. But my mom was tied to this man, and it hit me harder than I thought it would. Mom had wanted so much, not only for herself but for all of us. I only wished we could start over somehow, but that wasn't possible.

During that summer the reverend would gather us together and take the family, with the exception of Buddy Holly and Marty, to the local farm fairs. The Tabernacle of Worship Church owned a tent, which its members would set up for the reverend so that he could spread the word to the good people of the Pines and bordering areas. The tent had red, white, and blue stripes and to hear the reverend tell it, the tent was patriotic and religious at the same time; the religious angle had to do with each color standing for something—white for the pure soul, blue for the skies of heaven, red for the fires of hell. It sounded pretty farfetched to me. The white was closer to yellow and the tent smelled like mildew or cat piss, depending on the day. I had heard someone say that it was bought secondhand from a traveling carnival, the kind with games of chance and sideshows and broken-down rides. Our family would be paraded around the tent as proof positive that a good Christian life, which included a place in the Tabernacle of Worship Church congregation, could bring happiness and prosperity to anyone who would hear the call. We worked in shifts, handing out literature, asking for donations, advertising the times of the daily sermons, being available to answer questions. It was after one of the sermons, when I was alone with the reverend in the small back room of the tent, that he made his first move.

"Kitty," he said, "Dear Kitty."

My back was turned to him because I was counting the daily donations. I remember thinking that if I don't say anything he will go away and everything will be back to normal or close to it.

"Kitty," he repeated as he tried to put his arm around my waist.

I jumped across the room, as if I had springs attached to my white pumps. I started for the canvas flap that would get me outside, but before I reached it, he was in front of me, a grin on his face, his big white dentures shining under the light of a single bare bulb hanging from an overhead cord.

"No one will ever know, sweetheart," he said as he placed his hands on my waist. "It'll be our secret."

"Take your hands off me!" I said firmly.

"Call me Preston, darling," he said, not removing his hands.

"Now!" I said, reinforcing what I wanted, but he ignored me.

"Kitty, don't be like that."

Then I hit his drooling mouth with my fist, a fist that was as hard as a February snowball. The next thing I knew he was off me and I was outside looking for the others who, it turned out, had been sent by the reverend to the other side of the fair on an errand.

I would have thought that my total rejection of the man would put an end to his garbage, but I was wrong. He hassled me and Patsy on a daily basis, as if he was on a schedule. He even stopped bothering Marty about touching his daughter, only calling him a damned fornicator when he had to speak to him, during those odd moments when he wasn't busy trying to grab one of us. All that summer Patsy talked about quitting high school and leaving the reverend's house. She knew that it would be tough without a diploma and without extra training or a college degree, which no one in my family had ever got and my mother talked about constantly, hinting in the same breath that the reverend might cover the tuition. I tried to change Patsy's mind, tried to reason with her, but the reverend's little games seemed to push her closer to a final decision.

Then, after putting up with our stepfather's abuse for too long, Patsy and me and Marty devised a plan, something that would embarrass him, something that was juvenile but at the time seemed right. I was willing to try anything that might keep Patsy home and in school. I just sensed that she wouldn't make it alone at that age. We could have told Mom about the things the reverend was doing behind her back and could've tried to get at him through her, but we decided that Mom's questions would be met with the reverend's denials and claims of a conspiracy based on the fact that he had banished Marty to the wheelless van in the back yard.

Patsy was friendly with a girl from school, an aspiring actress whose name was Sue Conover, someone who had never been to our house and after our agreement never would. Sue was beautiful, blond, and talented, and when she was made up she looked like twenty-five rather than seventeen. We decided to offer Sue her first paying job as an actress and hoped that she would want the role. Patsy asked her to appear at the Tabernacle of Worship Church on Sunday morning. After the service she would introduce herself to the reverend, and she would tell him that she was in need of a private meeting concerning a problem of faith. We knew that the reverend, on occasion, would meet with individuals after the service and Sunday school to help them find their way on the path. Sue would appear at his office at the right time, convince the reverend that she was desperate, then try to entice him to make advances, which we suspected wouldn't be that hard. We figured that within fifteen minutes the reverend would be hot on her. At that point, we would call the fire company. With a little luck and good timing the firefighters would arrive to witness the reverend's attempted seduction of Sue Conover, who would claim innocence and make a scene. We had to pool money from our summer jobs to convince Sue that we were serious and Patsy had to agree to cover for her over the following weekend because Sue wanted to go away with her boyfriend for a few days. Patsy agreed to this, proposing that Sue would tell her parents that there was going to be a sleep over at the reverend's house.

When Sunday came, our plan went along as we intended. Sue Conover appeared at the church, as pretty as a beauty queen. After the long service, she approached the reverend and asked for a private consultation. He was his courteous, friendly self, calling her child and sweetheart. After Sunday school she appeared at his office, and the way she told it, he began to look her up and down as soon as she was inside and the door was closed behind her. In his little office the reverend only had one window, and in this window he had an air conditioner which on that warm morning hummed away. At the time we agreed on, Marty called the fire company. Within five minutes a truck was outside. We stood across the street at the convenience store drinking sodas, which we did every Sunday after church, and watched.

To hear Sue tell the story, the reverend was nearly on top of her when the truck arrived. She said he had put so much cologne on that she could hardly breathe. He stopped for a second, then ignored the siren, saying that it was probably going to one of the shacks down the road. When the volunteers entered the church and started up the aisle, he heard them, but by then it was too late. He fumbled with his greasy hair and clothes, all the while trying to calm Sue, who had started to cry.

Before the reverend could do anything about it, the firefighters were at the office door.

"Fire Company, open up," one of them yelled after hearing Sue and trying the locked door.

"Hold on," the reverend responded.

But Sue continued to cry, really laying it on.

Finally the reverend turned the doorknob and asked, "What's going on?"

"We got a call," the man at the door said as he looked through the crack, around the reverend and at Sue. She had unbuttoned her blouse a little and her hair was hanging on her face. She was still crying. "There's supposed to be a fire here."

"Does it look like we have a fire at the Tabernacle?" the reverend responded, trying to sound as official as possible in the face of a potential disaster.

"No, not exactly," the fireman replied as Sue pushed past the reverend and the volunteer and charged down the aisle.

Crying, she looked back at the firefighters and the reverend and exclaimed, "He wouldn't stop. Thank God, I don't—" Then she broke into some serious sobbing and made her way toward the exit—not the best performance the Tabernacle of Worship

Church had seen. That award was reserved for the reverend every Sunday morning, but it was pretty effective.

The reverend denied everything with a vengeance, saying, "With God as my witness in the Tabernacle, the young woman is troubled and was possibly sent here to darken our holy name. She tried to seduce me, tried to weaken my resolve as a man of God."

The firefighters took it in stride, knowing that with all the preaching going on over the TV, and all the high and mighty people falling from grace, that this situation wasn't extraordinary. Hell, it was to be expected and I'm sure it actually satisfied what they already knew about certain types who readily claim to be one thing but are the opposite. They were probably more interested in getting back to what they were doing before the call was placed than the goings on at the Tabernacle of Worship Church. That's not to say they wouldn't talk though.

After the trick was played and three local firefighters witnessed the flushed, half-dressed girl retreating from the church, me and Patsy and Marty thought everything would be hunky dory. Sue took her money and left town on the next Friday with her boyfriend. The reverend suspected foul play, but wasn't sure. So we let him know that we knew what had taken place in his office and that he'd better watch his step. But the reverend wasn't going to leave it without doing something. He talked to Mom about what had happened, telling her that Salome in disguise had visited him, that she had thrown herself at him, that the fire company had been called, that he suspected a trap, maybe even an attempt to blackmail the church's good name or the Hardwick family. He said they had to be strong and willing to defend whatever rights they had as spiritual leaders of the Tabernacle of Worship Church. And Mom agreed without any resistance. As usual, she never let on exactly what she thought. But she didn't consider pulling out, as far as I know.

Just when we thought our lives would improve because the reverend had truly backed off, the walls came down around us. After supper on Friday evening, while Sue was enjoying her getaway weekend with her boyfriend, a pickup truck pulled into our driveway. Patsy and me were helping Mom clean up the kitchen. The Virgin Mary was nowhere to be found, as usual. Marty was outside in the van sitting in the opening left by its sliding door. I can still remember the dust from the truck as it rocked to a stop. The dry cloud made its way by the kitchen door and through the blackjacks and toward the bottom and its huckleberries which were a good quarter of a mile behind the house. Buddy Holly, who was sitting on his bicycle near the door, started to whine when the driver emerged. He was always scared to death of strangers. The reverend left his lounge chair in the living room and came back to the kitchen. When he glanced through the screen door I could see that he didn't know the stranger. Then at the same moment me and Patsy realized that the stranger was Sue Conover's father. His face was red and covered with sweat. He looked like he had run to our house all the way from his place, twelve miles away, instead of driving. Patsy and me expected the worst.

"Is your dad or sister around?" he asked Buddy whose whining had decreased to a whimper, but Buddy Holly didn't answer and pushed his bike forward and away from the man until he was behind Mr. Conover's truck.

"Can I help you?" the reverend asked as he buttoned his shirt and stepped onto the back porch.

"My name's Ralph Conover," he said, extending a sweaty hand that was nearly as big as the reverend's head.

The reverend was nervous now. I could tell because he raised his hand to his mouth and cleared his throat for no reason. I knew Sue didn't use her real name the Sunday before, but the reverend might have found out from someone else, someone in the congregation or one of the firefighters. He had even asked us, but we pretended that we hadn't noticed the new girl in church, only heard about what had happened after. I couldn't help smiling. Mr. Conover was about six six and weighed close to three hundred pounds. I thought he was going to break the reverend's neck right there on the porch and me and Patsy and Marty had front-row seats.

"Preston Hardwick," he answered, shaking Conover's hand.

"Preston, Preston, Preston!" Buddy Holly, who had calmed himself, yelled from behind Mr. Conover's pickup, loudly ringing his bicycle bell with each word.

"Looking for my daughter, Susan," the man said. "She's a friend of Patsy."

The reverend looked over at my sister. His face grew pale.

"You all are having a sleep over here this weekend?"

"Sleep over?" the reverend repeated, looking at Patsy again, his eyes narrowing to form two little slits under his wrinkled forehead.

Mr. Conover suspected something was wrong. He peered into the paneled kitchen, then glanced along the side of the house. He saw Marty sitting in the open doorway of the van, his shirt off and his black hair hanging on his shoulders. Marty waved as he pulled a cigarette from behind his ear.

"Your daughter isn't here, Mr. Conover."

"Then she'll be back—"

"There isn't a sleep over being held here." The reverend's voice was tight, like a rubber band that's been twisted to the point where it crinkles one last time then breaks.

"My daughter said that you all were having a—"

"She lied," the reverend interrupted. "Patsy, get over here."

Patsy walked around the table, taking the longest route to the kitchen door and the two men. She flicked her hair behind her shoulder. I knew she was trying to come up with something that would save her friend and maybe herself.

"There's some explaining that needs to be done," the reverend said.

Patsy didn't say anything. I could see that Mr. Conover was getting mad, real mad. His already red face was getting even redder and had a touch of purple mixed in now; his temples were moving like he was clenching down hard with his teeth.

"Now!" the reverend insisted. "Mr. Conover says his daughter was invited by you to stay here this weekend."

"I don't know anything," Patsy offered, stalling as long as she could.

"Patsy!"

My sister looked at Mr. Conover, who wanted to know where his daughter was, even if she wasn't at our house.

"I was supposed to cover for her."

"Why?"

"She went away with her boyfriend," Patsy said in a defeated kind of voice. "She's all right, I'm sure—"

"Jesus H. Christ," Mr. Conover said.

"No, Jimmy is his—you know him. Don't. I mean—" she tried saying without any success, her humor lost on Mr. Conover.

But Mr. Conover didn't wait to hear Patsy's explanation. He was behind the wheel of his big truck faster than I thought possible for a man that big. Buddy Holly was still behind him though, sitting on his bike, taking it all in but never showing that he understood a word of it. When Sue's father started the engine, Buddy Holly smiled, probably glad that the stranger was about to leave, but not realizing that he was blocking his way. Mr. Conover looked in his rearview and beeped his horn and Buddy Holly returned the beep by ringing his bicycle bell. Mr. Conover beeped again and Buddy Holly answered the request by ringing his bell, as hard as he could. Frustrated, the man looked at the reverend who looked at Mom who went outside and told Buddy Holly to move, which he did after ringing his bell one final time. Mr. Conover's truck took off toward the street, dust flying a second time.

"Ralph, Ralph, Ralph," Buddy Holly stammered as Mr. Conover's truck shot past him.

Then all hell broke loose. By the time Mr. Conover's truck had disappeared, the reverend started to hit Patsy, who squirmed away from him and escaped outside, just like Marty had earlier that humid summer. Then the reverend promptly slammed the door and locked it on her.

"Stay out in the van with your no-good sinner brother," he shouted. "You're both going to hell."

Within a few days, Patsy announced that she wasn't returning to school in September and had found a full-time job and a place to live and that she was going to leave the reverend's house forever, adding that Mom would always be welcome in her house but the reverend would not ever set foot in her living room, even if he was deemed to be the second coming himself.

Patsy's fall toward death started at that moment. The day she left us was the day that marked the beginning of all the bad things that happened to her, except for the reverend's groping. Her job didn't pay much and was a dead end, but she probably knew that before she took it. Her rushed marriage failed, but not until she had a baby boy. Her need for money led her to start dancing at bars along the Black Horse Pike—bars like Downy's and other dives, then in the Philly and Camden bars like Minnie's Place, where Tiny Tim's ex, Miss Vicky, had danced once, and finally in Baltimore. I know the reverend reveled in all of this because it supported what he had been saying about me and Patsy and Marty, who ended up in prison for grand larceny, or because of mistaken identity if you let Marty tell it. Not one of us Sawyers were any good. My brother and sister were proof positive of that. And it was only a matter of time before I fell in the fire along with them. According to the reverend, my divorce had already put me halfway there. Buddy Holly was the only Sawyer who didn't seem to be damned by him, even though at times he was convinced that Buddy Holly was aware of more than he let on.

On the day of her funeral, Patsy's no-good ex-husband appeared at the cemetery with another woman. He didn't say anything to the few of us who were gathered there to listen to the reverend's praiseless eulogy. Patsy's ex didn't even speak to his own son, who I had decided to take and raise as my own. In a way it's better that he didn't say anything because Mom would have made it a double burial and that would have ruined it all for the reverend and the Hardwick name.

When we went back to the house, I didn't talk about getting together more often, exactly as I had promised myself. To fill in the space where this talk would have taken place, Mom and me cursed Patsy's former husband for the better part of an hour before Mom, who was still angry but more down at that point, disappeared into her bedroom. The reverend and her had stopped sharing the same room a few years before. I didn't know for sure about the agreement that had led to Mom sleeping in Patsy's old room, but I had a damn good idea what it involved. Mom would be allowed to keep her distance and her respectable position as the wife of a prominent man in the community and the reverend could be the married preacher and a good Christian family man, at least officially, as long as Mom kept what she knew or suspected to herself and put up with an occasional insult or two.

As I sat at the kitchen table with Buddy and Patsy's boy and considered my mother's situation with the reverend, I heard the notes of an old, scratchy C & W song gliding from under her bedroom door. The lyrics were filled with that special something that my dad always talked about: real heart-pulling stuff, he called it, words that skin life raw so we can see what it's all about. What had taken place on that day, as well as on so many days before Patsy's death, was all for the sake of things that really didn't matter in the long run according to that song, and I believed it.

Once Mom vanished into her bedroom, I suspected it was time to load Patsy's boy and myself into the car and get back on the Parkway. Mom would probably spend the rest of the day alone, playing old records, and healing whatever wounds needed to be healed. I had to go back to work the next day, and Mom didn't need me hanging around reminding her of things I wished we both could forget.

The Dromedary

E wan pictured his grandfather as the man pranced on hot charcoal pits, testing the floats and sand for soft spots and watching the color of the smoke as it left the flue holes and dissipated, to determine how fast and hot each pit burned. When business was good his grandfather had a crew of men who helped him build the pits with cord wood, turf, and sand, but it was always his grandfather who took the responsibility of being the firewalker, staying in the woods for two weeks at a time, watching and testing the ring of slowly burning mounds day and night until they had come to foot and could be cooled down.

As he gazed across the Avenue Hassan at the palm-lined oasis that bisected its middle for several blocks, Ewan thought for a moment that he saw the man, his face and hands black from charcoal, emerging from the green cover of the median. A firewalker, Ewan thought, forcing the apparition away, as the waiter carried another glass of fruit juice spiked with brandless gin to his sidewalk table, which was sheltered from the sun by an umbrella imprinted with tiny Moroccan flags.

Every day, after a tepid shower and spartan breakfast of sweet mint tea and a buttered roll, and then a bowl of kif smoked in the privacy of his hotel room, Ewan left the Palais Jamai, descending through the Bab Guissa into the medina with its souks and medersas. He was always startled by the intensity of the mid-morning sun when he left the shaded confines of his hotel and its balconies and ventured away from the close protection of crumbling walls into the open spots along the serpentine passageways of the marketplace, a twisting labyrinth of webbed streets and alleyways that reminded him of the sand roads and fingerboards of his home. Regardless of the heat, he always bypassed the tanyards at Chouara with their piles of animal hides and open, round vats of dyes where men and boys stood knee deep in stench and murky chemicals, working the raw hides with their feet. Instead, he navigated through the souk where his nostrils would fill with the scents of spices carried to the marketplace from the reaches of the continent. After this, life seemed to return to his sluggish, indifferent body, if only for a short time.

Ewan's father had learned coaling from his father, the man teaching his son what he had learned and the son making what he thought were slight improvements and alterations on his father's knowledge, but after World War II their livelihood was slowly decimated by big companies with commercial kilns and the country's move away from coal-heated homes and businesses. Ewan's father found a job with the forestry service and moonlighted when it came to coaling, helping the older man when he had time and imploring him to leave the woods for the comfort of a retirement village somewhere down the shore. As Ewan finished high school and it was evident that he would graduate second in the class, his guidance counselor pleaded with him to attend college. There wasn't a family business or trade to enter, she argued, confounded by Ewan's blank stares as she asked him about what he planned to do with his life. His grandfather had died when Ewan was fifteen, and his father, who had left coaling behind for good, was close to retirement after putting in twenty-five years with the state. Ewan's counselor thought college was the obvious choice. He would be able to find a profession since he didn't have one in mind, but despite her efforts, Ewan had no interest in attending college.

Once he had found his way to the Avenue de la Liberte, bypassing El Jedid and other diversions, he entered the green cab which always took him to the cafe in the Ville Nouvelle. After two weeks of delivering him to the same nondescript place every morning, the driver didn't ask in his fragmented English where Ewan wanted to go. At 1:30 the cab would return and carry Ewan back to the Bab Riafa and the old city where he would walk through the ovenlike heat to his hotel, a former vizier's palace. The driver, who was always soaked despite the car's air conditioner, collected his fare for the round trip and his tip at this time of the day and Ewan never asked him to return the next morning, but the dented and scraped cab always waited for him when he passed through the gate of the medina.

As Ewan rode in the back seat, watching the red tassels which hung from the head liner sway to the taped voice of a woman who sang meandering cadences in Arabic, he reconstructed the conversation that had acted as a catalyst for other conversations and other events; all of which, in a previously unforeseen way, had led him to Fez.

"How'd you like to make a fast two thousand?" Finley asked him one day from the other side of the bar at O'May's.

Ewan had heard just about every get-rich-quick scheme imaginable over the nine years he had tended bar there. He continued to wipe the counter, rubbing its surface next to Finley's bent elbow. Ewan had met the man through Andrea, his girlfriend. He didn't know much about him except that Finley kept a twin-engine Otter at Red Lion and lived somewhere in Indian Mills.

"I need somebody to pick up a package."

"For two thousand?"

"Yeah, in Florida."

"I'll pay for your ticket down. You rent a car and pick up the package, then drive to a hotel, stay overnight, and come back the next day—with the package. When you hand it to me, I'll hand you two grand."

"What's in it?" Ewan asked, suspecting that Finley was running coke.

"Does it matter?"

"Might."

"I only ask once," Finley replied in a rehearsed tone.

"Why don't you do it yourself and keep the cash?"

Finley leaned on the bar and lowered his voice. "There's less risk for me. And I'm willing to pay someone to take it. Plus you're dating Andrea and she tells me you're broke."

Ewan felt the back of his neck grow warm.

"Goin' once," Finley said.

"How risky is it?"

"Not very. Good flights, short hops sometimes. You get a night layover, all expenses paid. I've never had any major problems. Packages are disguised. Stuff is put in different containers. Sometimes you wear it. Standard issue. But if there is a problem, I'm history. You forget you ever saw me. You're high and dry, or fucked as they say."

"Guns?"

"No guns, no money. Just pick up the package. Afterwards, I'll give you a call at the hotel, and then you carry it back. You can even take Andrea if you want."

"Two thousand?"

"Cash."

Ewan stepped back from the bar for a minute and noticed a customer, who was sitting at the other end of the counter waving a dollar bill in the air.

"Well?"

"Hold on," Ewan said as he opened the cooler and removed a bottle of beer. He wiped moisture from the green glass with a bar towel.

Finley watched him twist off the top and place it in front of the man.

"Okay," Ewan said when he returned to face Finley. "I could use the money—"

"And the excitement?" Finley added, but Ewan didn't answer.

After high school, Ewan had spent three years working at a gas station and watching the world fly by as it swirled around the circle at Four-Mile. He sensed that he was waiting for the right opportunity to come but didn't know what that opportunity would be. He didn't take to the woods as one of his friends had, moving through the seasons, trying to juggle a half dozen jobs with the demand for his sweat. The world of his father and grandfather was alien to him in that he knew what they had done and what his friend was doing, but he couldn't find any interest in leading that kind of existence. He thought that his coolness toward their way of life might be caused by his lifelong familiarity with it. As the only son and the youngest in a family of six, Ewan had spent what amounted to years of his early life in the woods with his father and grandfather. Ewan learned everything he knew about the Pines next to them.

But with his informal education came a need to do something different. He didn't want to follow in his father's footsteps, even though his father thought that he could find a niche for his son with the state. Ewan respected his father and his devotion to the woods, but he didn't want to make his living there so he turned his father down. His father and mother, who had started to worry about their only son's future, weren't surprised, suspecting that a teenage boy who spent most of his free time inside reading wouldn't be interested in the woodsman's life. His parents' only surprise was that their son, whom they had determined to be very bright and what they both agreed was college material, did not want to continue his formal education.

Ewan's desire to work as a pump jockey, then as a mechanic staled by the time he was twenty-one and he took the first job offered to him, a position as a bartender at O'May's. He left his parents' house and rented a trailer which was located at the end of a sand road between Tabernacle and Chatsworth. His move precipitated the beginning of a string of relationships with local women: two hairdressers, a clerk who worked in a gift shop in Beach Haven, a waitress in the bar where he worked, a woman from Monmouth County who stayed in his trailer without complaint or desire to enter the working world. His high school sweetheart had attended college in another state, telling him that she would be back during breaks and, after four years of college, would return for good. But predictably this didn't happen. After a year of maintaining their long-distance romance, she moved on and eventually married an ambitious man from Indiana, someone who had convinced her that his home state was where they should settle.

During Ewan's years at O'May's, he resisted the temptation to go to Atlantic City where he heard that bartenders made good money and had to beat off cocktail waitresses who were funneled and refunneled through the casinos. He liked the uneven pace of O'May's, so he made a decision to sacrifice the money and temptations of Atlantic City for the peace of the small restaurant and bar not far from the gas station where he had worked and waited for three years. He watched his friends marry and divorce, leave the Pines, return, and, in one case, die. And he continued to wait, thinking that something would come his way.

Many customers at O'May's were people driving to the shore from the suburbs and from Philadelphia, and the bar was the traditional halfway point for most. In his conversations with these customers, he learned about their frequently disrupted lives. He decided that every customer who took more than a minute to talk with him seemed to be disappointed with life in some way. If the person had money, there was a predictable family problem: a wife or a husband had left or a daughter was pregnant or a son was an addict and thief and headed for jail. No one, it seemed to Ewan, had it all. So when he was in the process of ending a relationship or in the midst of yearning for a car he couldn't afford or wondering when his break would come, he remembered his customers. One thing people shared and couldn't seem to shake, he reasoned, was disappointment. Ewan decided that whatever he had would probably never totally satisfy him. And if satisfaction came his way, his curiosity about something else would probably ruin what he already had.

Like everyone else, he concluded, he would always find heartache and disappointment lurking around the fragile edges of happiness.

Then Ewan's life changed. His girlfriend left after they argued about the late hours he spent at work, a complaint that Ewan felt was unjustified because the woman had known what he did before she moved into his trailer. She had even met him at O'May's. He started seeing Andrea, who worked as a secretary for a landscaping company in Medford. Through her he met Finley who had had work done by Andrea's employer at his house in Indian Mills, a house that Ewan would later learn didn't belong to Finley. Finley's personal affairs remained largely his business. Ewan's conversations with him had consisted of bits of information and informal exchanges which lacked any content. But this suited Ewan who rarely felt he had anything significant to say to the man.

In Fez, with his high school knowledge of French and a few hastily learned words of Arabic, Ewan never attempted a conversation with the locals beyond simple requests to the cabdriver or the waiter at the cafe or the desk clerk at the hotel. In Ewan's mind, their interest in Americans was marginal. His tips were generous and they appeared to appreciate this. But he had nothing to offer them beyond these customary requests and payments. Ewan couldn't find the energy to move beyond that. His chief concern after a month of wandering with Andrea in the deep south of the country beyond the pass at Tizin-Tishka was the cafe and the small, umbrella-shaded table that looked out on the green cover of the avenue and the Place de Florence which was overrun by young loitering Moroccan men who called with defiant persistence from their benches to passing tourists. It was only during the hottest part of the afternoon that they dispersed and sought cool shelter, sometimes in the darkened reflection of the long line of palms.

After two months in Morocco, which was preceded by two months in France and Spain, Andrea had returned to the Pines, glad to be leaving North Africa, a place she described as a small piece of hell on Earth. They had been to Tangier and Fez and Meknes, then to Marrakesh and she had willingly crossed the Atlas Mountains with him and descended to Tagounit at the edge of the Sahara on the Algerian frontier. She was determined that they should leave North Africa together, but when they returned from Tagounit and the fonduk where they had stayed, Ewan only wanted to go back to Fez and not return home where an uncertain future awaited him. In Morocco he found the comfort of escape, away from who he was and what he had done. He was the outsider there, adapting to foreign surroundings, and in his daily confrontation with this world, he lost a part of his past.

Within a week, he had planned another trip south, wanting to push farther than they had traveled before, into Algeria and the Hamada du Draa and the Sahara to find the Blue People who emerged from the desert on market days in the small towns along the fringe of Morocco. In France, he had read about a man's search for mythical Smara, a place no European had ever seen and a place the man had found. Then the man died. But Ewan wasn't looking for Smara or any other identifiable location. As far as Ewan knew, he wasn't looking for anything except what he found beyond the country of dark cliffs and red rocks. He wanted to submit to the fluid succession of events that life offered without notice or interference. But on the morning they planned to leave for the desert, Andrea fled.

"I can't," she said as they stood with their two bags in front of the hotel.

Ewan looked at her and saw that she was finished and that if he wanted to leave Fez and head south again she wouldn't stay.

"I'm going back to the States," Andrea said, using the word like a veteran traveler. "My flight leaves in two hours. And you can still get a ticket."

"Oh."

"Tim."

"I'll get you a cab," Ewan responded, not wanting to argue or prolong her leaving, later thinking that his acceptance of it might have something to do with his taste for kif and the lethargic high it provided. "To the airport." He lifted his stuffed backpack from the curb and carried it into the lobby.

"Why don't you come?" Andrea asked when he returned. "Haven't you had enough?"

Ewan didn't say anything. Instead he watched a bellhop struggle with an elderly couple's luggage. The woman wore a hayek and shouted through the black material at her husband.

After several minutes passed and the argument ended, Andrea said, "What's done is done. You have to accept that. You can't change it. You can't."

"I have to stay." He gave her a passionless kiss. "Do you need any money?"

"But Tim." She took a long look into his eyes but found nothing there. "No, I'm fine."

Ewan fumbled for his wallet and before he opened it he said, "Take some more. You can change these dirhems at the airport."

"Tim," she pleaded again as she unconsciously reached for the money. "We can—"

"Here's your cab." Ewan sounded more like the doorman than her boyfriend. He didn't know what else to say. If she wanted to leave, he wouldn't try to stop her.

"Call me or write," Andrea said as she embraced him before entering the backseat. "I love you," she whispered through the open door.

When the cab moved away, Ewan didn't wave. He didn't know if he'd ever see her again. Her strained face looked through the back window of the cab, repeating the same words she had just spoken. Then she was gone.

"Goodbye," he finally said after Andrea had vanished around the corner. He returned to the lobby and quickly reviewed his plans to journey south, imagining new, more dangerous routes in Western Sahara. As Andrea's taxi made its way to the airport, Ewan decided to stay in Fez for another week, feeling that whatever waited for him in the south could wait at least that long. He wanted time to look over his plans. Ewan walked to the hotel's opulent restaurant and sat where he could gaze down on the old city, a heaped tangle of small, dirty white cubicles punctuated by minarets and towers. He ordered a cold drink from the waiter who scurried between the chairs and tables, always smiling and willing to please the hotel's unusual assortment of visitors.

Ewan had worked for Finley for a little more than a year. During that time, he had made seventy thousand dollars running for him. Mostly his trips took him to Florida or to Arizona. And as Finley had promised him, there was never a problem, at least never one that Ewan couldn't handle. Two thousand dollars a trip plus expenses was what Finley paid Ewan for three months. Then he increased the amount to three thousand a trip. After their first conversation, Ewan never asked questions about the contents of the packages and followed Finley's instructions without deviation. Both of them were satisfied with the other's role and both of them were making money.

During that year, Ewan tried not to think too much about the fact that he was running coke. His rationale was based on the premise that drugs were going to be sold and used. No one could change that. He smoked home-grown grass when he could get it, popped an occasional pill, and had tried coke once or twice. He knew that drugs could destroy people, but he had watched obnoxious yuppies and middle-aged executives and old Pineys drink until they fell from their barstools, each ounce bringing them one step closer to death. He couldn't see much difference between the two worlds. If he didn't run for Finley, someone else would, and someone else would make the money. As his earnings accumulated, Ewan started considering the possibilities that his new-found wealth created. He set a limit on the time period—two years—that he would work for Finley. After that he would be finished, and by his calculations would have about a hundred and fifty thousand dollars to play with, although he realized that he had to be careful.

But his two-year limit was cut short by events that were on the very margin of his work for Finley. Fearing arrest was always part of the job. Never knowing if a gun waited behind the next door worried him. At times he thought his heart would rip apart because of the stimulants being pumped through his body. There was excitement, just as Finley had mentioned. But there was something else waiting for Ewan, too.

As he sat at his table in the cafe, Ewan remembered reading something in high school about Morocco. He could only recall the opening few paragraphs about flies traveling between corpses on their way to burial and Europeans who sat at tables like his own and watched the processions over cool drinks and food. The flies, a regular nuisance around cafe tables, found the smell of rotting flesh more invigorating than what was on the tables. But eventually the flies returned to the cafes and their occupants, bringing with them the residue of death.

Europeans still haunted Fez and the other cities of the country. Ewan had watched them from a distance, and had maintained that distance with Andrea at his side. Europeans found the government's exchange rate acceptable and the price of services and flesh cheap. And with their numbers, they found a buffer between what they were and what Morocco was, inventing for themselves instead what they wanted the place and its people to be. With Andrea gone, Ewan's own buffer had dissolved and as the days passed, he found himself lonely and was tempted to join their ranks, knowing that with the Europeans he could avoid some of the harshness that he willingly let overtake him.

When he was eighteen he took a trip into the woods with his father, a trip that managed to resurrect itself one hot, thoughtless afternoon in Fez after he had smoked too much kif. His father wanted to show him a spot where his grandfather had used old railroad ties to make charcoal. That in itself wasn't unusual. Abandoned lines were frequently targeted for their ties, which burned long and even and made fine charcoal. It was the size of the project that was important. According to Ewan's father, this particular mound was larger than anyone in the Pines had ever attempted. Its fagan reached twenty-four feet into the air and the kiln held over thirty-two cords of wood. When they finally reached the opening in the woods, an enormous burned ring, turned varying shades of green and yellow by the passing years, was permanently imprinted in the sand-whitened ground. Ewan stood in the center of it, thinking that it was forty or fifty feet across. His father said that it had taken seven weeks for it to burn and another two before they could bag the charcoal. They had brought his grandfather food as he watched and walked and dressed and redressed the immense pit. He had slept only when Ewan's father was present, because his son was the only one Ewan's grandfather trusted to watch the smoke seep from the flue. And your grandfather, his father said as he surveyed the scene, still amazed by what had happened there, had stayed on the entire time, twenty, twenty-five feet in the air—firewalking.

On Ewan's last trip to Florida, Andrea came and brought along her twelve-year-old niece. The three of them flew to Orlando, rented a car, and headed for a hotel in Disney World. After spending a few days at the resort, Ewan planned to pick up Finley's package. Later that day they would return to Philadelphia. On their way to Disney World, they stopped to eat at a fast food place. Andrea's niece wanted to stay in the car and listen to the radio while Ewan and Andrea went inside to order the food and use the bathrooms. At the time Ewan didn't find the request unusual. Andrea's niece claimed she loved the song that was playing and they left her in the backseat happily singing the lyrics. As they recrossed the parking lot with a bag of cheeseburgers and french fries, a man with a pistol rushed to their rental car and before Ewan or Andrea could do anything but shout, he sped away with Andrea's niece still inside, side-swiping another car in the process. Two days later, just within the boundaries of an undeveloped section of Disney World, the police found her strangled, naked body.

After that, Ewan stopped working for Finley and then he quit bartending at O'May's. He moved through the predictable stages of guilt and depression about what had happened, finally deciding that the child's death was a pay back, that all of it had been some type of cosmic joke. He was the runner. He was in Florida because he chose to work for Finley. He was to blame because he had set the events in motion. Without his compliance, Finley's offer and his many trips to Florida and Arizona would never have happened. He wouldn't have been able to afford a trip to Disney World with Andrea and her niece. He even thought that Andrea might have dropped him, remembering Finley's early remark about Andrea and his lack of money.

When Finley heard about the carjacking over the phone he said, "You didn't pick up the stuff early, did you?"

"Hell no." Ewan replied, not convinced that Finley didn't think the man who drove away with Andrea's niece in the back seat had followed them, hoping to make a score and taking what he thought was his best shot.

"Good," Finley breathed, revealing his true concern. "They'll find her," he added, realizing that he wasn't reacting the way he was expected to. After a long pause he said, "I guess you're finished."

"Yeah," Ewan agreed faintly as he glanced at Andrea who was sprawled across the bed, her face buried in a pillow. She had been crying since her niece had disappeared.

"Everything will work out," Finley said halfheartedly.

But everything hadn't worked out. After the funeral and his decision to leave Finley and O'May's, Ewan was emotionally stranded. To those around him he looked like a condemned man waiting for his fateful day. He had plenty of money but had no inclination to spend it. Alone in his trailer or when Andrea came to visit, he wanted to do nothing but count the passing hours by watching soap operas and TV movies. He never followed what the actors said or did because he didn't care. They supplied a static barrier that helped block his constant return to Florida and what had happened there. On occasion he would accompany his father deep into the woods, riding beside him on the bench seat of his truck, helping his father keep check on the monuments of his past, and listening to his stories, but still thinking of the brief moment when the carjacker, who was never arrested, bolted for the car door and disappeared with the girl.

Andrea hung on, trying to bring him back and imagining that it would only take time. She wanted to have children. Before her niece's death, they had thought that they might eventually get married, maybe within the next year after he was finished with Finley. Now she was trying to recapture these plans and find a way to return to where they were before her niece's murder. Andrea had told him that he wasn't responsible for what had happened, that no one blamed him. But he had only shrugged, not offering to enter into a debate about a conclusion he had already reached.

After several months, Andrea convinced Ewan that they should leave the Pines and the things that only seemed to remind Ewan of what he wanted to burn from his memory. Maybe, she thought and finally believed, another place would bring him back. When she asked him where he wanted to go, he said away and he didn't care where. She suggested France, a place she had always wanted to visit, and he told her to buy the tickets. Andrea quit her job and they packed their bags, only delaying their departure to wait for passports.

Two weeks after Andrea had left him on the steps of the Palais Jamai, Ewan was still in Fez. His routine hadn't changed, nor had his intransigence. He still graced the same spot for part of each morning and early afternoon and he still brushed the flies away from the rim of his glass. But now he had noticed something different in his monotonous routine as he stared at the group of young men gathered under the palms of the Avenue Hassan. Around 11:30 each morning an elderly European man, dressed in a white linen suit and carrying a cane which hung from one of his crossed forearms, traversed the foliage of the median. His straw hat was pulled low, its brim riding just above his white eyebrows. He didn't look at anyone directly and his blue ascot never seemed to move against his rigid, creased neck. In one hand the man clutched several dirhams. He walked with even, firm strides through the others, who either ignored his presence or stepped before him. When his path was blocked, he stopped. If he waved his free hand the man before him moved aside and let him continue. It was only when the European turned and the man who blocked his way followed him that the European's progress along the avenue was reversed and the ritual ended.

On four consecutive days, the elderly man appeared and went through the same routine. Ewan asked his waiter about the man, but the waiter didn't know him and claimed that he never noticed him until Ewan pointed to him one morning just after the European appeared. For a reason which he later attributed to curiosity and boredom, Ewan decided to follow the European and his newly acquired companion. One morning he left his seat before the well-dressed man appeared. When the man split the throng along the avenue, Ewan followed him at what he thought was a safe distance. The man, with his new friend walking behind him, returned to a waiting cab which carried both men away.

The next day Ewan waited in the area where the European's cab had been parked. This time Ewan would not lose him; he had arranged that morning to have his punctual driver return early to the cafe, a request that didn't sit well with the man until Ewan said he would double the fare. When the European arrived and stepped from his cab, Ewan alerted his driver. Within five minutes they were following the other cab. Ewan expected the European to stop somewhere in the Ville Nouvelle and enter one of the numerous blocklike apartment buildings, but his cab returned to the medina and stopped before a gate that wasn't familiar to Ewan.

"Bab Chorfa," his driver remarked. "Not good," he said, shaking his head. "Tomorrow?" he asked, thinking that the change in routine had jeopardized their arrangement.

"Yes, for a few more days," Ewan said as he paid him and rushed to catch a glimpse of the European before he and his companion passed through the gate and into the medina.

After a few minutes of first catching a glimpse of the man's hat, then losing it as it disappeared down a narrow street with low reed awnings, Ewan was lost. The street was intersected by shoulder-wide alleys and crowded with men in hooded jellabas. He tried asking a few people who passed him about the European and where he was, but they ignored his questions. Oncoming mules laden with the products of the market were whipped around him, their drivers not interested in this haggard American who was obviously lost and who had no business being lost.

When Ewan heard the muezzin's call to prayer, he stopped asking questions and sat against a smooth stone wall in the shade, avoiding the trickle of sewage that wove its way between the worn stones of the road. The faithful would be entering the cool courtyards of the mosques and washing in the pools of intricately designed fountains before passing into prayer rooms. He closed his eyes for a moment, imagining himself standing outside a mosque's entrance. As a non-believer he could only watch the cleansing that rejuvenated some before the midday prayer. Flies buzzed around his face and the sun slowly shrank the margin of shade surrounding him. When he opened his eyes, the European was standing in front of him.

"My name's Spenser. What do you want?" the man said with a sharp British accent.

"Nothing," Ewan replied as he struggled to his feet. The European, who was several inches shorter than he was, held his straw hat in his hands while his cane remained snugly secure in the crook of an arm.

"You must want something." The man looked at Ewan's clothing for a second. "You're an American, aren't you?"

"Yeah."

"So?"

"I was curious," Ewan said, thinking that he should tell the older man why he followed him into the medina. He hadn't meant any harm. "I've seen you on the Avenue Hassan."

"Oh," the man responded, cutting the last sound of the word with his mouth just when Ewan thought it would continue indefinitely.

"I saw them follow you."

"And you're interested?"

"I don't—"

"Maybe you'd like to watch."

"That depends on what that means," Ewan said curtly.

"My boys," he replied, smiling. "Or my men, as you Americans would say."

"I don't think so."

"I pay them, and women, too. I don't get involved anymore. Although I do take an occasional picture, for posterity." Spenser glanced at the red and blue cotton band around his straw hat. "I'm like a director without a script. I tell them what I want and they improvise." He looked at his aged body. "No, this won't let me get involved. What would they find attractive about this wrinkled old skeleton? A kouros, I'm not. But there's no use, is there?" He laughed lightly and gazed at Ewan.

"Listen, I don't think—"

"What are you doing here, in Fez?"

"Nothing really."

"You must be here for a reason. The splendors of the place. To see the sights? The exotic flavor. The skin trade."

Ewan didn't answer.

"Are you alone?"

"Now I am."

"What's your name?"

"Tim Ewan."

"I knew someone by that name back in England."

"I've never been there."

"Can't say I blame you," the man remarked. "Well Mr. Ewan, any plans?"

"I'm heading south in a few days—Berbers—maybe Western Sahara or Algeria. Whenever I decide I've had enough of Fez."

"For what? That's dangerous business down there. I mean there's nothing past Marrakesh really. Nothing except—"

"Just to look around, to see what I can find."

"Oh, so you're an adventurer. That's what I am as well, except I do it here." Spenser chuckled. "They make good money, you know."

"Sir?"

"The people I employ. More in two or three hours than they could make in a week. I mean look at those poor souls along some of these streets, ten or twelve to a room, hammering away at something or the other for literally hours." He shook his head. "Horrendous."

"It's pretty rough by our standards, I guess."

The man hesitated, turning his hat by the brim in his hands, then said, "Where are you staying?"

"Palais Jamai."

"So you aren't short of money. That is, unless you plan to skip out on them."

"I don't think so," Ewan said.

"Have you had your afternoon meal yet?"

"No. I usually don't eat lunch."

"Well be my guest then. If you're in no hurry, we can go over to M'Nebhi. Have you ever been there?"

"No, I haven't."

"They serve marvelous native food: bstilla, couscous, tajine, and the like. And they have music and pretty dancers. A young man like yourself could appreciate that. Am I right?"

Suddenly Ewan found himself unsure of what he wanted to do. He didn't fully trust Spenser but he didn't find him unlikable. The one thing he was certain of was that he had a little time and was growing bored with Fez.

"Well, what do you say?"

"I guess there's no harm in it," Ewan responded, not convinced that his decision was for the best, but willing to accept it. He would worry about the consequences later, if there were any.

"Wonderful," the older man said as he replaced his hat and started to retrace his steps which would lead them out of the maze and into the razorlike sun. "Tell me about yourself and your family," Spencer said, tapping his cane on the paving stones once to mark the final word of his sentence.

"My grandfather was a firewalker," Ewan responded as he matched the man's progress, following him around one corner, down a flight of steps, and into a small open square which was graced by one shimmering olive tree.

"Aren't we all," Spenser replied without breaking his stride. "Aren't we all."

The Blue Comet

Omens are meant to be recognized, and denying this one basic fact can lead to unnecessary trouble. Accepting the likelihood that omens might carry with them some prophetic warning, even if we're not sure about the actual magnitude or truth of any particular sign, is enough, enough to avoid the bad shit that's out there, or at least most of it. But we usually ignore the signs. Why we've given the cold shoulder to omens has to do with our supposed understanding of the physical world, I guess. That's what I hear at school, anyway. Yet we only have to watch the nightly news to see that there are plenty of omens out there these days, more than enough to go around.

On that spring day, as I waited for my onetime friend to return with my mother's new car, the first of three omens occurred before my uncaring eyes. I had let Yancey borrow the car that morning. It was spring break. He was home from college, and his car wouldn't start. He was on a budget and he thought he knew what the problem was, but his parents both worked and there was no way for him to get to the store to buy the part. He lived down the street. I had seen him the night before and we were planning to get together that afternoon. He knew that my parents were away for the weekend and my older sister was in another state attending law school and that I would be cutting Friday classes, which I liked to think of as a senior privilege. Of course, Yancey agreed. So I gave him the keys to the month-old, shiny white coupe, loaded to the gills. I was still halfway drunk from the havoc of the night before. And the parts store was only a few miles away. Who cared if my friend Yancey was on the reckless side? I asked myself as he backed out of the driveway. I knew Yancey and his car were the survivors of many daring campaigns that had crossed state lines and, at times, defied explanation and encouraged bravado. The scars that covered his car proved this. But I was reasonably certain on that spring morning that my friend wouldn't let me down.

As ten minutes turned to twenty, then thirty to sixty, my attention focused on the sky. What had been a beautiful, clear morning, resplendent with sunlight streaming through the trees and windows, became dark, foreboding, portentous. For a second I forgot about Yancey and the car, and concentrated on the heavens. Masses of clouds shifted from one corner of the horizon to the other. Birds flew erratically from perch to perch. Street lights popped on, their sensors confused by the weakening light. Then hail started to fall, small pieces at first, hardly larger than wet snowflakes, but within minutes the hail grew in size and became heavy, unresponsive golf balls. The house shook. Limbs arched. Flowers collapsed. Any respectable auger, any reader of signs, would have seen this as a bad moment, a foreshadowing of something to come, a signal that all was not right in the universe, ominous with a capital O. But I saw nothing but hail. Zero. In a bizarre way, it was entertaining. I watched the ice fall for several minutes, noting with amused silence that it brought new dents to fragile surfaces, and then I went to the bathroom. When I returned to the kitchen, it was over. Within five minutes, the clouds parted and the sun returned. Order was reestablished. So much for divination.

Only after ninety minutes had passed did I start to worry. I phoned the parts store and asked the voice at the other end if anyone in the place had seen him. I even described his clothing: ripped jeans and a college t-shirt, black high-tops, hoping that someone had noticed him.

"Hold on," a distracted voice mumbled as I was switched to a taped message. I checked the yard for surviving pieces of ice. "Yeah," the voice said, interrupting the self-assured message about a great weekend deal on batteries. "Can I help you?"

A different person, I told myself. I reexplained my request, describing Yancey a second time.

"Hold on," the voice said, but I wasn't put on hold this time. I thought I heard a hand partially muffle the receiver. I could hear several guys laughing in the background. Someone said what I thought was the name Yancey. "Yeah, he was here," the voice finally said, still recovering from laughter. "About an hour, maybe seventy-five minutes ago. He was with another guy, I think. Didn't have his part though. But we'll get it by tomorrow morning."

Another guy? I asked myself when I hung up. Another sign? Not only had I let Yancey borrow my mother's car, but he was using it to pick up his friends. And the laughter at the other end of the telephone hinted that I was part of the joke, that someone knew Yancey and he was trouble. I was pissed. For a minute I considered taking to the streets. But I didn't allow my anger to alter my plans for the rest of the day. The fact that Yancey was abusing our friendship didn't shine in my eyes as a sign. Hell, I didn't believe that he had violated any sacred laws of trust. My disappointment was based on how long I thought he would take, nothing more; unless the unspeakable had happened and the car, its fenders crushed beyond recognition, was being lifted by a tow truck winch. I positioned myself behind the kitchen table so that I could see the street. As soon as Yancey turned into the driveway, I would be outside and in his face, just for the principle. I didn't want him to screw around when it came to my mother's car. One dent, one scratch, and my ass would be worthless for the summer. No ride, no life. I needed that car.

But my anxiety subsided just like the hail. After all, I reasoned, I didn't need the car for anything at that moment. And Yancey had never seriously let me down in the past. So with a little explaining on his part, I would let it go. We had been teammates and friends and I planned to attend the same state college as Yancey. A few extra minutes weren't worth the hassle. Anyone who knew Yancey realized that he was always late and rarely followed an exact, unalterable plan. He was a master of improvisation.

As my thoughts reached other topics, the glare of flashing lights, as they reflected on the glass of the kitchen window, caught my attention. My worst fears instantly clogged my throat: Yancey had totaled the car and the police were bringing him, along with the loaded tow truck, to my house to apologize, to grovel, to promise remuneration. Then an ambulance lunged into the Reddicks' driveway. Paramedics rushed from the cab and the rear of the ambulance. A gurney was pulled into the house. Before I could reach the low fence that separated our yards, the gurney reappeared with Mr. Reddick strapped into place, oxygen mask on his mouth, his almost bald pate shining in the sun like a wet coin. His wife, still wrapped in her flower-covered robe, followed him into the ambulance and they were gone before I could say a word. I knew that Reddick had emphysema, but medication and a little oxygen seemed to keep his problem in check. The day before, he had been working in his garden, his knees and hands deep in the manure-rich bed. A beautiful day, he had said cheerfully to me as I left the house for school. I had waved halfheartedly, feeling that classes at eight in the morning would prevent me from appreciating it.

I went inside and without thinking found a can of beer in the refrigerator—another mistake made in the face of a portent. I behaved so casually about Mr. Reddick's emergency and possible death; I was slightly disinterested, almost bored by his misfortune. I settled back and waited for Yancey, dismissing the Reddick incident as old age, ill health, bad luck. At that moment,

I didn't see how Reddick's sudden departure had anything to do with my life.

It was after one when Yancey appeared. I had downed a six and a bag of taco chips. But I was still on him when he stopped the car.

"What the fuck?" I yelled as he opened the door. "Where have you been?" I charged around the car, searching for a scratch or a dent or a ruptured tire, anything that I could find, but there was nothing. "Come on," I said. "What happened?" And the fact that there was nothing damaged, and maybe there should have been, slipped by me like I was in a coma. Now I respect the idea that omens can come in a variety of forms and that a positive occurrence, when all indicators point initially to an opposite outcome, can signal deep shit. "I thought something went wrong," I added when I reached him by way of one complete circumnavigation of the car. Yancey was heavier than me and a few inches taller. He had a perpetual grin on his face.

"Hey, chill man. I told you I needed to check on that part and when they didn't have it well—"

"What's that supposed to mean? Three fucking hours for a twenty-minute errand?"

As he reached into his jacket pocket and produced a small plastic bag, he said, "You don't mind if I bought a little weed for this afternoon, do you?"

"Where'd you find that?" Our town, which wasn't much larger than a thousand people, had been dry for months. Even the surrounding area had experienced a blight unknown in the recent past.

"What's the difference? We got it. I ran into an old friend. We're going to smoke it." He brushed his sandy hair from his forehead. "Okay?"

"I got some beer stashed inside," I offered after a slight hesitation, thinking that our afternoon and evening were made and quickly forgetting everything that had occurred that morning.

"Why don't we go out to the wreck? Drink some beer. Do some smoke. Wait for some women to show. Maybe get laid? It's spring, right? Bitches heading down the shore. We'll be waiting. If nothing is going on, we head down to Long Beach Island or over to Seaside or A.C. where something will break."

Even after being away from the Pines since the previous summer, with the exception of Christmas break, Yancey was somewhat of a legend when it came to women. He always seemed to find them, or they seemed to find him. He had played quarterback on the high school football team and he had slept with half the cheerleaders. If he wasn't on the field or in class, it seemed that he was in bed with his current girlfriend or on his way there. He was hot and anybody who counted knew it. To hang with Yancey was thought to be a guarantee of sorts when it came to the opposite sex. That's not to say that I or any of our mutual friends benefited on a regular basis from our association with Yancey, but the odds were in our favor when he was around. After drinking a little beer or wine or Jack and doing some weed or whatever else was available with Yancey, things happened. He always knew where to find a party.

Within twenty minutes, we were near the wreck. The two-lane road advanced before us for several miles, its tarred seams thumping beneath the tires of passing cars with rhythmic certainty until the road crossed the bay and dead-ended at the grey Atlantic. Near the railroad trestle surrounded by scrub pines, we turned onto the rutted sand road, the tires spinning free for a moment before they found more than loose, billowing sand.

"Looks like a few people have been back here today," he commented, opening another can of beer. His eyes followed the fresh grooves cut into the sand before the car. "Could be a bitchin' time."

I stopped the car when we reached the wreck—rusting, once blue and cream cars with a Statue of Liberty-shaped logo painted on their sides splayed along a single track for a couple hundred yards. The scene always reminded me of my toy train set that ten years before would never stay on its unevenly assembled track as the locomotive careened around the tinseled

90

Christmas tree and ultimately derailed as it crashed into a misplaced present.

"The Comet and its ghosts await," Yancey professed with a belch as he left his seat.

A few four-bys were gathered at the far edge of the clearing that quickly disintegrated into a green mass of briars, then gums and cedars. Yancey leaned against the hood and surveyed the scene. As I left the driver's seat to join him, another car pulled up behind us. Jerry Russell, who was a junior, was driving. His girlfriend Sheila sat beside him. Another girl, who I had seen around school, was crouched in the backseat.

"Hey man," Jerry said to me from the open sunroof of his car as he waited for his girlfriend to brush her windblown hair.

"What's happening?" I responded.

Jerry got out and his girlfriend followed him. He glanced along the jagged line of the wreck, as he swaggered toward us, pigeon-toed, holding a beer bottle in one hand.

"Gonna be a few more people here in an hour or so."

"From school?"

"Yeah." Jerry looked at Yancey.

"You know Yancey?"

"Yeah. Hey man," Jerry said as Sheila wrapped her arms around her waist and looked at the sky through her sunglasses. "Haven't seen you around," he said to Yancey.

"I've been away. College."

"Cool. Still playing ball?"

"No, I hurt my knee. Had to give it up."

"Too bad."

"Who's the girl?" I said, nodding toward his car. "She looks familiar. Isn't she somebody's sister?"

"Talton's."

"Ray?"

"Yeah. She's a freshman."

"She coming out?" Yancey asked alertly, probably thinking what I was thinking.

"Who knows. She's wasted. Been huffing some shit in a Pepsi can. Go see if you can get that crap away from her, Sheila. I don't want her hurling in the car like she did in Giberson's last weekend."

Sheila left Jerry's side, her arms dropping from her waist by the time she leaned through the open window.

"So, what's up?" Jerry said.

"Gonna drink a few brews, smoke some weed. The usual."

"Car number 33?"

"Only one to be in," I replied, knowing that car 33 was the cleanest of all the cars resting along the track. It didn't smell like piss and rotting wood and a thousand other unidentifiable odors, not as much anyway. "You got anything?"

"Just these Rockets. Couple of cases iced in the trunk."

I looked at Yancey who was still distracted by the thought of Ray Talton's sister.

"I tried to get some acid or coke, but nobody had any."

"Well, Yancey here is the man for finding some excellent shit."

"Really?"

Yancey glanced at us when he heard his name.

"Got something to sell?"

"You can do a few with us, if you want. But I don't have enough to sell." Yancey looked back at Sheila and Jerry's car, preoccupied with other thoughts. "That's if you put in a good word for me with what's her name."

"April."

"Whatever." Yancey looked at me, then Jerry. "April Talton. Christ, I knew her brother when she was in fifth grade," he remembered.

"She ain't no more."

"Fuckin' A."

We found our way to car 33 and made ourselves comfortable, swatting at the swarms of gnats that had hatched recently. Since my last visit, someone had built a decent-sized fire in the corner of the car, burning the last weather-beaten piece of walnut paneling left in the place in the process. It was still cool at night and

I had done the same more than once, but never inside 33. Traces of nickel-plated fixtures that connected long-gone fans dangled from the ceiling. One remaining fragment of what had been a wicker chair—part of the old train's seashore theme when it ran from New York to Atlantic City—had been smashed and scattered around the car.

Yancey rolled a mega joint and we smoked it. Everyone agreed that it was fine shit, mostly buds, no crap. Sheila and April were both standing outside now, near Jerry's car. I could see Sheila as she guided her friend back and forth, trying to get her blood circulating.

"What was she huffing?"

"Paint, I think. Gold."

"That'll fuck you."

"You know it."

"Maybe she'd like a little weed," Yancey added.

"I'm sure she would. She'd fucking inhale that whole bag if you let her."

"That depends," Yancey responded hoarsely.

Jerry laughed and said, "When she's ready, Sheila will bring her over."

We drank a six and smoked another bone. Jerry yelled through one of the broken windows to Sheila who was still walking around the clearing with her wasted friend.

"She doesn't want to come in," Sheila replied. "Her head's screwed up."

"Well my friends, that's life and—" he said as he faced us. Before he finished two cars entered the clearing. "All right. Party on, man."

Our small gathering grew by several people: Toady McNeil, the school's resident cyberpunk, and Zelinski and their girl-friends and a few other people, all out to get toasted and have a good time.

"A lot of staties out there today," Toady said as he entered our den. "Might be coming back here. Hey Yance." They touched fingertips.

A girl with long brown hair and cutoffs entered and sat next to Yancey without speaking. She had six earrings embedded along the rim of one ear. I didn't know her, but nobody bothered to introduce her.

"You think?" Jerry's face showed some concern, which wasn't cool and didn't win the respect of Yancey or me or anyone else.

"Probably just looking to write a few tickets," Yancey said. "A Friday and all. People from Philly going down the shore, trying to fly through Jersey as fast as possible."

"I don't know. They were back here a couple weeks ago, big time."

"He's right," Jerry added, "but they didn't bother anybody. That's what I heard."

"Yeah, I heard that too," Zelinski said, fingering a red pocket knife in one hand. "But nobody had anything except a few cans of cheap beer."

Sheila called Jerry from outside. She had been talking with Zelinski's girl.

"What's wrong?" Jerry said after ignoring her first attempt to get his attention.

"Let's go to the beach," Sheila answered. "Heather says the state police are coming back here." She raised her hand to block a sun already blocked by her sunglasses. Her bleached bangs rose above her stiff, ring-covered fingers. "Please," she added.

"Christ," Jerry complained.

"Please."

"Christ, Sheila." He paused as he faced us. "Well guys," he said apologetically, "duty calls."

"Yeah, Sheila calls is more like it," someone commented.

Toady smiled. "Heather's a fucking paranoid, man. You know?"

Everyone agreed, but Jerry was already on his way out, stumbling down the jerrybuilt steps. No one said anything for a minute. Green heads buzzed above us. Crows called from across the lunarlike clearing. Yancey started talking to the girl, Heather's cousin we found out, who had arrived with Zelinski, but wasn't from our part of the Pines. Even with Jerry gone, there were enough revellers left, enough for a good time, but it wasn't long, no more than an hour after Jerry Russell pulled away, that Toady and most of his crew decided to abandon the wreck. Our beer was almost gone, some of it vanishing in seconds as each of us did a shooter. And we had smoked all of Yancey's grass, a feat quickened by our number. Heather Bozarth kept talking about the police, about her parents, about getting arrested.

"Fuck 'em," Yancey said loudly for a second time, the first being audible only within the walls of 33. "The police, parents, everybody."

This comment reinforced to the others what had been known directly or through friends about Yancey. He wasn't easily intimidated. He rarely, if ever, backed down. He could be a tough ass, but I knew that part of this behavior wasn't without reason. Flaunting these traits in front of women and guys who thought they were bad, or that their reps were awesome but actually weren't, was the perfect scenario for Yancey and he played it to the max.

"I'm staying," he pronounced with authority, waving his hand and passing judgment on all potential deserters.

"Me, too," I foolishly added. "I'm with Yancey. Fuck 'em."

The girl beside Yancey looked at him. The others started to stand.

"I'm staying, too," she said.

"Suit yourself, Terry," Zelinski said.

"Tell Heather."

"Yeah," Terry slurred. "Tell her."

Yancey put his hand on the girl's knee.

"You'll give me a ride back to my cousin's?" she asked him.

"Sure," Yancey said. "Sure."

"I'll give you a ride," I responded. "It's my car."

"Whatever."

Toady led the others outside as Yancey whispered something to the girl, leaning close to her ear, his hand still on her knee.

"Terry," a voice called from beneath one of the empty holes which at one time had been a window. "Terry."

"Yeah?"

"You're really staying?"

"Yeah, I don't feel like going to the beach. I'll see you tonight."

"Remind her about the beer," Yancey said as Terry got up.

"Could you leave what's left of my half of the case?" she asked as she was framed by the windowless opening.

"Okay." Heather paused, uncertain of her cousin's decision. "You're sure?"

"Heather," Terry said firmly.

After they drove away and the swelling cloud of dust that the cars left behind settled, we began to drink Terry's beer. Terry told us she had been in the hospital the winter before because of depression. Her mother was getting divorced for the second time. Her father was an alcoholic and was living in Arizona. Her stepfather, a man who had promised to be the perfect match for her mother, had turned against both his wife and stepdaughter and eventually forced them out of what he called his house. Now Terry and her mother were living in a one-bedroom apartment outside of Egg Harbor City. Her mom was a cocktail waitress at one of the casinos.

I had allowed myself to consider the possibilities. My fantasies ran from having Terry reject Yancey for me to having Terry share herself with both of us. But even in my condition, I knew they were only fantasies. Yancey was in charge. And once I had learned something about Terry's recent distressed life, my desire turned cold. But Yancey used all of his powers on her. Eventually he convinced her to take a walk in the woods with him. A botanical expedition was what he called it. When Terry stood, her head tilted forward and one knee collapsed. Yancey had to support her with his arm.

"God," she said. "I'm trashed."

Yancey winked and led her outside. "Don't wait up," he said humorously, guiding the girl by placing his hands on her slender waist.

"No later than midnight," I replied, contributing to Yancey's lighthearted mood. "Or you're grounded."

Then they were gone. I was alone, surrounded by the rusting hulk of the car and dozens of beer bottles and cans. I looked across the clearing. An enormous horse fly tried to bite my arm. The four-bys were still clustered at the far end of the wreck. Another truck and a car had arrived, along with two bikes. Music was playing now. Occasionally, someone would emerge from the car and walk to the edge of the woods to take a leak. They looked like college people to me. The few women I saw looked older, their distant voices more confident than the high school girls I was accustomed to. One was wearing a bathing suit. For a moment I considered walking down to their party and introducing myself. But I dismissed the thought. Without Yancey I feared I would look like an ass and that would ruin my chances. With Yancey I might be successful. At that very moment he was living up to his reputation, although I had to admit that for Yancey, Terry was easy money.

After twenty minutes, Yancey returned alone.

"Where's Terry?" I asked before he was inside.

"Back there. She got sick after we did it. Really sick."

"Too bad. She's really wasted."

"That's an understatement."

"How was she?"

"A piece of ass," he said as he opened one of the last two beers. "She'd probably do you if—"

I hesitated then replied, "No thanks. Not what I had in mind."

Yancey smiled and said, "Fucking liar."

I looked away.

"She'll be okay. I told her to finish getting sick and come back after. We don't need her hurling in old 33, do we?"

"She's all right?" I said as I watched the gathering around the last car, suddenly imagining that Terry had been in the wrong place on that warm spring day.

"Yeah. She'll be fine."

"She can sleep it off in my mother's car, if she wants," I said, trying to reconcile what I was feeling with what had happened. "Did she want it?"

"Hell, yes." Yancey said, slapping me on the back. "You know me."

I opened the last beer and rested my head against the wall. Listening to the music, Yancey positioned himself so he could watch the party at the far end of the wreck. Ten minutes ran by us without another word.

"Looks like a good party over there," he finally said. "A fucking slammin' party."

"Yeah," I responded, closing my eyes.

"What time is it?"

"It's past four."

"Shit, we got to get moving."

"What about Terry?"

"Fuck her."

"We can't leave her."

"Hell, I don't want to leave her, not yet. I mean let's go down to the end there. You know? See what's happening. Maybe I know someone over there. Looks like they have plenty of shit."

"I was thinking the same thing."

"Fuckin' A." Yancey moved toward the sprung door. "We'll leave your mom's car open for Terry. When she's feeling better, she can wait there or come down and join us." He bounded outside and faced the trees behind the wreck then cupped his hands and shouted, "Terry, we're going down to the party at the end. Car's open."

There was no response.

"Terry?"

A groan came from my right as I descended to the ground.

"Did you hear?"

Another groan.

"Okay, let's go," Yancey said, pointing with his finger.

"Do you think she heard you?"

"Yeah, fuck her."

Yancey walked along the side of the railway car, then ducked between 33 and the next car. I tried to pinpoint where Terry was. I saw something move, and then I heard a retching sound.

"You coming?" Yancey questioned impatiently from the other side.

I looked over my shoulder once more, trying to fathom why I was concerned about Yancey's conquest; then I was beside him, shoulder to shoulder. When we reached the end car, Yancey didn't waste any time.

"You mind if my buddy and I join you?" he said to the first person he encountered.

"No problem," the man replied. "Jenkins is making a beer run. Got any cash?"

"I've got a five," I said.

"Me, too," Yancey added.

We placed the money in Jenkins' hand as he emerged from the car, his fingers wrapped around a wrinkled lump of green bills. The money seemed to grease our entrance into the party. We were contributing members, not hangers. Introductions were made. Most people weren't from the Pines. A few were from Cherry Hill or someplace like it. As I had expected, many were in college. When Yancey was introduced to a woman who attended the same college, I knew we were made. I thought Yancey would work his magic and I might be on the road to something real, something I could even brag about around school.

"Your name sounds familiar," Sarah, the woman from Yancey's college, said to him after a moment. "But I never met you, right?"

"Not that I remember. Big place." Yancey offered in his friend-liest voice. "But you have now." He smiled and leaned forward, almost imperceptively.

She shook her head and I noticed how her loosely tied red halter top moved with each turn of her neck.

"Sarah, right?"

"Yeah." She paused, raising a finger to her temple, still attempting to remember why Yancey was not a stranger to her. Finally she shrugged. "It'll come to me. I forget sometimes, but eventually I remember."

"I do the same thing," Yancey said, hoping to find common ground. "My mind goes blank. Then it clicks back into the groove. You know? It's like totally off."

We spent a few hours drinking and talking. No one had any weed. At one point I left the group and returned to my mother's car, a fact I tried to keep hidden from the others, to find Terry asleep on the backseat, exactly where I hoped she would be. When I returned I tried to make conversation with Sarah's girlfriend Angel, who was from a faceless town in North Jersey within spitting distance of New York, as Yancey continued to talk to Sarah. I could see that he was working on a double score, something that would only enhance his reputation in the eyes of his admirers. I never established if Sarah or Angel was attached to any of the guys there. They both knew Jenkins and his friend Dave, who was from Toms River. Jenkins was going part-time to the same college as Sarah and Yancey, but was a few years older. Dave was along for the ride. The others were connected in different ways. Later that night, they planned to go to A.C. to lose some money, as Angel put it.

Near seven-thirty, as I was struggling not to betray my age and inexperience to Angel and her friends, Dave produced a pistol and started shooting empties that he had placed on a pile of sand and gravel about twenty-five yards from the railway car. Before long, another gun was produced from a glove compartment. The shots increased for a few minutes, most missing but some finding their mark, shattering bottles and sending empty cans reeling across the sand. Members of the party watched from the confines and imagined protection of the car with its long row of broken windows. Then Dave suggested a quick-draw contest to his shooting companion. "To the death," he added.

"Best of three," his intended opponent, whom I now realized was Jenkins with a ball cap pulled low on his forehead, suggested as he raised a beer can to his mouth and gestured with his weapon.

"Done," the other man said.

My heart sank as both men reloaded. This wasn't fun; this was crazy. Everyone was drunk or halfway there. I wanted to say something, but didn't because no one else seemed impressed by the thought of two men firing at each other before our bloodshot eyes. Then, to add to my amazement, a couple of people started to cheer.

"Those two," someone outside said. "When are they going to grow up?"

"Who won last time?" another voice asked nonchalantly.

"Dave," the other voice offered.

Last time? I said to myself, without thinking.

The men assumed their positions, staggering to spots that were about seventy-five feet apart. Their arms bowed slightly; their hands were poised near, but not too close, to their pistols, which were tucked inside their waistbands.

"I told you to be out of town by sunset," Dave threatened, looking for a second at the darkening sky.

"Go to hell," the other man countered.

"No, amigo that's where I'm sending you," Dave twanged as he reached for his weapon.

As they spoke I felt I had to say something, even if the others were convinced that there wasn't anything wrong, even if it ruined whatever chance I had of impressing Angel. I looked at Yancey, but he was engrossed in the drama before us.

As they drew, I shouted, "Don't!" But my feeble cry was obliterated by pistol blasts. Dave fell to the ground, grasping his side. Everyone clapped, cheering Jenkins. "Jesus," I said.

The next few seconds seemed to hang before me for an hour. When the clapping stopped, Dave stood and brushed off his jeans. The other man bowed, brandishing his weapon over his head.

"It's a game," I muttered softly. "They're using blanks."

"What did you think?" Angel said, staring at me as if I were in first grade. "They're not morons."

I regained my composure, hoping to rejuvenate my standing with the woman.

"You know?"

"I've seen the real thing," I said, using a tragic tone. "People get killed when the bullets are real."

"Maybe they deserve to," Angel responded, "if they're that stupid."

The next duel was much like the first brief skirmish, but Dave was the victor. The final exchange would decide the outcome of the contest. Both men squared off, fired, and Jenkins was the clear winner. The other man raised his hand to his bare chest to feign injury, but after a slight hesitation he dropped to the ground and grabbed his shoe.

"Son of a bitch," Dave yelled. He struggled to a sitting position and awkwardly placed his foot on his lap. Blood soaked one of his hands as he removed his leather sneaker. The other man stumbled to his side after deciding Dave wasn't clowning around. "Fucker, you shot me," he yelled at his opponent.

"Man, I had blanks in here," Jenkins said, confidently shaking his gun.

"Well then, what do you call this?"

They stared at Dave's bleeding wound as everyone gathered around the gunslingers to see what had happened.

"Where's Thomas? He's the vet."

Then Thomas, whom I hadn't noticed before that moment, pushed his way through the knot of people. He knelt next to Dave and wiped the wound clean with the bottom of his striped shirt.

"Well?" Dave said impatiently.

"I think we need to cut it off," Thomas said with a professional aloofness. "Not only the foot but the entire leg. It seems
that the knee bone is connected to—"

A few people laughed, breaking the tension and postponing
Thomas' diagnosis.

"Come on, Thomas."

"You're one lucky fucker," the future vet pronounced. "The
bullet only grazed you. We'll clean it and wrap it up and it'll stop
bleeding."

Dave looked away from his foot and his damaged shoe.

"I'll buy you a new pair," Jenkins said.

Dave glared at the accommodating desperado, but didn't
acknowledge that his offer was accepted.

"Really," Jenkins repeated. "Tomorrow, first thing."

Dave lunged at the man's legs, but the others kept him from
reaching Jenkins.

"It was an accident," the other man said. "I'm fucking sorry."

Dave reached for him again, but Jenkins moved away and
returned to the wreck. Within a half hour, the two were laughing about what had occurred and slapping each other on the
back, ignoring their close call with something more serious.

When darkness came, the party broke. Bats appeared, their
courses erratic and unknown. Peepers started to call, sounding
like a million shrill bells being rung in overlapping harmonies.
A few people disappeared, deserting the main group in the
night, keeping their intentions and destinations to themselves.
Yancey and I decided to stick with Sarah and Angel and a few
others, including Jenkins and Dave, who were still going to A.C.
Everybody was wasted by then, but it didn't deter anyone from
the prospect of driving for miles on narrow, uneven roads. I still
didn't know if I would have any success with Angel, having just
as much difficulty reading women as omens. But as we talked
and I moved closer to her, she didn't readjust the distance
between us. Yancey wasn't faring as well with Sarah. On one
occasion just before we left the wreck, I noticed her shy away

from him, suggesting to me that Yancey might have to work harder if his goal was to remain within reach.

Yancey and I returned to my mother's car. For a reason unknown to me at the time, Sarah rejected Yancey's offer of a ride to A.C., deciding instead to go with Jenkins. But Angel came with us, ignoring Sarah's decision not to ride with us, and this small gesture assured me that something was going to happen between us. Yancey got in the back seat with Terry, who was still asleep. A bottle of pills rested on the floor, and Yancey casually said once the doors were closed that they were downers, adding she'd probably be out for the rest of the night if she took a few on top of what she already had in her system. Angel sat next to me, and although she wasn't hard against me, she didn't hug the passenger side door.

"Who's she?" Angel asked, nodding toward Terry's sleeping form.

"A friend of a friend," I said. "We have to take her home later tonight."

"Oh," she replied. "Must have been really binging to be out like that. You're sure she didn't take many of those," she added, looking at the bottle of pills which still rested in Yancey's hand.

"Don't think so." He held up the bottle in the available light, shaking the contents slightly. "Doesn't look like it to me."

Our group formed a caravan, headlights casting skewed, temporary shadows along the sand road. We were last in line. When it was time to turn onto the main road, the group continued to follow the single set of railroad tracks instead.

"Where are they going?" I asked Angel.

She shrugged, apparently not knowing where she was in relation to where we had to go.

"Just follow them," Yancey said from the backseat.

"Yeah," Angel affirmed. "Jenkins knows what he's doing."

So I followed, not thinking about anything except pleasing Angel.

"What's back here?" she said after a quiet minute passed.

"Woodmansie. Hidden Lakes."

"Then Pasadena," Yancey said. "Used to be a big factory or something, years back. Nothing much left. Clay pits. It's outside my range."

After rocking along the sand road for a few miles, the caravan stopped. I looked through the window. Nothing but the black night and black shadows. Then we got out.

"What's going on?" I said to Dave, who hobbled out of his truck.

"Just a little adventure," he said.

"Yeah, you ever been back here?" someone asked from the other side of the caravan.

"Not really."

"It's fucking terrific. You know there used to be a pottery back here and there are these underground pits, kilns really. It's like walking through a mine field, only in the dark. One wrong step and down you go."

"Cool," Yancey said.

The idea didn't sound too fantastic to me, but when Angel agreed with Yancey I kept my mouth shut.

"After this we'll go to A.C.," Sarah commented as she came into view. "Listen," she said quietly, "just go along with it. Jenkins and a few other guys are doing it on a dare. They're blitzed."

"Count me in," Yancey said.

"Me, too," I volunteered, not wanting any part of the dare, only wanting to seal my supposed hold on Angel.

We gathered at the edge of what used to be the factory site. I recalled driving by the partially destroyed fence and the piles of rubble more than once. But there was no reason to get out, no cause to look at piles of sandstone and bricks. A few shacks stood not too far from the abandoned ground, but they weren't visible from where we waited.

"All right, this is how we do it," Jenkins instructed. "Everybody who's in, form a line across here." He motioned with his hand. "Stand about twenty-five, thirty feet apart.

Yancey, you stand over here. Dave over there." He pointed at me. "You stand next to your friend Yancey."

Everyone blindly followed his instructions.

"Now we walk across that field where the factory was. If you go down, someone will pull you out. The holes are only seven or eight feet deep. If you make it to the other side, you get a prize."

"What's that?" I said.

"You get to fuck me," Jenkins said.

A few participants snickered. I should've known that the prize was the recognition of doing something dangerous and doing it without second thoughts, something Yancey seemed to understand. I promised myself that I wouldn't say another word.

"Okay, let's do it," Jenkins bellowed like a sergeant ordering his men to take an enemy position.

The line moved forward. I stumbled once, even before I entered the kiln field. To my right, Yancey was keeping pace, even a little ahead of the line, exactly where I suspected he would be. The ground was soft in places, as if it was supported by wire springs or much softer soil. Someone at the other end of the line cursed as he fell. For a second I thought he had found a pit, but I saw his dark silhouette reappear and catch up with the man beside him. Then I noticed that Sarah was in line next to Jenkins. And why shouldn't she be? I considered silently. Somehow I knew that she was involved in this crazy ass idea.

Then Yancey went down, disappearing into an unforgiving pit with one long scream.

"He's down!" I yelled as I moved without caution toward the spot where he had walked an instant before.

The ground was softer as I left my prescribed course, and after taking three or four quick steps, the sand opened and I was history. I landed on my ass with a hard thud at the bottom of a brick-littered kiln. I didn't know how far I had fallen, but estimated the distance to be a good fifteen feet, not the seven or eight feet described by Jenkins.

"Shit!" I said loudly as my hands automatically checked my body. "Shit!" I said again, waiting for the others to appear. "Hey," I called. "Anybody out there?" But there was no response. I tried to focus on my surroundings, but couldn't see beyond my hands. Then I noticed that I was sitting on the hardened carcass of a dead deer. I rolled away from the animal and its broken antlers, which were probably shattered as it tried in vain to climb free of its manmade trap.

"You okay?" a voice which sounded like Angel's said.

"Yeah, just get me the hell out of here," I pleaded, but with a harshness that showed my anger. Something slithered over one of my legs and I jumped to my feet. "Hey!" I said again, but nobody answered.

"You break anything fucker?" I could hear Jenkins ask. At first I thought he was talking to me, but I then realized that he was talking to Yancey.

"My leg," Yancey bellowed. "I fucked up my leg."

"Excellent," Jenkins said.

"You know," a voice said loudly, a voice which I quickly assumed was Sarah's. "It took me most of the day, but I remembered."

"What in the hell are you talking about?" Yancey asked, obviously in pain.

"Why your name sounded familiar."

"Just get me the fuck out of this hole."

"You play football, right?"

"Yeah, used to. Why?" he said.

"You tried out and didn't make it."

"I hurt my knee," Yancey said. "We can talk about it after you get me out of here!"

"Shut up, scum bag," Angel interrupted.

"You went out with someone on my dorm floor—Paula Merino?"

"I don't remember," Yancey said. "I go out with a lot of people."

"You don't remember? Five two, bleached blond hair, about a hundred pounds?"

"No."

"Fucker," Sarah hissed.

"Let's cut his balls off," Dave shouted; then he ventured, "Let's pull him out and shoot the son of—"

"No fucking guns," another woman's voice interrupted. "You wanna go to fucking prison?"

Dave was quiet for a moment.

"You're on the list, jackass," Sarah said harshly.

"I don't know what you're talking about. Just get me—"

"The list, scrotum. You're on the rape list. It's in all the dorm bathrooms."

"I don't—"

"You raped Paula, asshole."

"Let's get him the hell out of there and cut—"

"I didn't rape her. You even said I went out with her."

"Fuck you, dipshit. What's that supposed to mean?"

"That she wanted it. We both did. Now I remember."

"That's not the way she told it. You're on the fucking rape list, hot shot. You got her a little buzzed and raped her. She didn't have a choice, you bastard. She trusted you!"

There was a pause in the exchange. I could hear the sound of peepers and crickets and a sudden squeaking hinge, all of which dropped into the hole above my ragged breathing. Then, filtering down to me, I thought I could hear the people standing above Yancey whispering to each other.

"What the fuck is going on?" I yelled, but there was no response. "Hey!"

Suddenly, a rope dropped into my shaft.

"Put this around you" Jenkins said.

In a few seconds, I was standing next to him and Angel and another guy.

"Is Yancey—"

"Still in the hole."

"Let's get him out," I said, glancing toward the kiln that held him. Dave, with his bandaged foot and body turned to one side, was laughing and pissing into the opening.

"Cut that shit out," Yancey complained from below, but Dave only bellowed something unintelligible at him as he continued to spray the gaping hole.

"Fuck Yancey," Sarah said. "You're lucky Angel's here or you'd still be down there, too." She pointed at the hole behind me. "And then what would you have done?"

"You'll have to get the bastard out," someone said from beyond the people around me.

"But we're taking the girl with us. After we tell her about your pal, she'll want out." Angel said. "Where's she live?"

"Egg Harbor." I paused, considering what I should do. My mind was swarmed with conflicting emotions. "It's my mother's car," I blurted. "Please don't trash it. Please," I pleaded, realizing I was whining and that maybe they hadn't even considered wrecking the car.

Angel looked at me, her eyes widening slightly in the darkness. I didn't know if her reaction was one of surprise or sympathy or amusement.

"Egg Harbor. It's on the way to A.C.," Jenkins mumbled. "No problem."

"Do you want to come with us?" Angel said calmly as if nothing unusual had happened. "And leave the fucking dirt bag here?"

I glanced at their faces, first looking at Angel then the others, and sensed that they would judge me by my answer. If what I heard was true, I didn't want them to include me in Yancey's league. But I had lost the appetite for the chase and I didn't think Angel, beyond her insistence that I be removed from my confinement, would be interested in carrying on beyond the point we had reached in our momentary friendship. Some things are better left behind, I thought, so I declined, hoping that Yancey could repair what damage had been done. Ultimately it would be his word against Sarah's, and at that fragile moment loyalty, it seemed, might survive regardless of truth.

Whitman's Tomb

And then they left, taking the rope with them and leaving me and Yancey and my mother's unblemished car not too far from the wreck and at the edge of a deserted, forsaken place, surrounded by all the seen and unseen omens in an impassive universe.

Missing, Again

Curtis Sim ordered another Scotch as he watched the boats sway in the current. He quietly checked the edges of his beard as he counted twelve boats tied in their slips: none over forty feet, most under thirty feet. He knew many hadn't been moved in weeks and were the idle toys of people who had other more pressing things to do, people with 'I'd rather be boating!' bumper stickers. The boats were protected by stretched and zipped brown or blue waterproof covers which prevented anyone from looking around their decks and cabins—a deterrent to theft, their owners probably thought. Curtis knew better.

He couldn't remember seeing the river so high, but as he studied the surging current he recalled another time when he had read from his cell in the county jail about a high-water mark being broken. The peeling beige walls of the cell were covered with terse poems and autographs and rough drawings of Christ and naked women. Curtis deftly added a boat to the montage, creating a visible reminder of his crime. That was in 1964, during his second visit to the grey, fortresslike structure constructed of stone and concrete that the county sheriff's department called a detention facility and the inmates called a shithole.

A shadow drifted over the trees that crowded the far shore, a distance not over two hundred feet, and for a brief moment the bar gained another degree of darkness. Curtis lifted his glass from the counter and considered sitting on the new deck, which reached to the water's edge. There was a small service bar on one end where an idle bartender stood. The setting sun struck the tables and their striped umbrellas at an oblique, yet inviting, angle. The few patrons sitting there seemed very relaxed. But then Curtis realized that Janet might not see him there and his plans for the evening would be ruined.

He glanced at the painted snapper shells that hung above the bar. Each had a landscape or a hunting scene painted on it. The varnish that sealed the work to its base had turned dust-yellow and the coloring lent itself to the pine panelling that covered the walls of the bar and the dining room. The crossed, stained beams of the open ceiling added a lodgelike touch to the building's plain decor. As he glanced around the interior, the only addition that Curtis noticed since his last visit was the collection of framed pictures that hung on the walls of the dining room.

For a Thursday evening, the restaurant was crowded. He gazed at the diners, noticing that only a few appeared to be under sixty. Their bald and white-haired heads created a shifting sea of flesh and hair as they lowered their faces for another forkful of food or to study the menu in the low light of the room. An adjoining space was used as a dance floor and Curtis guessed the band scheduled to play that evening didn't cater to a younger crowd. Curtis loved to dance, loved to take the floor with his partner and shake to the music. In high school, before he quit, he was voted the best dancer of the junior class. But he hadn't danced in several years, at least with a partner. In his cell he would sometimes move to the vibrations of his Walkman, his gyrations more aerobic than dance. And he had never danced with Janet, but he planned to remedy that as soon as she arrived and they ate dinner. By then, he thought, the musicians would be well into their first set and Janet would be in his arms.

His beard, a brown-blond tangle of hair that resembled but didn't match his own, was purchased a month ago from a mail order catalog by his sister when his most recent escape from prison was still in the planning stage. On the morning of his escape, she had left it, along with his clothes and money, in a gas station washroom not far from the prison where he was incarcerated. His entire family knew that if Curtis was in jail, he was thinking about how to get out. And at various times most of his family had helped him with the mechanics of an escape. Not only clothes and money, but cars and plane tickets had been left for him by family members. His brother Clayton had done time for hiding him on his property three years before.

Curtis ran in place in his cell for hours each day, patiently waiting for an opportunity to test his wits against the best the state could find. Escaping had become second nature to him, as normal as getting a haircut or brushing his teeth. After fleeing he always gravitated back to his old haunts and his birthplace, the place where his mother and father had reared five children with varying degrees of success. Curtis ignored the dangers involved. He ignored the predictability of his logic. His escape always began with a brief and some would say illogical trip back to the Pines. Then and only then would he decide where to go. As his eyes returned to the river, he was leaning toward California. But Curtis knew that he would eventually be caught and returned to the prison in North Jersey or to another institution from which he would plan another escape, his eleventh in eighteen years.

Many people said Curtis Sim was indifferent when it came to jail and his sentence because he always found his way to freedom, even if it was only a temporary freedom. Within their praise Curtis found satisfaction, even though it was satisfaction based on an unconventional accomplishment. An impromptu fan club had formed in his hometown. During one of his more spectacular escapes, the club had t-shirts made with his mug shot on them. Across the top of the picture was the word "Missing" and along the bottom border the word "Again" was printed. At first he was amused. Several thousand were sold. But after thinking about it, Curtis was convinced that having his picture worn by people had hurt his chances while he was on the lam.

He had hijacked trash trucks and driven them through gates, worn women's clothing and posed as a visitor, jumped from a moving car, wrestled unsuspecting guards to the ground, shimmied down coils of sheets and along drain pipes, cut through bars with smuggled hacksaw blades, and he had swallowed handcuff keys as well, all in the cause of freedom. One time he had pushed a pack of dogs to exhausted confusion as he ran in tight, overlapping circles that he eventually crossed to freedom. Only a stolen car that ran out of gas prevented him from eluding his pursuers.

He had written to his parents, who had received a certain unwanted notoriety because of his crimes and his subsequent escapes, that he was in control as long as he was outside running and could depend on his intuition and intelligence, but dead as long as his jailers controlled him and were able to regulate his movements. His parents understood his need for freedom but were unable to understand his taste for crime. They realized that Curtis' brothers and sisters weren't always perfect citizens, but they hadn't made a career of breaking the law and of breaking out of jail.

Each time the door opened, Curtis expected Janet to appear in the long hallway which led the newly arrived customers past the bar to the reservation desk. He hadn't seen Janet in eighteen months, but he had faithfully written to her every week for five years, whether he was in jail or on the run. And Janet had been consistent with her replies. Originally, she had answered a personal ad that Curtis had placed in the newspaper. He had asked for someone who cared about the fate of those less fortunate and who understood what it meant to be truly alone to write him. He preferred someone who lived in his part of the state. Three people responded. Janet was the most interested and the most sensitive to his predicament. Curtis imagined she was vulnerable as well. So he cultivated his friendship with her, thinking that it might prove to be worthwhile beyond the diversion it provided while he was behind bars. He suspected that Janet needed whatever she found in their correspondence. He had witnessed prison romances and observed women who somehow were convinced that their boyfriends were innocent victims and that love could change the hearts of parole boards. After a year of letters, Janet visited Curtis at the prison on several occasions. Their relationship had never been viewed outwardly as anything but platonic by either of them, but Curtis suspected that given the proper circumstances their friendship might grow into something more passionate.

After escaping twice from the facility which held him, Curtis was transferred. After this transfer, Janet had only seen him once. She still wrote the same caring, concerned letters that she had before, but her desire to visit him, at least in Curtis' mind, had lessened. Her explanations of distance and time had failed to convince him that something wasn't wrong. But Janet denied it. Now Curtis was hoping to spend a day or two with her before leaving the state. For a moment he had permitted himself to think Janet would come with him, and they would flee to California together. He stared across the river, finding comfort and an awkward peace in the idea, but knowing it was an idle daydream.

Curtis had often thought about her as he rested in his cell, about how she moved up and down the peaceful stacks of the library, about her love of literature, about the tedium of her profession as a cataloguer. Janet was single and had never married. At forty-one she was alone except for her cat, but she never admitted to being lonely. She said in one of her letters that her interest in Curtis stemmed from her convictions about injustice and the condition of the American penal system. As the months accumulated, Curtis decided otherwise. She was searching for something and Curtis suspected that maybe she had found it in him. Her cause was his rehabilitation and eventual freedom, not through deception and escape but by hard work and due process. Curtis knew that most people on the outside, including Janet, thought of life in prison as dehumanizing and something to be avoided. Curtis didn't necessarily disagree with that, although with his frequent flights outside the walls, prison had become more of a nuisance rather than a burden.

When he telephoned Janet, only three hours after his latest escape, she was startled.

"What do you mean, you're in Burlington?" she said.

"That's a fact."

"But how?"

"Better not to ask about it. Let's just say I've taken a leave of absence."

Janet didn't say anything. Curtis closed his eyes and saw her twisting a pencil in her fingers and looking beyond the glass enclosure where her desk was, despite the fact that he had never seen her office. She would be disappointed that he had escaped again.

"What about dinner tonight?" Curtis asked when he felt his freedom might prevent him from seeing her.

"What about the police? Isn't it dangerous?"

"No, I don't think so," Curtis said, thinking about but not mentioning Lt. Mullins, the trooper who was stationed at the Red Lion state police barracks and who would be in charge of the manhunt for Curtis in his section of the Pines. The beard would throw off Mullins only for a moment, Curtis thought as he rehearsed his possible flight across the deck and into the river. He had to be prepared for any possibility. Those few seconds of indecision on Mullins' part would be enough for him to stay out of jail for another day or maybe a week or even a month. Lt. Mullins was a doggedly persistent man who had recaptured him twice, once in the rows of blueberries near his parents' house and the other time in the trunk of a wrecked car in the Friendship junk yard. Curtis thought that both times Mullins was lucky. Mullins even admitted that luck had something to do with it. But so did Curtis' predictable nature. Mullins understood that Curtis was still playing the same games he had played when he was eighteen and in jail for the first time.

Finally Curtis said, "I mean life is a risk, right? Driving a car is risky, right?"

"That's true," Janet answered apprehensively. "Everything is, I guess."

"Then it's a date?"

"I—"

"Sweetwater. Around seven-thirty." Curtis returned the telephone to its cradle before Janet could say another word. He didn't mention the beard because he was curious to know if she would recognize him.

During his first jail sentence, Curtis and a friend had broken out of the county jail four or five times. They routinely bought two six-packs and went to a local bingo game; most of the churches and fire companies held them as fund raisers. After bingo, they drank what remained of their beer. By early morning the two returned to the jail, creeping along the stone rear wall of the yard where hangings had taken place a little more than fifty years before. Curtis had thought this nightly adventure would continue for the entire ninety days of his sentence, but an off-duty deputy spotted him one evening as Curtis leaned over his dozen bingo cards and tried to keep pace with the priest rhythmically calling the numbers as the balls emerged from the round wire cage.

His boyhood friend and cell mate had died in 1967 after stealing a boat much like the ones that Curtis watched bobbing beyond the glass windows of the restaurant. Curtis had spent the day flounder fishing with him after his friend met him with the boat in Waretown. His friend had said that the boat belonged to a relative. Curtis knew he was lying but didn't care. He had nothing to do on that Saturday and no reservations about his friend borrowing someone's boat to amuse them. They fished and drank beer until late in the afternoon and then his friend wanted to continue their drinking at a bar that was located on the bay near Mystic Island. After an hour boat ride, his friend steered the craft into a slip in front of the low-slung building. It was hot; the humidity folded around them like a damp blanket. The grass around the bar was littered with piles of marine scrap surrounded by purple and white petunias.

Without announcement, Curtis' friend stripped off his shirt and dove into the water of the empty slip beside them. When he floated to the surface, Curtis thought he was trying to get him into the water. When his friend's head didn't turn away from the water, Curtis was certain of the ploy. If Curtis entered the still, brown water, the other man would pull him in, wrestling with him until they were both drenched. But after a minute passed with only one arm twitching slightly as it rose and fell next to his friend's side, Curtis realized he was hurt.

He waded into the water, suspecting that there might be submerged pilings between those that were visible at high tide. A small weather-faded sign forbidding swimming was nailed upside down to a post next to the vacant slip. When Curtis reached his friend, he saw blood trickling from the top of his head. Curtis pulled him to shore and ran inside where an observant waitress had just finished placing a call to the emergency squad. His sometime cell mate didn't survive the ambulance ride to the hospital and Curtis, unable to convince the judge that he was unaware of his friend's boat theft and had no part in it, found himself in jail again.

His string of arrests and sentences had progressed from that point and turned into one rushing stream. His time on the outside shrank. Before Curtis realized it, he was classified as a career criminal, someone who would never be a contributing member of society, only a threat to it. But Curtis didn't care about the opinions of those who chose to keep him behind bars.

When Janet finally arrived, she was forty-five minutes late. Curtis had nearly convinced himself that she wasn't coming. He imagined his telephone call had frightened and even angered her; something Curtis hadn't wanted to do. As she glanced around the bar and restaurant, Curtis watched her, counting the seconds pass before she recognized him. She was taller than he remembered. When she had visited him in prison, she was always seated on the other side of a thick sheet of plexiglas when he entered the room. Now, when her eyes met his, he looked down at his drink. She had eliminated the four or five customers who sat at the bar and the older diners in the other room, but it had taken her almost a minute. His fake beard was about as effective as Curtis thought it would be.

"You're late. I almost thought you weren't coming," Curtis said as she sat beside him.

"I got lost," Janet replied. "I made a wrong turn or something. I was almost in Egg Harbor."

Curtis ordered her a drink. "It's really good to see you." His tattooed forearm fell next to her fidgeting hands.

"I was a little surprised when you called," Janet whispered. "I thought we had—I mean I didn't think you'd be able to escape from—"

"There isn't a jail built that's escape proof. I've told you that. Hell, fellows even made it out of Alcatraz. That place up there is filthy. I just had enough of it."

Janet didn't answer.

"You seem nervous," Curtis said, feeling that her anxiety was predictable. Visiting me in jail was easier and safer, he thought.

"No, I'm just tired and a little hungry."

Curtis knew something else was wrong. This wasn't the same woman who had written him letters filled with what he interpreted as affection or the same woman who had visited him in prison, carrying in a large bag whatever he had asked her to bring. He knew she must be disheartened by his escape, but there was something more than that bothering her.

"Your dress is pretty. It looks really nice on you," Curtis offered.

"Thanks."

"You're uneasy about meeting me. You can admit it. This ain't like seeing me in jail."

"Yeah, I suppose you're right."

"Why don't we get something to eat? Another drink and something to eat," Curtis added. "Maybe that'll relax you. Let's not talk

119

about jails and the rest of it. Let's just pretend we're here having dinner like everyone else and that the other stuff doesn't exist."

Once they were seated at their table with its center post wrapped in coiled rope, it seemed to Curtis that Janet was more at ease. They looked at the menu. Curtis suggested the snapper soup, something the restaurant was known for, but Janet wasn't interested.

"I never touch turtle soup in a restaurant myself," Curtis said, trying to say something that would accommodate her reluctance. "Not many people around who can make it as good as my daddy."

Darkness overtook the river as swallows and bats vied for insects. Lights flickered on along the dock behind the restaurant. The current stilled a little. A few boats found their slips after an afternoon of fishing. The benches that were placed at intervals along the slips were occupied by people who had eaten but weren't ready to go home.

"I thought we'd go down to Atlantic City after dinner," Curtis said when their salads arrived. "I haven't been there for—"

"Do you think that's wise?"

"I don't know why not. No one knows where I am."

"They're probably looking for you."

"Always," Curtis said as he smiled. "But then I'm fucking Houdini, right? An escape artist. And a dangerous outlaw, too, if you listen to certain folks."

Janet didn't reply, her silence palpable.

"That's what you said once, remember? The Houdini part. In one of your letters."

She nodded her head.

"Curtis Houdini. Maybe I'm a reincarnation. Maybe he's right inside here," he said, striking his chest firmly. "Who knows?"

"Anything's possible," Janet speculated. "But I wouldn't count on it. You're always getting caught. Houdini wouldn't approve."

Curtis frowned. He pushed away his half-eaten salad.

"But you have the escape part down. That much is true. Time and time again. No one would argue with that."

120

Janet slowly finished her salad, her eyes lowered. A waitress brought their main course and removed their used plates. Curtis ordered another drink as the woman rearranged their glasses.

"You never said anything about my beard."

"It's different."

"You didn't recognize me."

"No. But I haven't seen you for a while."

"Does it look natural? It must look pretty believable."

Janet looked at it closely, then said, "Not bad."

"Not bad?"

"It works—for a minute or so. Then I knew. In a way, it's exactly what I expected."

"That's what I thought. The minute or so part at least. That's all that's important."

As they ate, the band arrived, and after a few moments of shuffling equipment and tuning their instruments they began to play an old song from the 50s.

"You'll dance with me, won't you?" Curtis asked, his feet moving under the table.

Janet nodded as she chewed.

Curtis asked her about her job, her family, her health. Her answers were friendly but short, too short for Curtis, who had lost his appetite and run out of things to say that didn't relate to prison or his escape. After they finished eating and Janet refused dessert, Curtis thankfully led her to the crowded dance floor.

"You know I haven't done this in a couple of years," he said to her as he pulled her close to him. When he felt her back stiffen, he loosened his grip. His hand moved from her hip to her waist.

"Neither have I," Janet said as she looked at the other dancers.

Then they swirled slowly around the wood floor, nudging other couples. Curtis was delighted with Janet's ability to follow his rusty footwork. She had never impressed him as being a dancer.

"Where'd you learn how to move?" he asked, watching her eyes as they shifted from one side to the other.

"That's not important," Janet said. "What's important is what you're doing."

"What do you mean?" Curtis rested his cheek against her head. "I'm doing what I've always done, except now I'm doing it with you. Tonight, we'll go to A.C. and tomorrow I'll be back on the road. Maybe I'll see you again in a few weeks. You know I'll keep in touch."

"Where are you headed?"

"Florida," Curtis said, thinking that Janet didn't need to know everything. "But that could change. Maybe I'll go north," he added, keeping his cheek against her hair as he inhaled the scent of her perfume.

They walked back to their table when the song ended. Curtis would have stayed on the dance floor until the band had finished its set, but Janet wanted to sit. The waitress had left coffee on their table, and Curtis impatiently watched Janet add three packs of sugar to her cup before stirring the hot liquid.

"Okay, what's wrong? I mean really wrong. Not this nervous shit," Curtis finally blurted.

She looked away from her coffee and attempted to describe what she was feeling. "I really—"

"What? I mean you didn't have to come if you were scared but there's some—"

"That's not it. I'm not frightened."

"What then?"

Janet looked at him, examining his face as if she had never seen him before and would be asked to remember each detail. Then she closed her eyes and asked, "How did you get here?"

"In a car."

"Where did you get it?"

"Where do you think?" Curtis answered defensively.

"From a couple at a convenience store in Livingston?" Janet pronounced softly as she opened her eyes.

"Yeah. That's where I was. Where'd you hear that?" Curtis glanced around the restaurant. The table next to them was empty. The diners who still filled most of the room continued to eat. He really didn't want to discuss the details of his escape in the company of so many people.

"On the radio. On the way here. That's why I was late."

"How did that make you late?"

"Well, I was upset. I missed the turn like I said. For a minute I thought about going home and forgetting about you."

"What else did it say?"

Janet's eyes filled with tears, but none fell down her cheeks. She waited for them to disappear, blinking several times, and then she said, "A man was shot in that store, the store you robbed before stealing the car from those people. He was hit in his abdomen and he's in critical condition."

Curtis tried to think of something to say that would change what he thought Janet was feeling.

"Well?"

"It was an accident. The guy behind the counter pulled a pistol on me. I only had my finger in my jacket pocket. He thought it was a gun. When I saw the piece, I lunged at him. It was a reflex. When I hit him, the gun went off and he went down," Curtis said. "I couldn't help it. I didn't want to hurt anybody. I only wanted a few extra dollars. Betty could only scrounge up one fifty. I needed a little insurance."

"Damn it, Curtis. How long did you have left?"

"Three years, four months, before this escape."

"And the robbery and the shooting and the car theft and—"

"I get the picture," Curtis responded swiftly. "The last thing I need is you lecturing—"

"Can't you think of anyone but yourself? I mean other people have put a lot of time into—"

"Mr. Sim," a garbled voice said over the restaurant's PA system. "Telephone call for Mr. Sim."

Curtis looked around the dining room again, but he didn't notice anything unusual. One man raised his head quizzically then returned to his meal. Curtis stared at Janet who turned her eyes toward the river.

"What in the hell?" he said. "Maybe my trip is going to be shorter than I thought." He stood, still waiting for Janet to return his gaze. "You don't have anything to do with this, do you? No one but you knows I'm here."

Janet shook her head, but Curtis wasn't sure that she was denying his question or trying to understand what had happened earlier that day.

"Curtis Sim, old buddy," the voice said on the other end of the line when Curtis took the telephone call at the bar. "Long time, no see."

"Who's this?"

"Hell, I'm insulted. After all this time."

"Mullins?"

"Right. Now I feel better. For a minute, I was starting to think that it was over between us."

"What can I do for you?" Curtis said as he watched Janet leave their table and walk to the ladies room.

"Well, you can come outside and give yourself up. I've got twenty troopers with me out here. And they don't want any trouble."

"And if I don't?" Curtis said, buying as much time as possible so that he could decide on his next move.

"Then we'll wait. We let you finish your dinner. Now why don't you return the favor and let us all go back to the barracks. Those people in there don't need to get caught in the middle of your mess. Just come on out and we'll take you home."

"Did she have anything to do with this?"

"She?"

"Janet."

"Don't know the lady," Mullins said, but she's a good looker from what I could see. I guess you had big plans."

"Yeah, right."

"So Curtis, what's it going to be? Peaceful without anyone getting hurt or ugly with even more time."

"How's the clerk from the store?"

"Still alive the last I heard. But that could change."

Curtis left the phone on the counter, then slipped around the bar and into the ladies room. It was a small room with a sink, two stalls, and one high window.

"Janet," he said after pushing open one door and finding the stall empty. "Janet!"

"What?" she said from the other enclosure. "What are you doing in here?"

"That was Mullins on the phone. They're outside."

"Oh."

Curtis thought she was crying, but without seeing her he couldn't be sure. He turned the light off.

"What are you going to do?" she asked when the room went dark.

"I'm out of here." Curtis reached above him and opened the glazed window. He pulled himself up to the sill. "Just tell me one thing," he said before slipping through the opening. He could see her faint outline below him, still sitting on the toilet.

"What?"

"Was it you?"

Before Janet could answer, Curtis dropped to the damp ground next to the building. He didn't want to hear her answer because it might ruin what little faith he had left. An air conditioner hummed nearby. He could see the police cars along the drive and in the sandy parking lot behind the restaurant. His car was impossible to reach. The troopers were fanning out along the perimeter of the property.

Within ten seconds he had crept along the foundation and onto the dock. The boats were bobbing again in the swelling tide, their polished trim glistening in the weak glow of the walkway lights. He tried to move from shadow to shadow, certain that the electric lights from the restaurant and deck didn't provide enough light for Mullins to see him. Just before he dove into the water, he looked over his shoulder.

"Sim!" a voice shouted. "Sim!" the voice, which he now realized belonged to Mullins, said a second time.

Then Curtis laughed, making sure that Mullins heard him, making sure all of the troopers knew that they were dealing with Curtis Sim.

Without pause, gunfire exploded from the the periphery of the dock; bullets zipped through boat covers and windows and the sheds that stood near one end of the structure. People who still sat in the benches dropped to the ground to find cover. And as metal lashed the sweet, humid air, Curtis was in the cedar water, still wondering if Janet had led Mullins and his troopers to Sweetwater.

As he kicked deeper, Curtis imagined he had waited to hear Janet's reply and she had said no and she wanted to come with him. Then he wished that he had met Janet at another time and in a different life, far from prison and the Pines. Maybe I am Houdini, he thought as he heard the pop and fizzle of bullets underwater. If so, I'll come back and take Janet away and make her forget who I am. And then he realized, as he found the river's strong channel, that he would never see Janet again.

The Art of Dying

H aven't had snapper soup," he paused, gazing at the outline of her shoulders, noticing the gentle shift of her muscles as she swung the ladle from the battered soup pot to a white bowl beside it, "since I drowned him in the cedar swamp."

She leaned the spoon against the inside wall of the pot and lifted the bowl from the cluttered counter.

"What Jack?" A strand of brown hair was caught in the corner of her mouth. "I'm sorry." She had been coaxing the cat at her feet to move, nudging it with her foot. She hadn't heard him enter the kitchen and sit at the table behind her.

"I can't eat that," he said, shaking his head, as she placed the bowl in front of him. "I can't."

"Why?"

"Because of him."

She wiped her hands on the yellow cloth apron that hung from her neck and said, "What are you talking about? Are you feeling all right?" She stood over him, catching his glance for a second.

He looked away from her eyes. They seemed so blue and impartial in the fluorescent light. Second-guessing her had always been impossible. He never could be certain what she was thinking by looking into her eyes even though he had known her since childhood. Instead he tried to distinguish the outlines of the green scrub pines that stood in the black yard beyond the kitchen door.

"I never told you because I didn't know what you would think. Hell, you don't even like me killing bugs in the house," he said clumsily, running his fingers through his fine hair. He hesitated. "You cared about him." For a moment he thought that he could find a more eloquent way of explaining it, but now knew he couldn't. He wanted desperately for her to be receptive. "I left Pap back there, Marge." Then he realized it, as if he hadn't thought about it a thousand times. He looked away from the kitchen door. It wasn't her acceptance he wanted, but her approval. His eyes followed her as she dropped into the chair. She appeared to be testing its strength, its ability to support her.

"But you told me he disappeared, that you went to his house to take him to the hospital and he was gone." She repeated the exact words that he had spoken to her and everyone else over six months ago.

He felt an unpleasant surge of blood rush up his neck to his thin face. His temples began to ache.

"I thought he'd be dead by the time I got to his place, but he wasn't. I don't know why I thought that. Maybe I wanted him to be dead. I know I wanted his misery to end. I just couldn't take him to the county hospital. He was past that." Jack waited for a response but her face was blank, unyielding. "I left him in the cripple and he drowned."

Jack had claimed that his grandfather vanished. The young man even helped the rescue squad organize a search party. But his grandfather was never found. Someone in the old man's condition could have easily become disoriented in the dense stands of pines and hardwoods or the soft bottoms of the cedar swamps that surrounded his house. Everyone accepted what appeared to be the dreadful conclusion.

A few seconds passed. Dripping water beat a steady but short-lived rhythm in the sink. She reached for the bowl in front of him and stood, not thinking about what she was doing, only running the single word through her mind. Drowned. Drowned! Her eyes fell to the grooved linoleum floor as she turned toward the stove. Drowned! She stopped, her back rigid. The dead man rose before her. Jack's voice continued in the background—starting, hesitating—as he tried to decipher her reaction to his confession. But she didn't hear.

"And I don't want to be wedged into some goddamned four-by-eight piece of cemetery dirt surrounded by a lot of people that I couldn't stand when they was alive." Pap stopped and moved his fingers along the chest buttons of his dirty khaki shirt. "They were so damned petty when the blood was pumpin' through them, just think how irritatin' they'll be after a dozen or so years in the ground. You know I just want to rot in peace, that's all, Marge." He was still for a minute. "And I understand that," he finally said. "Yes, sir."

"Understand what?"

The coffee wasn't hot yet but I could smell it. He liked a little chicory in it.

"That—whatever you call it." He pointed outside in the direction of the back field. "Those cedar logs fixed in the sand—that sculpture—Number Eighteen. Isn't that what you named it?"

"Yes." I handed him a tin coffee cup. "Number Eighteen."

Pap's fingers were stained and burned from smoking his cigarettes until he couldn't hold them. The olive blanket slipped from his bony shoulders and fell onto the cot. Since the cancer came he couldn't get warm at night so he pulled his cot closer and closer to the wood stove. It wasn't far. There were only two rooms and an outhouse. I thought that he looked like a bad photograph of someone that day. He hardly resembled his old self. He rose cautiously and walked to the door, his unlaced boots sliding on the bare plank floor. He bent over once from the pain.

"Jesus kill me," he mumbled to himself, then pushed open the door and faced the neat, bushy rows of blueberries and Number Eighteen. "All those years. All that money and the work you did at that college. I didn't know nothin' except what those bitches made at church meetings—them tiny square pot holders and those damned plaster cats painted yellow with big orange eyes."

I could see Number Eighteen over his shoulder—the light brown logs standing aslant, lifting above the green, orderly rows of blueberries, set against the pines and blackjacks, and only washed evening sky behind the top few convergent feet. I had asked him two summers before if I could use the wood that was stacked behind his place to build something, although I think I used the word create. I don't think Pap was impressed with the idea, but he said that he had no objections. Jack was his namesake, his favorite grandchild, and I knew that's why he said yes.

"It means everything in a way. Isn't that it?" He looked at me with a dying effervescence on his face.

He would be gone in three short weeks.

"But if you ain't lookin' at it right it don't mean nothin'."

I nodded.

"Took one hell of a long time to figure it. Practically my whole life, I guess. And that there is only one part of the picture. I was sittin' out back day before yesterday and it hit me. Sent a shudder through me and all of a sudden I knew, knew what you've been sayin', Marge, to Jack and your parents and my daughter and even her husband when he was still livin' and anybody else who'd give you a minute to spare." A trace of a smile touched his mouth. "Now I suppose you're doin' the same over at that high school, tryin' to tell them kids about all this and how important it is." He coughed, mucus thick in his throat. "It's beyond words nearly. The difference," he looked through the doorway again, "between that and some boat model made of popsicle sticks is that Number Eighteen will git inside you, do somethin' to your spirit, make you squirm a little and maybe even make you think about life and death and what in the hell we're doin' here, and where we're goin', too."

I nodded again, but he didn't notice.

"Yes, sir. You jest can't say, man that's nice. Maybe it took me a lifetime, but you know, Marge, I've never been the schooled type. I've been workin' these woods here since I was a boy. I never had the time for much else. But it's better now than never, I'd say." He was quiet for a minute as his chest rattled. "You got to take some time and study it. Try 'n feel it like when you're trackin' a buck and you know that he'll be able to smell you in a flash. You got to think ahead of him, see where that buck's gonna go." He coughed again, wincing from the pain. "It's like a beautiful day, a summer mornin', I think. The world's alive. You step outside and smell the air, look at the sky. You hear the birds. Then you git this feelin' inside. And you can hardly explain it because it comes and goes so fast. But somethin' is happenin' inside you—way down deep inside. And if you grab it, you're part of that mornin' too, jest not someone lookin' at it. All of a sudden you're bigger than you, if that makes any sense." He lifted his arm, searching for support. "Surprised?"

"No, Pap. I'm not surprised." I reached for his hand. "You're right," I said quietly.

He was tired. I helped him back to his cot, and I put the coffee cup on the table next to him. I watched him lean back exhausted from the talk and movement. He stared at the ceiling, a phantom drifting away from me. Then I covered him with the blanket. His eyes were closed before I left the house. It was getting dark, and I could hear the peepers as I drove along the sand road between the head-high blueberries. When the truck hit the tar, everything dissolved into the cool, nighttime swish of spring air.

"It's the turtles, Marge." Jack had waited patiently for her to say something, anything. "They're probably from the bog that's fed by the cripple when it rains. That's where Wescoat gets them."

The bowl slipped from her hand and shattered on the floor, throwing soup across the kitchen.

"Hell," she said as she automatically fell to her knees and began to wipe the liquid with her apron, gingerly piling the pieces of the white bowl to one side. The cat rushed eagerly to her.

He knew that she didn't want to hear any more, but he continued to justify the drowning by explaining why he couldn't eat the soup.

"They eat red meat. The big ones—the alligators—even pull ducks down." He listened to the insects hurling themselves against the screen door then bouncing away repeatedly as if they could only sense the bright light in the room and not the physical barrier that prevented them from reaching it. He saw that he would have to tell her, that merely recalling the final act wouldn't be enough. Slowly his mouth started to move, forming the fragile sounds that would hopefully convince her that he had done the right thing, that his grandfather had wanted it that way.

"I stopped the pickup where the road dipped and curved to the left. For almost two hundred yards before that I could see the cedars up above the other trees. The day was over but the air hadn't cooled much. It was probably the first real warm day that spring. The sand was almost hot. Every few minutes I looked through the rear window at him on the thin mattress that I pulled from his cot. With the gate closed no one could see him. I had carried him in my arms from the house. I don't imagine that he weighed more than eighty pounds by then. Ma said to take him to the hospital, but she wouldn't come with me. She couldn't stand seeing him that way. He was delirious, lost in what Aunt Dell used to call the shadowland—not here but not delivered—struggling with his worn hands, trying to grab hold of anything that would anchor him here and keep him away from the emptiness. He opened his eyes just as I put him down on the truck bed and he looked right at me. For a second I thought he was coming round even though his eyes were still filmy and yellow. He opened his mouth. His false teeth were out and his gums were dry and shriveled. He groaned hoarsely as he tried to say something. I moved my ear closer to his lips. 'Dead,' he said without a breath. 'Dead.'

"It got darker when the truck entered the swamp. The road firmed up and mixed with some gravel. The trees were tight in against us, growing a foot or two apart for half a mile. Water sat in pockets surrounded by mounds of peat and ferns. The bugs were bunched in clusters here and there. I could hear the cripple running hard, and them damn frogs were banging like mad back in there. He shrieked once behind me. I glanced back at him, the outline of his skull showing blue-grey under his skin, and knew that I couldn't take him to the hospital, couldn't let them hook him up to some goddamned machine and fill him with drugs that he refused to take in the first place, just for a couple of more days of lifeless breathing.

"I turned the engine off and got out. By the time I reached his feet, the gnats and early skeeters had already started to light on him. I lifted him and stepped off the road into the swamp, threading my way between the tall cedars toward the sound of the water. Pap was quiet then. No more moaning, almost as if he knew that it would be over soon. The ground was soft and my feet sank beneath the water. I looked up once. A white moth floated down out of the branches, but it was a splinter of light that caught my attention. It creased the top. The branches were so dense and tangled up above me that it looked like a gigantic dome or something, all hollow and still. But that bit of light made it through the tangle and hung there, just above us.

"Then I reached the cripple. It had swelled to about twenty feet across from the rain. I stepped in. It was only knee deep. I cradled him against me and wondered why he hadn't been taken without the pain and suffering. I stepped farther into the water. It was cool and the color of light molasses. When it was waist deep I stopped, knowing that it wouldn't get any higher. The water wet his backside and feet. I wanted to get it over with. I looked down at him and started to sing for some reason, the same hymn that Grandma used to sing to us when we were little. My voice got clogged and I started to cry. I raised my pitch, letting the notes rise out of my stomach. I went through it once, then again, the tears still coming. Right at the end I lowered him until he was free of my arms. He seemed to stay up over the water for a second then he spun once, ending with his face down. He butted against a stump and disappeared. I waited there for five or ten minutes, thinking that he might come up but he didn't. Then I walked out to the pickup, drove home, and reported him missing." Jack exhaled, letting the air escape resolutely through his nostrils.

"What have you told your mom?" she said with a low voice as she carried the pieces of the soup bowl toward the counter.

"Just what I told you before. Nothing more."

"She has no idea?" Marge extended her arms, her hands still clutching pieces of the broken bowl. "Christ, Jack. He was her father."

"I know that." He paused, lowering his eyes for a second. "I'm not sure that it makes a difference now. Not that she wouldn't care."

"You did?"

"Of course."

"But you—" She grimaced, her arms falling to her sides. "God."

They faced each other, not speaking now. A long time passed, and it was punctuated by nothing except the incessant ping of the insects on the screen. Marge dropped the jagged pieces of the soup bowl on the counter then returned to the table. She mirrored her husband's anxious gaze, thinking, for an instant, that she understood. But she still heard the same interminable word over and over.

Life at the End of the World

"Imagine," Loftis says as he reaches the draped corner of his office. "Imagine—imagine that she wants you." He touches the plant there; its fronds are brittle from the furnace's heat and they rattle against the loosely gathered cloth behind them.

The other man closes his eyes.

"You can imagine that?"

"Yes. Yes, I can."

"But you can't have her, not yet." Loftis leaves the corner, and with his slipperlike loafers pads to another part of the room: the wall where his still aviary allows dozens of fragile glass eyes to stare down at them.

"Why?"

"Because she's married, because she might not be well, because you're not sure."

"But I do want her."

"Not yet."

The man rearranges his thin legs. His forearm rests lightly on his lap. He feels tired and wants to fall asleep, but he knows Loftis won't permit it.

"Can you see her?"

"Yes."

"And she's beautiful, isn't she? She's young, lovely."

"Yes."

"And thinking about her, about her mouth and breasts and how her legs would wrap around you, makes you ache."

"Yes. I want her. I've already told you that."

"But you can't have her."

"No. That's what you've—"

"And she's intelligent, isn't she? You know she won't bore you. When you tire of one position or fantasy or conversation, she'll be waiting with another. You can see that. But maybe she's too intelligent."

"What do you mean?"

"Because she knows you want her, knows what kind of man you are, knows what you've done in the past."

"But I haven't told her much. Not about my life, at least."

"But she knows. You don't have to spell out every detail. She has an extra sense—call it intuition or whatever—but she knows. She even thinks she could make you love her, despite everyone and everything."

"How could she make me do that?"

"Remember, she sees your weaknesses. She's like you to an extent. You're—what's the word? Pegged. You're so easy for her. And don't forget that she wants you as well." Loftis turns and looks at the other man whose face tightens. He pauses, then sits near him.

"That's good," the man says. "I like that."

"Yes," Loftis agrees. "It's mutual. Sort of a level field."

"And I can—"

"No." Loftis' voice is resolute and doesn't betray his sympathy. "Now imagine that you not only want her, but you love her. Imagine that your desire hasn't been satisfied—you haven't slept with her—but suddenly you find yourself loving her, just as she's planned."

"She's still married."

"So?"

"What about my wife?"

"She's dead. She dies suddenly, just as you find yourself in love with this woman."

"And my children?" the man whispers, his eyelids flinching.

"Nothing has happened to them. They're still around. But they need a mother, just like you need this woman."

"Will they love her?"

"Yes, they will, in time. She knows how to make children love her, too. She understands so many things. She even knows how to please you before she has."

"I believe that."

"But not yet."

"Why?"

"Because of her husband. You see in this delicate situation, she still has feelings for him, even though you're in the picture now."

"But she wants me."

"Yes. She finds you handsome. Sexually, you appeal to her. And she's tired of her husband, tired of going to business functions and playing the well-behaved wife, tired of her husband's politics. She has an artist's soul and this soul is being slowly crushed by him. They don't really have much in common, except his money, and the fact is that she has made him love her, too."

"So before she met me, she loved her husband more," the man says.

"Before she met her husband, she made others love her as well," Loftis answers.

"But she doesn't love him as much, not now."

Loftis' eyes drift from the man to his cluttered mahogany desk where a brass censer allows a thin line of smoke to coil above it and form a waferlike cloud near the top shelf of his bookcase. "Imagine that she finds herself still loving him, but in a different way. He's been good to her; he's helped her. When he met her, she was in trouble with another man. Actually, at that moment, she was very ill and he took care of her. He loved her, just as she wanted. But she didn't want to fall in love with him, although she finally did. She let her guard down."

137

"Like with me?"

"No, she hasn't said that she loves you. We only know that she desires you."

"But what about her husband? You said that she loves him, but in a different way."

"She loves him like a brother. Yes, imagine that her affections for him have changed, that now she loves him, but it's without heat, without passion. She'd do anything for him, but when he touches her body, nothing happens. When he's fucking her, she feels nothing, thinks nothing, except this is wrong. She is convinced that something is terribly wrong."

"Now she wants me."

"She always has, even from the first time she saw you. But now you seem to be larger, more important to her. It's as if you've become her salvation, her only link to her senses. She finds herself thinking about you—incessantly. When her husband is on top of her, she thinks of you. When her lips touch his body, it's you she's touching."

"And now I can—"

"No, you can't."

"Why?"

"Because there's a problem." Loftis clears his throat, hesitating as he finds his next thought. He notices a scratch on one of his gold cuff links and tries to rub it away with his thumb. "There's one very significant problem. Let's just say if she lets you have her, she's afraid she'll never be able to go back to him. He might find out, one way or another. And then she'd lose everything."

"Their money?"

"His money."

"But I have some money," the man reasons.

"Not enough, not enough to keep her happy, or to keep her in your bed forever."

"But she'll love me. I'll work harder, earn more."

"Maybe."

"What about love?"

"Do you mean fairy-tale love or the kind of love we find in life?"

The man is quiet. His mouth is dry, but then his mouth is always dry when he visits Loftis. He drinks from a glass of water then returns it to the table beside him. He contemplates the woman leaving him before he even has her. When he senses Loftis' impatience, he shakes his head.

"So, you admit that she might not stay with you. That's good. Recall that she made you love her. She knows men and what they want and what they'll do to get it. And, it seems, she can will this blind pursuit into being with hardly any effort—a particular smile or laugh, the way she looks at someone, the manner in which she crosses and uncrosses her legs."

"You're right."

"She controls you, doesn't she?"

"I'm not sure."

"Making a man love her suggests that she has some power."

"True. But controls me?"

"That's part of the reason why you're here, right? It's part of what we're dealing with. You're obsessed with her."

"All right. She has some control over me." The fingers of the man's left hand stretch outward for a moment; then he clenches them into a fist. "Let's get on with it."

"Now." Loftis' voice drops several notes. "Imagine that you call her one night. Tonight. Tomorrow night. It doesn't really matter. You don't have to worry. Remember your wife is dead. And you know her husband is working late, making money for her to spend."

"Fine."

"Well, what do you say when she answers the phone?"

The man opens his eyes and stares at the ceiling. A fan hangs above him. He recalls the motor's low, hypnotic hum from earlier sessions. Suddenly, he doesn't want to listen anymore. He wants to leave. After all, visiting Loftis wasn't his idea in the first place. He had never heard of him a few months before. His shoulders stiffen as if he will stand; then they fall back.

"Focus!" Loftis demands.

The man's eyes close for a second time despite his intention.

"Tell me whatever comes to your mind. Just let it out."

"I say that it's me."

"Don't you mention your name?"

"She knows it's me by the sound of my voice. We haven't talked on the phone much, but she knows. I want to think that she was waiting for me to call."

"And?"

"I tell her not to talk. I've prepared a little speech, but I don't say that. I tell her what I think—how I want her, or how I love her. I might say that I want to fuck her."

"Do you say fuck or make love?"

"Both. I mean, I'm thinking one but saying the other."

"Is she surprised?"

"No. Actually she laughs."

"Why? When you ask her, what does she say?"

"Something about her husband, that she's married, that she wants children. Then, I don't know what to say. I thought she wanted me. I feel like an ass. I'm sitting alone on my bed. My kids are asleep. The night light in my son's bedroom is shining like a damn full moon across the hall."

"But what are you thinking? I mean what is your inner self saying?"

"Inside I'm saying get rid of him."

"Her husband?"

"Hell yes," the man swears. "I don't give a shit what he does as long as he's gone. I want him to leave, to find another woman, to go away so that—"

"So you can have her."

"Yes."

"Do you tell her this?"

"No. I apologize. I'm confused. I'm not sure that she still wants me. I'm not sure about anything. All of a sudden, I wish I had never called."

"But you do ask her. You need to know what she has in store for you. You've already admitted that she has this power over you."

"All right. Yes. Finally, I ask her what she wants from me." The man stops, unsure of her reply.

"And she says, in the most innocent voice, 'Just you,'" Loftis offers, then rises. His hands clasp behind his back. He feels the pull of his vest on his white shirt and silk tie. "She still wants you. But she doesn't tell you when or where, only that she does."

"I ask her to meet me."

"But she's worried about her husband finding out."

"Yes."

"So you say that you'll see her tomorrow or the next day and hang up?"

"Well, I can't. My hand is in—I want to hear her voice for a few more minutes."

"No!" Loftis orders. "You hang up."

"Okay. I hang up and I look around my bedroom for a minute. I think about what she said and then I get into bed."

"And what about your hand?"

"It's still there."

"So you fantasize that she's next to you?"

"Yes."

"And after you're finished, what happens?"

"I fall asleep without finishing. I can't do it without her."

"Like now?"

"Yes. Christ—"

"All right. And then you dream, dream about her and how you need her. You are desperate. You don't understand it. You don't think you'll ever understand. There are other women who would come willingly to you, attractive women who would fuck you and demand nothing."

"That's true."

"But no one else will do."

"No."

"When you begin to dream where do you find yourself?"

141

"In a building, an enormous building."

"Is it day or night?"

"Night."

"What type of building is it?"

"Office. A lot of hallways and cubicles. A few larger rooms with conference tables. Computer terminals. Paintings on the walls that I can't see. Green, leafy things in the corners. More hallways and doors and desks. I'm lost, or that's what I'm feeling."

"Are there any lights on?"

"No, it's dark. But I do see one patch of light, one small sliver close to the end of a hall. It's coming from beneath a door, an office door."

"Can you hear anything?"

"No."

"But you walk toward the door."

"Yes. I don't know why but I get closer and closer to it as if I'm floating. And the hallway seems to be getting smaller. I have to lower my head so I don't bang it."

"It's a dream."

"But I'm weightless. I need to see who's in the room. I look at my feet and they're not moving, but I am. For a second, I try to stop. And then, when I reach the door, the light goes out."

"Do you go in?"

"Yes."

"Without speaking?"

"Yes."

"Are you carrying anything?"

"As soon as I go for the doorknob, I realize I'm holding a knife—a knife from my kitchen. And then I'm standing inside the room."

"Just like that?"

"I don't remember walking inside. It's dark and there's no one there, no one I can see. I don't know where he's gone."

"Her husband."

"No."

"It's his office building. He works there."

"I don't know that. I've never been there."

"Trust me," Loftis suggests. "It's his office."

"If you say so."

"Go on. You're inside—"

"Then I look around this room, her husband's office, but I can't see anything. I almost turn on the light but I pull back from the switch because I feel something damp, wet really."

"What?"

"At first, I'm not sure. But for some reason, I touch my face and there's blood on it. Then I realize that it's all over my hand, too. I'm bleeding."

"Do you panic?"

"Not at first. But after a few seconds, I start to sweat; my heart begins to feel like lead. Then I go spastic. I run down a hallway, but I'm having trouble seeing because now there's blood in my eyes. I want to find a telephone. I want to get out of the building. But I can't. I can't find anything. I'm bleeding to death, I say to myself. I'm going to die. I can't believe what's happening. I'm actually dying."

"Then you wake. You open your eyes and you're safe."

"Yes, just as I'm ready to collapse, I sit up. I'm sweating, drenched."

"You're afraid."

"Yes."

"Of what?"

"Of what I might do."

"You'll do anything, at least in your dreams. But you're not dreaming now."

"Right. That was a dream and this isn't."

Loftis glances at his pocket watch, tapping its beveled crystal with a fingernail. He raises his head, and his mouth puckers for a second before saying, "Now, imagine her husband is gone. He's vanished. You don't have to murder him. He's disappeared. It's as if he never was. And she has his money. There's no paycheck, but the other assets are still there. There's been no divorce. But once he's declared dead, there will be more money

143

from insurance settlements. Eventually his pension will kick in. She will be rich."

"And I get her."

"Oh yes. You finally have her. She's in your bed every night. And she is incredible, truly what you've built her up to be. She's always willing, always ready to spread her legs for you—insatiable. She tells you that you are the best lover ever. You believe everything she says. And you fuck each other unconscious every night."

"I want to marry her," the man concludes.

"I know."

"I want to make her mine."

"When you tell her that, do you use the word mine?"

"Yes, I do. Then she confesses that that is what she wants, too."

"And she confesses that she loves you, that she'll never love another man, that the two of you are destined to be together, forever. And after her husband is officially history, you marry her."

"Yes, that's what happens."

"And you begin your life together."

"And my sons?"

"They end up loving her like you do," Loftis says. "They're still young, so they forget their real mother to a degree. After all, she's been dead for a while, and your new wife is their mommy now. You've even forgotten your other wife, haven't you?"

"Yes."

"Even her name?"

"Yes."

"And she's made it so easy."

"Yes. I never think about the other one. Never."

"So a few years pass. Your life together is wonderful. And she is still beautiful, still desirous, still anxious to please you. She gets pregnant and brings another child, a girl, into your family. Since the husband was declared dead, you have plenty of money. Everything is perfect."

"Yes. I'm with her. Nothing can change that now."

"Wait!" Loftis presses the toes of his feet into the Bohkara on the floor and glares at the unaware man. "Not so fast."

"But we've made it. We're happy. We're together."

"I know."

"We're in love."

"But wait a minute. Hold on now. Imagine that five years pass. You're what people call settled now, like you were with your other wife. Imagine that you meet a woman at work or at a dinner party or in the grocery store. Wherever. When you meet this woman, she makes you remember something. It's something that you can't put your finger on, maybe something you've forgotten. Your life has been filled with happiness. You are so content. Your wife is still lovely. Your children are healthy and smart. The neighbors marvel over your family. What a lucky man, they say to each other. A few envy you. A few want your wife for their own."

"I don't like—"

"But this woman. Let's talk about this woman. There's something about her. She's so different, unusual, and you feel like you've been with her before. You find yourself being seduced by her despite your efforts to resist. And then suddenly, you're numb. Your everyday routine crumbles under this numbness until you feel like you're sleepwalking through the events of your life, the events you previously enjoyed so much. At night, in bed, your cherished wife still makes love to you. She tells you to do whatever you want to her. Your pleasure seems to be her only concern. But you imagine that this other woman wants you, too, that she has to have you, and that she's what you've been looking for, or what you've been missing—without consciously knowing it, of course. You simply never realized it. That's the amazing part. You thought you were happy and now you're positive that this new woman will bring you everything you've been missing. But you can't have her, not yet."

"But what about my wife?"

"She dies suddenly, just when you figure out what the other woman wants. Your wife gets cancer. No, she's killed by a truck as she crosses the street. It's tragic, but she's gone. Dead."

"But—"

The telephone buzzes.

"Think about this other woman," Loftis says as he excuses himself.

The man can't hear what Loftis is saying into the receiver. He is still pondering why he can't stay with his new wife, why this other woman has appeared, and why he wants her. Apparently, there is no escaping her because he is mesmerized by her.

When Loftis returns to the man's side, he says, "What have you decided?"

"About the woman?"

"Which woman?"

"Not the new one. I'm still wondering about the one I wanted, then married. We were so happy together, so—"

"Yes," Loftis says without emotion. "You were happy. But she's dead, remember?"

"But why?" the man counters.

"You think about that and we'll continue on Thursday." Loftis walks back to his desk and scribbles a note to himself under the man's name.

"Okay, I guess we're out of time," the man says as he stands and passes the aviary with its silent wings. "Next week with the new woman."

"Yes. And the dead ones as well," Loftis replies as he follows the man to the door.

When he leaves the building, the man tries to recall where he has left his wife's car. He walks along the curb dotted with buttonwoods. He thinks about the women, especially about the new one and how she has managed to replace his perfect wife. As he gazes along the roofs of the parked cars, a cool gust floods the space around him. Particles of sand rise from the gutter and sing as they strike metal. Futilely, he raises his hand and lowers his shoulder, trying to protect his face, trying to protect himself.

After Summer Passes

Everyone in the township knew that Judge Pope's courtroom antics bordered on the theatrical and that his unpredictable outbursts usually were designed to attract attention, both inside the courtroom and on the street—attention typically thought of in legal circles as unwanted and even damaging. The bench was never used by the judge to camouflage his most personal opinions, even when those opinions were bound to create controversy and calls by his detractors for his resignation. Many were convinced that his frequently outrageous pronouncements were carefully designed to bring him publicity. According to his opponents, this craving for attention was caused by emotional problems stemming from the judge's youth which was spent as a foster child, the offcast son of a reluctant father and an uncaring mother. But this was nothing more than speculation.

Because of his aggressive behavior that could turn from unyielding firmness to acidity in the courtroom, threats against his life were commonplace. To defend against an assault he kept loaded guns in his office, in his car, and in several rooms of his home, despite the objections of his second wife whose six-year-old daughter from a previous marriage lived with them. After lis-

147

tening to his wife's complaints he always promised to buy trigger locks for his weapons or to hide the ammunition, but he never did, knowing that a trigger lock or hard-to-reach ammo would prevent an immediate reaction if faced with an armed intruder. With a quick response he might save himself and his wife and even his six-year-old stepdaughter. Without it, someone might get hurt.

The judge's own children, Ben and Liddy, were older and had been raised around firearms. Each had been trained by the judge. They knew the value of a loaded pistol and how any one of their father's harsh decisions might bring an angry felon or a disgruntled family member into the house. But their knowledge of this possibility never resulted in any deviation from their normal activities because they were confident and ready to protect themselves, just as their father wanted them to be.

When another startling opinion or sentence was issued in his court, most people acknowledged the fact with a shake of their heads and went on with their everyday business. When the judge took away a paralyzed man's motorized wheelchair for improperly crossing a township street, a few shouted discrimination and insensitivity to the plight of the disadvantaged. When he sentenced a young man, who was still in high school but had turned eighteen just before his fall into crime, to 412 hours of community service in an orphanage for smashing pumpkins during the week before Halloween—one hour for each pumpkin according to the young man's personal tally—his parents objected. But Pope countered with an additional fifty hours just to make his point, and then he fined the parents for their belligerent remarks made in his court. When three men, who in a drunken spree had ransacked a small country church and destroyed its organ were brought before him, Judge Pope responded by standing on his bench and shouting obscenities at the bewildered men, ranting vehemently about the sanctity of holy places and about spirituality and eternal damnation. Then he sent them to jail for four years.

Everyone knew that the judge cared less about the condition of the church and more about the destruction of the organ, an instrument that he had played with devotion since childhood. He had even donated organs to churches in need, creating for himself what he imagined was an unbreakable link to God. Pope's love for the instrument consumed his free time as he played his repertoire of show tunes from the fifties and sixties. If the judge had an audience—dinner guests or visitors staying at his home, or even an appreciative maid—he would perform for hours, building up to his salsa version of "I'm Gonna Wash That Man Right Outta My Hair," complete with marimbas and maracas.

"That," Judge Pope always whispered after the last note faded from his Lesley speakers, "was my dear departed wife's favorite." And then without prompting he would burst into a spirited encore, his slippered feet frantically working the foot pedals, his substantial bald head rolling from shoulder to shoulder.

There wasn't a person in the township or the county who would admit that Judge Pope fit any previously imagined stereotype. He was a homegrown original and although his antics did cause embarrassment, the majority of the residents and administrators of the township were unswayed by outside attempts to force a change or by internal disagreements about the judge's competence. His supporters, who were always outspoken, stated, after a show of hands in his favor, that the judge would have his position for however long he wanted it and that the township was lucky to have such a tough-minded individual to protect the interests of the township's residents. After all, his proponents usually concluded, the township was a safer place with Judge Pope to protect them.

So when the judge embarked on what was a thinly disguised personal vendetta against Victor Wisdom and his family, no one objected. Wisdom lived on a piece of ground, about thirty-nine acres according to Wisdom's estimate, closer to forty-nine according to the assessor, that bordered the judge's property for a few hundred feet. Long before the judge had built his sprawling home for his new bride, a house that bore a faint resemblance to Graceland, complete with wrought iron gates decorated with black eighth notes, Wisdom had settled on what was left of an old dairy farm. Once Wisdom's rancher was built—the old farmhouse had passed the point of resurrection—the man started to buy army surplus whenever he could afford it. His family's living expenses were always deducted from his small salary as a self-employed auto mechanic before he considered new purchases. But with what little money he had, Wisdom had managed to accumulate lines of rusting jeeps, fuselages of airplanes, an old locomotive engine, and whatever else caught his eye.

In addition to his fascination with surplus, Wisdom bought other discarded items, everything from wrecked cars to cast-iron kitchen sinks to boxes of soiled books and newspapers. By the time Judge Pope became Wisdom's neighbor, the junk man had gathered twenty years of relics, as he referred to them, on his property. Wisdom even claimed to possess a Gutenberg Bible, a prize according to him that was found hidden inside a World War II tank, which he had purchased in the early sixties. He said that it was illegal booty, and perhaps an unknown printing, even before it was liberated by a tank crew who had never returned to America or who had lost track of their weapon once home.

Within a few months of moving into his new home, Judge Pope had incited his neighbors, all owners of new estate homes bordering Wisdom's property, and as a group they approached the township authorities about what they felt were numerous violations by Wisdom of zoning ordinances and environmental laws.

"We're going to practice a little neighbor control," Judge Pope said to his wife, Sandra, one evening after Ben and Liddy had left the room. "Wisdom's pigsty has a negative effect on our property values. Plus he's breaking the law. Let him clean it up or get the hell out."

Sandra, finding her husband's tactics questionable and her neighbors' ire suspect, replied, "But we can't see his place really, with the trees and all. No one can."

"However, it does border our properties. If someone came to look at a house on this road, he would ask about Wisdom's place and what would the owner say? 'We can't see it, so we ignore it.'"

"Ben isn't going to like it, Dicky," Sandra reflected as she stood. "Not one bit. He's going to think that it has to do with Maggie, that this is a different way of dealing with her."

"He isn't going to find out, not yet anyway," the judge said as he switched on his organ.

Notices were sent to Wisdom by the township, the state, and the EPA. After opening the first round of letters, Wisdom threw the rest away, dropping them in a trash can he kept near the kitchen door.

"What a country," he complained to his wife. "A man buys land, builds a house, raises a family, has a little business, and the government is at the door. I've never asked those bastards over at town hall for nothing. Never." He shook his fist. "Just let me catch one of them snooping around and I'll—"

"Victor," his wife said. "I don't know why you're so upset. These zoning requirements and the rest are the laws. They're not going to change them for you. They let us go this long. Why don't we do what they ask? Straighten the place up. Build a fence. Don't fight them because you can't win."

"Never," her husband responded. "I'll go back to Europe. I'll disown America. I'll tell them to go screw—"

His wife left the room before Wisdom could finish, knowing that he wouldn't return to Europe and secretly hoping that he would get rid of most of the junk that had accumulated on their defunct farm for the past twenty years. His initial attraction to surplus and junk was easy for her to accept. With so much land there was space away from the house to deposit it and his obsession remained out of sight. Now they were surrounded by it and she found herself stepping over fenders and batteries and piles of discarded newspapers just to get from the front door of their house to her car.

"You'd think I'd get a little more respect around this township," Wisdom shouted from the other room. "I pay my taxes. I speak seven languages. Back home that meant something. Hell, I can put together an engine blindfolded. I can build a house."

After the letters, came a summons to appear in court, Judge Pope's court. No one seemed to remember who had first raised questions about Wisdom's property and no one in the township appeared to be willing to suggest to Pope that he find another, more impartial official, to hear Wisdom's side of the story.

"You know I've got a Gutenberg Bible," Wisdom announced in Pope's courtroom after being convicted of zoning violations and fined. "That makes me worth one hell of a lot. I'm good for whatever fines you can come up with."

"Three hundred dollars or thirty days," Pope repeated, using the same tone with which he told Wisdom that he could no longer continue to collect junk on his property and that he needed a license to do business there and that the EPA would act against him if he failed to properly dispose of any hazardous chemicals found on the property.

"I don't have it off hand." Wisdom said. "Three hundred in cash," he repeated to himself. "But I'll get it."

"Forty-eight hours," Pope said. "You might sell that Bible of yours," Pope added sarcastically. "Would bring a pretty penny. And don't forget. Ninety days from today, your property must be free of refuse, free of wrecks, and free of surplus materials, or completely fenced. If you opt for the fence, you'll still have to cease the acquisition of surplus materials and remove the articles in question within a reasonable amount of time. And dispose of any hazardous materials. And obtain a zoning variance and a license to do business of any kind on your property."

"But your honor—"

"Next case," Pope declared, lifting his gavel.

When the judge returned to his chambers, he whistled a song from *Oklahoma* under his breath. Wisdom would be gone within a year, he predicted. The fence would be far too expensive. And Pope was certain that Wisdom would decide to sell out and move farther back into the Pines where the junk man would hope to be left alone. Pope recognized that for Wisdom there was a principle at stake. It was brought on by Wisdom's frontier mentality, a mentality that was over a century too late. The judge even thought about buying Wisdom's property and dividing it into large lots for more estate homes. Pope would control enough building credits to make thousands of dollars on the property and in turn be able to protect his rear property line.

All of this might not only result in Wisdom's departure and a profit for Pope, but in the separation of his son and Wisdom's daughter, Maggie. That relationship, according to the judge, wasn't going to continue beyond high school and had already progressed too far. When Ben went away to Duke to major in pre-law in the fall, Maggie Wisdom, who was a year younger than Ben, would become part of his past. If Pope had his way, Maggie Wisdom and the rest of her family would become part of the township's and the county's past as well.

The day after Wisdom unexpectedly paid his fine, Judge Pope started receiving threatening notes, some crudely printed and others formed by cutout letters from the newspaper. Each note contained the same message: I'm Going To Get You! Pope had received dozens of threats in the past and knew that threats were part of his job. But no one had ever been as persistent as his new but as yet unknown nemesis. In response the judge cleaned and checked all of his weapons, readying himself and his family for any scenario. Pope suspected that Wisdom was behind the threats, but he couldn't prove it, not yet.

"Our best protection," he told his wife one night as they got into bed, "is this." He pointed to the loaded 9mm on his night stand. "It won't take much to eliminate the bastard if he makes a move. Maybe that's how we'll get rid of him. Bam. Right between his eyes."

Sandra looked nervously at the pistol, then her husband. "Just don't shoot at anything you can't see. It might be Debbie or me walking around here in the dark. Sometimes, I have to pee at night and so does she."

"Don't worry," Pope assured his wife as he pulled the sheet to his chin. "I've been through this before."

When Ben heard about his father's attempt, along with their aroused neighbors, to have Victor Wisdom put out of business and have his fields cleared, he was angry. He knew that his father usually got what he wanted, even if others had to suffer. And if his father thought he wouldn't succeed then he would devise another plan, more aggressive than the first and usually more costly in terms of whom it would affect.

"What in the hell is going on?" Ben asked during Sunday dinner after hearing about his father's vendetta from Maggie that morning.

"I don't know what you're talking about," his father responded as he cut his steak into bite-sized pieces.

"Mr. Wisdom is what I'm talking about. Maggie told—"

"Oh, here we go," Liddy said, rolling her eyes. "Maggie this and Maggie that."

Ben looked at his sister then back to his father and said, "Well?"

"Can't we talk about this after dinner," Sandra offered. "When everyone has eaten. After we digest our food."

"No, we can't!"

"Ben, you'll watch your tone when speaking to your stepmother."

"Oh, Maggie," Liddy continued. "What will we do? How will we live without—"

"Shove it, Liddy," Ben exclaimed. "That butcher boy of yours over at the Food and Save is no hot catch, is he? What's his name? Artie? Dad doesn't know about him, does he? That he's married? That he's thirty years old. That he's—"

"Ben Pope!" Liddy shouted as she stood. She threw her napkin on her plate. "That's none of your goddamned business." She was shaking and grabbed the back of her chair with one hand. Her head moved from her father to Ben to Sandra like a marionette whose strings were being jerked.

"Liddy!" Judge Pope said. "We'll have none of—"

"Artie, cut me a nice piece of rump roast and make it tender," Ben chimed, his voice a fifth higher than usual. "And what about the sausage? I like mine—"

"Fuck you, Ben Pope," Liddy said as she fled the room. Her fork fell to the tile floor. Debbie slid from her chair and picked it up.

"Liddy!" her father called, but Liddy was already charging upstairs to her bedroom. "I'll deal with her later," he said to anyone who wanted to listen.

"Mommy, Liddy dropped her fork." Debbie placed it next to her stepsister's plate. Sandra patted her daughter's forearm and forced a smile. "There," Debbie added as she returned to her chair and her food.

"Now Ben. You were saying," his father asked as he continued to measure and cut his steak.

"Why are you trying to hurt Mr. Wisdom? I don't—"

"Nobody is trying to hurt him, son. He's the one who is sending me the threats. Week after week. And he's guilty of numerous violations. I'm, I mean, we're just trying to do what's right."

"Bullshit."

"His place is an eyesore."

"But it was like that before these houses were here. Christ, he's been out here forever."

"That was fine as long as no one had to deal with it. But things change and we're here. He has to comply with zoning regulations, with—"

"It's Maggie, isn't it? That old Jersey Klan shit. Just like your old man and his old man."

"No. Maggie," Judge Pope lifted a small cube of steak to his mouth, "isn't worth the trouble. But you are. That's what I've been trying to tell you. Maggie is a Piney, son—white trash, of questionable stock. And trash is only good for—"

"Go to hell!" Ben yelled. He stood, scraping the legs of his chair on the floor, and left the room.

"You could have been a little less blunt about her," Sandra said once Ben was out of earshot. "He does care about her even if you don't."

Judge Pope continued to eat his steak. When he saw that his wife was waiting for a response, he looked at his plate and thought about the new sheet music waiting for him in the next room.

"The best defense, is no defense, I suppose," Sandra said when she realized that her husband no longer wanted to discuss Ben or the Wisdoms.

After another minute of silent chewing, Judge Pope asked, "What was Ben saying about Liddy and what's his name?"

"Artie. You know I'm the last one around here to know about what Liddy is up to."

Once Pope finished his steak and ate a piece of peach pie with a scoop of vanilla ice cream, he went into the living room and sat at his instrument. He ran his finger along the keyboard. He looked at the floor next to his organ. "Where's the Lemon Pledge?" he called to his wife who was in the kitchen loading the dishwasher.

"I'll bring it in a minute. I forgot to put it back," Sandra answered. She looked under the sink. "Debbie honey take this to Daddy for me," she said, holding the can where her daughter could reach it.

In the heat of late July, as Judge Pope counted the days left in his original decision about Wisdom's property and the threatening notes which he had received since Wisdom's day in court, an auction sign appeared near the drive that led to Wisdom's house and junkyard.

"Did you see it?" Pope gleefully asked Sandra over his car phone. "Big and white with red and black letters. Beautiful, simply beautiful."

"What?"

"The auction sign over at Wisdom's place."

"No, I haven't."

"Has Ben said anything about it?"

"Not a word."

"Try to sound him out for me. I want to know what he knows before I talk with him."

"All right," Sandra said without commitment. She didn't want to get in the middle of her husband's disagreement with his son.

"Maybe this is the beginning of the end," Pope speculated before he hung up.

"Maybe," Sandra replied, not as concerned with Wisdom's auction as she was with the ever present threats against her husband and his insistence that he would meet force with force if necessary. "I hope you're right," she added, believing that Wisdom was sending the notes to her husband, but sending the notes without planning to act on their repetitive message. Sandra thought Wisdom only wanted to harass her husband, a reaction to what the man saw as an earlier injustice.

"Do you know anything about the auction," Sandra asked Ben later that day, trying not to pry or to sound threatening. "I heard there's a sign over at the Wisdom place."

"I don't want to discuss it," Ben replied, making what would be his only comment concerning the auction and the events to follow, events which would reverberate outside his relationship with Maggie.

After the auction was held, a for-sale sign appeared on the Wisdom property. When Judge Pope saw it, he was euphoric. He called the real estate company and placed a bid on the property, a bid that was technically issued by one of his paper companies. Within two days, the agent called Pope to tell him that his company's offer had been accepted.

"Where are they going?" Pope questioned the agent, trying to appear as concerned as possible. "They've been residents of the township for decades."

"Didn't say," the agent said. "He's not an easy man to talk to, if you know what I mean."

"Really," the judge responded, permitting a hint of surprise into his voice. "I know he likes his privacy. He's a different sort."

"The only problem is that he wants to close as soon as possible. He said he wants to be out by the end of August."

"That's no problem. The sooner the better. I'll call my bank and arrange it."

Pope tried to hide his happiness around his son, not wanting to alienate him before he went off to college. The judge's early speculation had become reality and he couldn't believe his good fortune. Not only had he succeeded in getting rid of the Wisdoms, but he would make money on Wisdom's property. With any luck, his actions would force an end to Ben's relationship with Maggie Wisdom as well.

But with his fortune came misfortune. The threatening notes continued to plague him. The last few had drops of blood smeared on them. He had a lab run a test on the red blotches to determine if human blood had been used, but the test came back negative. A chicken was the most likely source of the fluid, the report read. This made sense to Pope because the Wisdoms kept chickens on their property.

Along with the bloodied notes, Judge Pope began to hear things during the night. He had always been a sound sleeper, but the noises which had started with creaking doors and what he thought were grunts, had made him restless. The judge had left the bed with his pistol clutched in his hand on more than one occasion, thinking that he would encounter Wisdom lurking in the halls of his home, but he was unable to find anyone.

"I can smell him," the judge said one evening when he returned to bed. "I can smell the son of a bitch."

Sandra pretended she was still asleep. She held her breath every time her husband left the room and she had told her daughter not to leave her bed during the night without calling her first.

"The next time, I'll get him," the judge swore as he returned the 9mm to his night stand and removed his slippers. In his sleep, he dreamed a new plan.

For the remainder of the week Judge Pope left his bed at midnight and waited for his adversary in a first-floor closet. Each night he stayed in the cramped space until dawn, trying not to fall asleep, which he succeeded in doing only half the time. Then, just as he was about to abandon his routine, thinking that Wisdom had decided any intrusion into what the judge liked to consider an armed camp was too risky, someone appeared.

Pope had fallen asleep around one o'clock. Liddy was still out, but by the time the judge woke, she was upstairs. The closet where he sat was directly beneath her bedroom. He could hear her tossing in bed. Ben hadn't left the house that evening. Hopefully, Pope imagined, Maggie Wisdom and his son had reached the logical conclusion to their relationship.

When he woke it was 2:30. Sipping from a squeeze bottle of cold coffee and trying to regain his alertness, Pope listened. For a moment he heard movement in the upstairs hallway, which he thought was someone using the bathroom. But rather than ending in the bathroom, the motion continued down the steps. The judge placed his ear against the closet door, straining to hear who it was, thinking that Ben or Liddy was going to the kitchen for a late-night snack. But there was something wrong. The footsteps were heavy and shuffling, not the noise of bare feet or slippers. The judge opened the door slightly, turning his head so one of his eyes could see through the small opening. In the shadows of the first floor, he saw a form, larger than Ben or anyone in the house, a form that he was suddenly convinced belonged to Victor Wisdom.

He leaped from the closet just as the shadow reached the kitchen. "Stop Wisdom!" Pope shouted. "Stop or I'll shoot!"

The person reacted to his challenge by ducking around a counter.

Pope rushed into the kitchen with his pistol steadied before him. As he reached for the light switch, a bottle of wine came flying toward him. When the judge lowered his head to avoid it, the intruder scrambled for the kitchen door. Pope fired once, knocking the man to the floor.

"Jesus Christ!" a voice winced. "You fucking shot me."

Pope switched on the light. The man was holding his leg and crying.

"I can't believe you—"

"Who are you?" Pope demanded, startled that Wisdom wasn't on the floor before him. He still held his pistol on the prone man.

"Artie Sellers, that's—"

Before the wounded man could finish, the rest of the family appeared in the kitchen.

"Are you all right?" Sandra said to her husband as she wrapped her robe around her. When she saw the wounded man writhing on the floor, she wasn't sure if her question should have been directed toward him rather than her husband.

"Yeah. Did you call the police?"

"Yes. They're on their way."

When Liddy reached the kitchen, she tearfully dropped to Artie's side.

"The fucker shot me," Artie exclaimed. "Your old man put a bullet in me."

Liddy looked at her father. "You're crazy," she said angrily. "Couldn't you see it was Artie?"

"We've never met," Judge Pope replied. He watched Artie's blood trickle from his leg to the tile. It formed a round red pool which contrasted with the white floor. "You'd better rig a tourniquet so he doesn't bleed to death."

Pope left the kitchen for the living room, where he would wait for the police. Ben watched his father as he passed him in the hallway. He wasn't surprised that Artie had been shot and was sprawled on the kitchen floor. He knew that Liddy had been entertaining the man in the house for weeks. Ben didn't like it, but felt that Liddy would eventually realize that it was foolish and dangerous. Ben's only surprise, as he glanced at Artie, was that his father hadn't killed him.

After the shooting and after the judge's explanation of it, his opponents in the township and around the county once again began to question the judge's competence. But it was determined that Artie had been an immediate threat to the judge's safety and had failed to identify himself. No charges were filed against Pope by the state or by Artie, and after a week the issue had resolved itself in the same way other controversies involving Pope had: it disappeared. He was impervious. A few people still reminded others about his misdeeds and his behavior, but the judge still remained on the bench and still persisted in voicing his opinions and finding ways to impose unusually harsh sentences on the unfortunates who stood before him.

And the threats continued to arrive each week and even with the police investigating the matter, Victor Wisdom was never any more than a suspect. Without any violence directed toward the judge, the police concluded that the notes were a prank. Until Ben was ready to leave for college, the content of the notes never changed.

During breakfast one August morning, just days before Ben was scheduled to depart for Duke, Judge Pope scanned the newspaper as he sipped his coffee. Buried at the bottom of page 17 was a short article that caught his attention. Sotheby's had sold a Gutenberg Bible for an undisclosed amount of money, which was rumored to have broken a previously established record. The book had been owned by Mr. Victor Wisdom, but the new owner, a businessman from Japan, was unidentified.

"Unbelievable," Pope said, rereading the article, thinking that his eyes had deceived him.

Ben entered the kitchen just as his father finished the piece for a second time.

"Did you know about the Gutenberg?"

"Yeah," Ben said as he peered into the refrigerator. "I heard."

"How much did he get?"

"Don't know," Ben said, carrying the orange juice to the counter.

"He hasn't talked about it?"

"They're too busy packing, I guess. Since you closed on his place."

"Where's he going?"

"Don't know," Ben said. He left the room with a glass of orange juice in one hand and a doughnut in the other.

Pope returned to the paper, realizing that Ben knew everything but wasn't prepared to tell him at this point. Maybe after he gets over Maggie and the rest of it, Pope thought as he turned to the comics, hoping that college would have a lasting effect on Ben's sense of loyalty. Maybe then he'll realize who his friends are, Pope concluded.

The evening before Ben left for the university, Judge Pope received his last note from his unknown enemy. As he left the municipal complex for home, he found it tucked under one of his windshield wipers. It read: I Got You! Pope placed it on the seat next to him, and as he drove home, he glanced at it when he could. He had no idea why the message had been changed. As far as he was concerned, his summer had been sweet with success. Before he entered his house, he dismissed the last note as being the work of a confused mind.

"I had an interesting conversation with Fiona Wisdom this afternoon," Sandra said when he entered the kitchen. "I ran into her in the supermarket."

"Oh," Pope responded, thinking that Fiona Wisdom might answer a few of his questions if he cornered her. He sat at the table and looked through the mail that Sandra had left there.

"She thanked me, and you actually, for buying their place. She said that she was ready for a change."

"Did she mention the Gutenberg?"

"No. But she did say that her husband was retiring, so they must have made quite a bit on it along with their land and the auction."

"Well as I said before, good riddance."

"She also said she was sorry about Ben's decision. She said she knew that you must be upset."

Judge Pope looked at his wife for the first time since she had started talking.

"She said that he's changed his major to comparative literature."

162

"What?" Pope dropped the circular that he was holding.

"Did you know anything about that?"

Pope jumped to his feet. "Ben! Ben!" he yelled, entering the hallway.

"He's over at the Wisdoms' place. He's helping them finish up. They're leaving tomorrow."

Pope returned to the kitchen, stunned that his son had not asked him about changing his major. "Comparative literature?"

"That's what she said."

"What in the hell is he going to do with a degree in comparative literature? Shit. Teach?"

Sandra poured her husband a glass of iced tea and placed it in front of him, trying to anticipate how he would react to what she had to tell him.

"I'll handle this when he comes in. He'll be pre-law." Pope lifted the side of the cold glass to his perspiring forehead. "Did she say where they're going?"

"South."

"Where, Cumberland County? Salem County?"

"No, not in Jersey."

"Where then?"

"North Carolina. Chatham County, I think she said. Yes, Chatham County, North Carolina."

"You're not serious."

"That's what she told me. They bought a place on a lake. She said that Ben could spend his weekends there. Maggie might even go to Duke next year."

Pope didn't wait for more. He sprang from the kitchen into the living room. He grabbed a pistol that he always kept in the hollow organ bench. But when he tried to load a round into the chamber, he discovered that the pistol was empty. He raced upstairs, searching for his 9mm, which he found in the master bathroom. But when he checked the magazine, it was empty, too.

He leaned against the wall, and he tried to think of another scheme that would save his son from Maggie and the rest of the Wisdoms and comparative literature, but the only thought that

163

came to him was that the note, which still rested on the front seat of his car, and all the notes before it weren't the work of Victor Wisdom or of another unseen perpetrator. They were the work of his son.

Love's Labor

Without broaching the subject, or even acknowledging that anything out of the ordinary was being considered, each agreed to the seduction of the other. They crafted this silent pact, ignoring always-heard warnings about the pitfalls and duplicity of such arrangements because forethought didn't occur in any recognizable form until they had moved toward a place that would only allow recollection and afterthought.

"I don't want to see you hurt," Natalie said to Karen one afternoon over lunch, sometime before it occurred. "I don't like what he's doing to you."

Once Karen had floated in the cedar water of the Oswego, her black hair streaming away from her head in loose, chaotic curls, her chalky limbs stretching toward unseen boundaries. She passed through a warm, shallow spot where the August sun had turned the water tepid, or was that her response? She remembered her body arching receptively, her breasts finding comfort in the warmth of the copper-colored water where the sun had penetrated it and had reached the sandy bottom. She wanted to stay there and thought about kicking, but as she opened her eyes she was startled by the sky that was spread above her like another pool, inverted and bottomless. Her desire to stop vanished and the turgid current carried her weightless form to another spot, another temperature, other thoughts.

"Frank doesn't really love you," her friend continued. "From what you've said, he takes the entire relationship for granted. Always has. Typical jock. He'd rather play with the boys."

A young, attractive woman just out of college, she had married Frank sixteen years before, preparing to become a teacher, thinking with an idealist's heart that her new life with the man she had dated from late in their freshman year would somehow satisfy most of her notions about what married life should offer. As their college years had unfolded, the only significant flaw in Frank that Karen detected was his lack of interest in anything other than the latest sports statistics. On occasion his blasé attitude about world events, events that Karen cared about, spilled over into their life, not affecting their faith in the relationship and pending marriage, but sometimes deadening the current which love had created between them. Like many men of his age, sports played a significant and at times messianic role in Frank's day-to-day life. His enthusiasm for the game, which changed from season to season, and the team, which also changed, never waned. But this single fact hadn't been a deterrent for either of them.

Their marriage marked the beginning of a short period of closeness which, when Karen glanced back at her life and examined it for the one sign that would indicate the shift to the permanent ambivalence in their relationship, occurred just before their second anniversary. With hindsight she saw the approaching malaise clearly: his continued obsession with sports, his frequent visits to the local bar, his participation in a softball league, a pool league, a basketball league, the occasional bet that exceeded rational limits, his adolescent attempts at serious conversation. During those years, none of these interests had led her to believe that, somewhere deep inside his growing but still muscular frame, Frank didn't care about her, didn't still love her and, in his own way, cherish the idea of their life together.

But then, after four years of marriage, they began discussing children. Karen had returned to graduate school and had finished her master's. Frank had been promoted, rising to the head of a small department in the accounting firm where he worked. With his new position came a higher salary and longer days. The few hours every week that they had shared disappeared. Work, watching games on TV, playing softball or pool or basketball, and hanging out with his teammates at their favorite bar occupied all of his time. When the subject of children was first mentioned by her over dinner, he said little as she tried to analyze how she felt. After she had the baby, Karen patiently reasoned, she wanted to stay home with the infant.

"Could we afford to do that?" she asked sincerely.

"I'm late," Frank mumbled as he stood, inhaling one last mouthful of food and finishing his high-protein drink. "Batting practice."

"But—"

"We'll talk later," he said as he backed out of the kitchen and into the hallway, leaving his chair in its customary position far from the table and his plate where Karen had placed it.

As she cleared the counter of dishes, he returned with his uniform on. She didn't look at his lightly freckled face as he kissed her on the cheek.

"I won't be too late," he said, grinning with the same youthful charm that had attracted her to him in college. "Shouldn't be anyway," he added as he passed though the back door. She heard the car start and then there was quiet, punctuated only by the measured intervals of a battery-driven clock hanging above the refrigerator.

At that point, Karen decided that she would wait for her husband to readdress the issue. She wouldn't prompt him. After all, she thought, he said that they would talk. He had to realize how important this was to her. Two months passed, then three. But despite her earlier approach, he never said a word relating to children. She knew he was busy, that his new position had brought with it new pressures. When her patience reached its weakest point, she mentioned having a baby again.

"Maybe in a few years," Frank said. "Things are too crazy now. I wouldn't have any time for it. Every damn thing that goes wrong at work falls on me. I mean—"

"How many?"

"Two or three. I don't know." Frank touched her hand and she was astonished by its lack of warmth. "You're young yet. Do you really want to throw away all those years in college? I mean think about all those classes and papers. What about your grad work and the community college?"

So the years passed. Karen had come to regard his dismissal of having a child with mixed feelings. Her husband's schedule, although far from the ideal that she had envisioned early in their relationship, gave her the freedom to do with her spare time what she wished. If she wanted to go to an auction or a lecture or to go shopping, she didn't need to make special arrangements or to worry about Frank feeling abandoned or even about whether he was available and willing to accompany her. He never was. And they had money in the bank, which she could spend whenever the inclination hit her. With a child, constraints would be placed on her. She began to see Frank's lack of interest in their relationship and his daily activities as a signal that he wouldn't be a good father. He might not be willing to change, she rationalized, predicting that having a child could drive them apart rather than bring them together. And his refusal, she imagined, was probably a reflection of his disinterested nature, something she had known about for years and had halfheartedly accepted. But now the word disinterested had taken on a broader meaning.

Then, when she least expected it, Frank began discussing the possibility of her having a baby, and it was she who was uncertain. Karen had survived into her mid-thirties without becoming a mother. Motherhood was overrated, she had started to think, always remembering her sister's various problems with her children. Being an aunt and not a mother had its advantages. She had access to her niece and nephew, but when she was finished and exhausted, she could return the kids to their parents. Her job, her freedom, her relationship with her husband, their money—all weighed on her. She decided they could afford to wait another year or two. She still had time and she wanted to be absolutely certain that they were doing the right thing.

After that—Frank had sensed her lukewarm response to his suggestion—the subject was mentioned from time to time, but for some reason, one of them found an excuse to postpone any action, until finally they reached the conclusion that they wouldn't have children and that other things could take the place of a family. And for a while they were comfortable with this agreement. Then, on the eve of her thirty-eighth birthday, they argued about what she had thought was their mutual decision. But her husband, for some reason, had changed his mind.

"Frank said it was my fault," Karen told Natalie. "Can you believe it?"

"I can believe anything. My first husband was the same way. For seven years he said nothing but me, me, me. Nothing worth repeating at least."

"It's partly my fault, I suppose."

"No, it isn't, Karen."

"Well, I did put him off."

"Only because of him, because of his needs, not yours. You wanted a baby for years but didn't push it because of him." Natalie stirred her spritzer with a swizzle stick and Karen noticed how the bubbles clung to the inside of the glass. "What are you going to do?"

"It's too late. I don't want to risk it now. God, I'll be forty soon."

Natalie reacted to her friend's comment with silence.

"I know," Karen reasoned after she didn't respond. "Women are having babies into their forties without complications."

"True."

"But I'm pretty sure that that's not for me. I'd be in a wheel-chair by the time I had grandchildren."

"Have you thought about adoption?"

"Frank doesn't like the idea. He thinks people will say there's something wrong with him." She shook her head as she continued to look at Natalie's glass. "Can you believe it? He's worried that his buddies will think he's sterile or something."

A year had evaporated since their supposed decision had been made, a year that Frank evidently had spent reconsidering his resolution to remain childless. Whenever a stray comment was made by a family member or friend about his lack of children, Frank would either not respond or lay the blame on Karen's side of the bed. This was part of his solution, Karen had thought at the time, his way of dealing with the fact and denying his role in leading them to where they were. Frank liked to add that he traveled light, especially if the questions came from teammates or drinking partners. This casual remark only hurt Karen, although she understood that Frank and his buddies often said things to each other that weren't mirrored in action or grounded in any kind of truth. In her mind it was part of some type of macho jargon that, once uttered, rated a superior ranking in the hierarchy of the club. Not once in her presence, to the best of her memory, did Frank commit himself to a serious explanation concerning the reasons behind their childless marriage, but Karen wasn't surprised.

Not that Karen could be considered truthful, in the strictest sense, when it came to what she imagined some people thought. She had failed at what many considered an elemental task. Marriages, like well-tended gardens, were supposed to bear fruit. She knew there were whispers and looks of pity and resignation cast her way across summertime picnic tables and during holiday gatherings. Without realizing it, she had started to search for other women who had made the same choice. She listened to their reasons, nodding her head in agreement. From what Karen heard, she developed a rehearsed response: a fragment, an anecdote, a horror story—some of it inherited or altered, some of it not. Whenever necessary she used her set speech, as she tried to downplay the self-created significance of her childless state. Not having a child as an heir wasn't an important factor, she would always conclude. She had no desire to foist her genes on another. She frequently referred to other childless friends, who actually were little more than acquaintances, implying that the decision was being made on a daily basis and that if more people had the courage to do the same, the world would only benefit. But in the minds of many of her family, which included women who had produced three, four, and even five children, this comment was a kind of religious and genetic heresy that could only be met with bewilderment.

"Leave him, Karen. You've put up with his shit for too long," Natalie pronounced, as she stood. She read the check without looking up and said, "Maybe you won't have children; maybe you don't want to have children. But maybe you can find somebody who would have wanted you to have a baby if you had met ten years ago. Who knows? There are plenty of divorced men with young children and Frank, well, he's a jackass. You know he doesn't really want a baby. He only wants to use all this to control you."

Karen bit her lip. The air blowing from the vent was cold and seemed to be directed at their table. She wanted to avoid the draft, wanted to step away and move around the room until she found a warmer place, a pool where the current ran soft and warm. She closed her eyes, picturing her weightless body in molasseslike water, her limbs still stretching, now well beyond their capacity, until they touched an unknown shore.

"Don't listen to me," Natalie concluded, waving the spotted check in the air. "It's the wine. You know me and wine. A few glasses and I say things." Natalie moved away from the table and Karen left the tip, digging through her cluttered, overly stuffed bag, as she searched for and then found loose change. "But I'd drop the bastard," Natalie confessed over her shoulder, "double time."

Elliot passed Karen several times a week—going to the post office or the grocery store or the pharmacy. She always smiled. Sometimes he said hello. At other times he was preoccupied. His work wasn't selling, at least not selling enough to make a comfortable living for him. He had hoped after a show in New York and two in Philadelphia, and the sales which followed, that his income would continue to grow, but it hadn't. Despite his earlier success, his income quickly fell. Moving to the small town where Karen and Frank also lived was part of his strategy to keep his expenses down and his intensity high. And he had succeeded in doing both. But without a few more sales a year, his plan would need revising.

Elliot's ex-wife, a woman who hadn't been willing to wait for his success, had been trying to locate him, contacting their former friends, sending postcards that never reached him. He was convinced that she needed money and had heard about his shows. She probably assumed that she was entitled to half of the money he made from any work he completed during their disastrous relationship, even though she had spent an hour a day telling him to give up and accept the fact that he would never make a living as a painter. Real estate is the way to go, she had always said. Big money in real estate. You can paint on the side. It can be your hobby, something you can do full-time again when you retire.

Elliot had picked the small town because he thought he could escape her there. He wasn't from the Pines but a friend had suggested it would be a good place to get away from whatever problems plagued him. And it was the perfect place to avoid a woman who didn't like to leave the city. Even if his former wife found him, he didn't have any money to give her, but Elliot suspected that she wouldn't believe him and that she would drag her lawyer into it, which would only add to his dislike of her. At least they hadn't had children, he always reminded himself. That had been their only blessing.

Within his dwindling success, Elliot was forced to consider other means of income for survival and to even reconsider, if only for a brief, blurry moment, what his wife had said about his future. He gave up his apartment and moved into his studio just off Main Street, an arrangement that suited him but proba- bly wouldn't please the owner. After a few months of living sur- rounded by his work and the debris of his creative activities, Elliot realized that he needed more money even though he had sacrificed his small apartment. Although he had an MFA, Elliot had avoided teaching because he thought it would be a sacri- fice, not only of time but of talent. He wasn't sure that he want- ed to toil over another's work when he had so much of his own to worry about. But those ideas were for the perfect world, he concluded as he opened his electric bill and was shocked by the amount of power his studio had consumed in one cold month.

In January a part-time job at the local community college miraculously appeared and with some reservation, Elliot started teaching. The first time he saw Karen at the college, he didn't say anything. Looking back on the occurrence, he was sure that he hadn't recognized her. It wasn't until the next afternoon in the post office that he stopped as he passed her for the hun- dredth time.

"Didn't I see you at the college yesterday? My name's Elliot."

"I know," Karen said, extending her hand and speaking her name.

He didn't know why it sounded so unusual when she pro- nounced it, but the ordinary name sounded lyrical when she said it. He liked that, although he didn't give it any considera- tion beyond his first impression. Those beleaguered thoughts wouldn't come until Karen became more familiar to him.

"How are you making out?" she asked.

"Okay. I'm only part-time."

"I know."

"I paint—that is, when I'm not teaching. I'm a painter." Elliot felt that he had to emphasize the point now that he would be in the classroom. He didn't want to lose that part of his identi- ty, even on a part-time basis.

When Karen walked away from him, she said that she would stop by his office to see how he was doing. She thought it was professional courtesy and in the past she had said it to many of her colleagues, especially if they were new to the college.

"Or my studio," Elliot added, pointing across the street to the building where he worked and felt more comfortable. But he wasn't certain she had heard him.

To Karen, the word painter carried with it hints of the exotic—Gauguin working under the South Pacific skies, Matisse in North Africa, O'Keefe in the sun-racked desert. Perfumed would be a way she might describe the word if she had to. Her trips, sometimes with Natalie, sometimes alone, but never with Frank, to art museums in Philadelphia and New York were spiritual flights to isolated islands where she could luxuriate in what she saw as meaningful and leave behind the daily dose of statistics which bombarded her.

As an undergraduate she had considered the possibility of becoming a writer rather than a teacher. She had heard the saying, 'Those who can create, do; those who can't, teach.' She had never believed it, not completely, but as soon as she had met Frank, her dreams of living an artistic life as a writer faded, until there was nothing left, only an idle memory or two of compliments paid to her by former professors and an unexplainable taste of almonds that appeared immediately after she thought about her one-time aspirations.

So Karen taught composition and literature to students who had little interest or patience. She had hoped to infect them with the same love for the written word that she possessed, but this rarely happened. In the classroom, she tried to deliver what she thought were the most inspiring lectures, but she finally conceded that she wasn't any competition for all the forces behind video games and action movies and the vast sports industry. Her students had been lulled into a bizarre biotech world where they acted as receivers. They took in monumental amounts of quasi-information but had no way of processing it unless, it appeared to her, the information had to do with a new product.

For them the act of receiving and reacting had taken the place of analyzing and understanding. Often Karen's mind drifted as her voice provided the required lecture, drifted above and through little eddies and lenient golden streams, drifted over water-bent reeds, waiting for a bright, dedicated student, waiting for Frank to change, waiting for a wind that would blow her to another place.

On subsequent meetings, both at the college and in town, Elliot began to notice isolated things about Karen which he initially dismissed as observations that an artist would normally make during the course of any particular day. One morning she wore a silk scarf covered with a Florentine pattern, which was tied loosely around her neck and shoulders. Nothing unusual about that, he thought after seeing her and returning to his office. But the colors of the scarf and the delicate line of her neck combined with her thick black hair as it cascaded from every angle and lay in the most innocent way on the silk and her willowy shoulders were overwhelming. Another day, this time in town where two-hundred-year-old buildings were sheltered by enormous buttonwoods, Elliot saw Karen leave her parked car and found himself rushing to greet her before she could escape his attention. When she turned from the street to face him his name passed her lips. Nothing more. He remembered how she had said her name when he first met her. She had an odd way of turning the second syllable and making the name sound so musical, as if an instrument had created it. When his eyes found her slightly parted lips, faintly red with lipstick, and the white edges of her teeth, he knew it wasn't the sound of his name but the mouth that spoke it which was so enticing.

And then one day as he stood in her office doorway, she sat in a chair next to her desk which was normally reserved for students. She draped one of her legs over the arm, the material of her slacks rising slightly, her foot dangling above the dull carpet while her other foot remained firmly on the floor. Her hand fell to her elevated knee as she talked about something that had happened the day before. With this ordinary act, Elliot found himself startled by her leg's motion and the hand that rubbed the raised knee. He tried to concentrate on what she was saying, all along wondering with a baffled amazement about the significance of such a small and regular occurrence as the way she sat before him.

This continued through the winter with the same unexpected intensity. He became certain that he wanted to paint her, but wasn't sure how she'd react. Her husband might not like it. And she knew the owner of the building where his studio was, a relationship that he hadn't asked about but one that could prove to be problematic if he offended her. He was still an outsider and didn't want enemies or the hassles they might cause. It was at that time, just as the winter had become a tedious and unavoidable nuisance, that their relationship changed without announcement.

"I really want to see your work," Karen said one morning over the photocopy machine that the English and Fine Arts departments shared. "If your offer still stands, that is."

Elliot was staring down through strands of his long blond hair at her feet and her velvetlike red shoes, which were closer to slippers and not really red but crimson, Alizarin Crimson, and he was thinking about how the shoes fit her slender feet and how rich the color was against the aging off-white floor tile.

"In your studio," she said as she shuffled through her handouts, trying to decide how much of the college's money she should spend on materials that almost all of her students wouldn't read.

"Yes," he said. "My studio."

"When?"

"How about Friday?"

"About three?"

"Four would be better. That would give me time to clean up."

When Karen looked at him, he noticed her eyes were bloodshot.

"Don't bother," Karen said. "I don't mind a mess, as long as it has a purpose." She gathered her papers together. "Four, right?"

"Yes," Elliot replied, catching her glance, which was somehow different than before, as she left the small, closetlike room.

Karen's suggestion that he forget about cleaning didn't alter his plans. On Friday afternoon he rushed home early, found his vacuum cleaner, which hadn't been used in three months, and started his assault on the studio. He didn't touch his work area except for unwashed dishes and empty beer cans and other half-discarded trash that had found their way to the floor. But he did his best to remove the accumulated months of dust and neglect from the area where he cooked and slept. He had moved his tattered, makeshift living room furniture to his studio when he gave up his apartment, but had never actually arranged it until that afternoon. He found a corner of the studio that was free of clutter and canvases and tried to create a living area.

When Karen arrived carrying a bottle of wine, she tripped on the door plate as she entered the studio. When the bottle slipped from her moist hands, Elliot caught it as she tried to regain her balance and not hit the wall which faced the open door. The wine was her gift to him for allowing her to visit his studio, not to buy a painting but to look and even judge, although she wasn't sure that her opinion should be offered or if Elliot would care.

And Elliot didn't plan to ask her to pose for him, not then. Karen started to trace the line of finished and half-finished canvases that rested against the walls of the studio. But as she commented on how she liked one painting more than a previous work and hinted at her reasons, he did ask her, blurting out the request or offer to pose, which, he wasn't sure.

"I would like that," Karen replied instantly, without thinking about it. When she heard herself agree, it was as if she had planned to do it since they had spoken the first time. But then other considerations appeared in her mind. What would Frank think? What would she have to do? How much time would it take? She squinted, trying to clear these half-formed concerns from her mind, as she felt her feet lifting from the floor. The normally tense muscles in her back relaxed, and something refreshing ran over her body and around her face. She looked up, searching for the sky which would be a swirled blue like a bird's egg, but found only ceiling. "Yes, I would," she said again, more to herself than to Elliot. "When?"

As a child and even as an adult, Karen had considered herself shy. Her sense of self was linked to the thought that her shyness was an indication of her desire for privacy. But she wasn't an introvert. At times, she simply needed to remain outside the pack and inside herself to find balance in her life. With Frank her shyness remained in place. Frequently, she dressed and undressed away from his eyes, until she assumed that he was no longer interested in what she considered a mild form of voyeurism and even a prelude to lovemaking.

Now, by the time she was ready for bed, Frank was asleep or still out with his friends talking, amid backslaps and whoops, about other conquests that for Frank seemed to be more satisfying. The years that had accumulated on their deflated marriage had deadened her shyness to a point. By her thirty-eighth birthday, she didn't experience any acute sense of invasion when he walked in on her as she was taking a bath. She dressed and undressed before his usually uninterested eyes without self-awareness and without thoughts of intimacy. But when Frank started showing renewed interest in her, her shyness returned and she presented her body to him with an innate reluctance.

Contrary to her need for privacy and to her surprise, she posed for Elliot for nearly a year. During that time they were colleagues, then friends. She found herself displaying her body to him, limb by limb, as if she were making love to him over that extended period of time—this month her legs, next month her breasts. Elliot hadn't even planned to paint her nude, not at first. He photographed and sketched her. One week he asked her to remove her skirt so that he could achieve a particular pose. Later he asked her to remove her blouse for a different pose. Her shyness, something that she admitted to without hesitation, completely dissolved. She didn't try to explain it because she never imagined that there was anything unnatural about what she was doing. With Frank's attention, there had always been a message that played itself again and again in her mind, reminding her that she was shy and that she had always been shy and that her husband would find anything but her shyness amusing. And then after months of removing one garment, then another, Karen and Elliot became lovers.

When Elliot thought about his relationship with Karen, the entire process had amounted to one prolonged yet inadvertent seduction, a seduction which they had willingly accepted after the fact and without qualification. His desire to paint her only increased as the year passed. His wish to understand the inspiration she provided dwindled and he finally decided that he could destroy what was transpiring in his studio by over-analyzing the motivation behind the process. By the time they became lovers, Elliot estimated that he had asked her more questions than he had any woman, including his former wife. He had a need to know her, beyond her physical self, because he felt he was painting more than that.

Their sessions were filled with the verbal give and take of people who are curious due to their respect for each other, not because of hidden or selfish motives. Karen talked about her prior ambitions to write and to live her life as a writer. But she confessed that she lacked inspiration and that she had taken the easiest path, the one that she thought would lead to security and away from the uncertainty of a poet's life. Elliot suspected that she still had the desire but lacked the support and atmosphere to test herself. He had prompted her to show him a few essays and some poetry that she had written, work which she said lacked the magic she associated with any successful piece of writing. But when Elliot disagreed, Karen seemed to be encouraged, and he thought her confidence grew simply because someone, anyone, had taken an interest in the work she had all but abandoned when she married.

On the days when they needed time away from the studio and away from bed, Karen took Elliot to the lakes of her imagination and childhood: Atsion, Oswego, Absegami, where they swam in the tannin-stained water, let their feet thread through the yellow-green eelgrass and made love in the lake or near the shore under the gnarled limbs of pitch pines and cedars. Before reaching the lakes, they always stopped to buy sandwiches and something to drink at an out-of-the-way store. One bright afternoon as they left the business, one of Karen's neighbors inexplicably drove into the gravel parking lot. When she left her car, which she had parked on the opposite side of the lot, the woman waved and shouted hello. At first, Karen panicked, thinking that her husband would discover what she had been doing, but within that same worry she thought that she shouldn't care because she loved Elliot and Frank loved other, less human things.

After a year of painting Karen and of watching the canvases take over more floor space in his studio, Elliot's fortunes improved. An important New York gallery offered him a one-man show. The gallery's owner was particularly interested in the pictures Elliot had done of Karen.

"Why should that be a problem?" she said coolly when Elliot explained the owner's fascination with the series.

"Frank?"

"I agreed to do it. I didn't think you'd keep them here forever. What would be the point?"

"You're positive?" For a second, Elliot felt that he had betrayed a part of the intimacy which they had shared.

"Absolutely," Karen said, considering the repercussions that would follow if Frank found out that she had posed nude.

"I don't want to force you to end—"

"Let me worry about that." She shook her head. "I'll deal with it."

She had told Frank little about Elliot. Frank knew that she was interested in art, knew that Elliot taught at the college and didn't seem to think anything about it when she had mentioned Elliot's desire to paint her, except that Karen was an unusual choice, one Frank would not have made. Her husband had been more concerned about being late for practice or a game, she couldn't remember which when she tried to recall the scene a week later. She understood that Frank wouldn't understand her decision to pose without clothing in a variety of positions, positions that she would have avoided only a year before and positions Frank had never seen. But now Karen was faced with a new dilemma. Her affair with Elliot had progressed effortlessly and without consternation. They hadn't discussed a future together on more than one or two occasions. Karen liked to think that Elliot was too possessed by his work and his need to avoid his ex-wife and her lawyer to seriously consider committing himself to another woman and marriage. And he had commented that Karen's getting a divorce could be ugly because she and her husband had accumulated bank accounts, investments, a house, two cars, and a truck—the baggage of a lifetime it had seemed to Elliot when he said it, thinking that Frank might turn out to be a bigger ass than either of them could imagine.

On the day before Elliot's opening, Karen wished him good luck and went home. She could feel the cold hallways and rooms close in on her before she arrived. Again, the bittersweet taste of almonds lingered in her mouth as she thought about writing, then about Frank. Was it Elliot she feared now and not her husband? she considered. His show might affect their affair, their entire relationship from artist's model to artist's lover to what could become the artist's latest conquest. Elliot had told her that he would call her the next evening, after the opening, to tell her how it went and she agreed, suspecting that any change in him wouldn't present itself for several days or possibly weeks. Frank wouldn't be home and even if he walked in as the phone rang, Karen felt confident enough to talk to Elliot in front of him, partly because Elliot was the man who had elevated her to a previously unimagined status, something Frank could never do, and partly because Frank didn't appear to suspect that a woman who had refused to sleep with him for nearly a year could be sleeping with anyone else.

When Elliot called the following evening, he was jubilant. His work was selling. A museum was interested in one of his paintings, a painting of Karen. He told her he loved her, which was the first time he had said those words outside the imaginary limits that his mattress formed, and that he wanted to go away with her to the Caribbean so he could rest and paint and so Karen could write.

But Elliot found her response to his plans guarded. When he hung up, he thought that maybe his exhilaration had gotten out of hand and that Karen wasn't ready, although she had openly considered leaving Frank for a new life. Then he assumed that Frank had finally discovered what had been going on under his uncaring nose. Elliot saw Frank standing before her, shouting that she would have to leave, not because of her unfaithfulness but because of the embarrassment he would face when his teammates found out that Frank had failed to control his woman and that he had been a willing accomplice in his own disgrace. After considering and reconsidering this scenario, Elliot decided to call her again just before midnight, hoping that nothing had happened and that Karen would be able to decide what she wanted without Frank's interference. But when the phone rang, her husband answered.

The next day Karen had lunch with Natalie. It was exactly fourteen months to the day that she had posed the first time for Elliot.

"And?" Natalie said as she leaned forward, her gold bracelets tapping the glass table top.

"That's it. His show's a hit. His paintings are selling."

"What about the paper?"

"They're going to run a feature on him from what he told me. Although he doesn't want them to mention that he has been painting me—by name I mean."

"Painting you naked, you mean."

"Yes. But that's not realistic."

"Have you told Frank?" Natalie whispered. "This is pretty heady stuff," she added. "A museum—"

"Not yet."

"I'd let it go. Don't say a damn word about it. Let Frank find out from one of his buddies."

"I don't know."

"Screw him. What's he ever done for you except take you to ball games and slap your rear end when the joke's on you?"

Karen thought for a minute, trying to assemble a list that would vindicate her husband.

"Well?" Natalie pressured.

"Not much, I guess."

"He'll know that you're his lover. He'd have to be stupid, really stupid."

"I don't care," Karen admitted to her friend. "I don't care if he knows and his teammates know and everyone else in the town knows. I'm glad that it all happened. And I'm willing to live with it whatever that means."

Natalie wasn't accustomed to seeing Karen so unreserved and open. Her friend had always constrained her emotions.

"It doesn't matter," Karen resolved.

"Did he ask you to leave Frank?"

"Yes. Yes, he did."

"And you're going."

"I didn't say that."

"You can't be serious."

Karen looked at her friend, knowing that whatever had passed between them about Elliot and her affair had remained a secret. She thought about Frank, alone in their house, walking from room to room, searching for something. She imagined it was her, but then she suspected that he was looking for his misplaced glove or another pair of clean socks. Suddenly, she hoped Frank had a lover.

"You're not going to stay with—" Natalie repeated.

"I'm pregnant," Karen said bluntly.

"Mother Mary and Joseph." Natalie touched her lips with her fingers. "Whose? Elliot's?"

"I'm not sure."

They didn't talk for a minute. Natalie looked at her friend, who took another forkful of salad streaked with French dressing and quietly chewed it.

"But I thought you and Frank hadn't been doing it since—"

"Only once, at the wrong time over a month ago. He came home drunk and I was asleep. Before I could stop him he was finished and rolled off me."

"Did you tell Elliot?"

"No, not yet."

"Don't," Natalie said. "Forget it happened. You don't love Frank. Maybe it will work out. It can't be that that one time, when you were doing it every day with Elliot, could end up being Frank's great moment."

"I don't know."

"Do you want to have it?"

"I haven't thought about that, or I've tried not to."

Natalie reached across the table and clutched Karen's hand.

"I have to tell Elliot. It's a mess, but one I have to live with."

"No, it isn't," Natalie said, knowing but not admitting that it was. "Leave the jackass. Go with Elliot. Tell him what happened if you need to. If he loves you, there won't be a problem, right?"

"I can't be sure of that."

"Get out now," Natalie said. "Now, before Elliot leaves, before you know whose it is, before Frank finds out that you're pregnant."

As Karen drove home from the restaurant, she reconsidered her entire relationship with Frank. After going over everything of significance that had occurred between the two of them, she didn't arrive at an unforeseen conclusion. Frank, although what some women would call a good guy and a good provider who still liked to play games, was probably faithful if indifferent, and he amounted to more than many women had or hoped to have. Their arguments about children had hurt their already declining marriage and now she knew that Frank's latest year-old problem with not having children was the last in a lengthy line of failures between them. It was true that with Frank she had her freedom and that Frank, although uninterested most of the time, could be funny and even considerate if he tried. He had been easygoing if anything, although Karen's rejection of his rare advances had made their precarious relationship even more strained.

When she reached the asphalt driveway that led to their house, she turned off the engine. She let her head fall back on the seat, bending her neck slightly. Her affair with Elliot had come easily; it was already under way and a part of her life before it became real to her. Now there were complications that might finally end what she and Elliot might call, in some distant future, the best year of their lives. Her head throbbed and she rubbed her temples with those same fingertips that Elliot had observed and painted again and again. For a moment, she felt her past pulling her back into those cold, stagnant halls and into the unrelieved tension there. But somewhere inside the pain that was caused in part by her confusion, she felt her body slip effortlessly from the car seat and down the driveway, away from the house, their possessions, Frank's world of games, and into the azure water of the Caribbean.

Laurel Fades

The voice from the adjoining apartment said:

"An ancient olive tree casts its gnarled, fantastic limbs over the high ochre cliffs at the entrance of this small Greek isle's harbor. Its roots disappear into solid rock, and its leaves create the only shade on this barren peninsula. Its fruit is said to be miraculously sweet and to not need curing. When local fishermen put to sea and pass the spot directly beneath the olive tree, they make the sign of the cross, asking to be blessed before sailing out on the Aegean."

Ransom moved his flabby arm away from his ear. The skin fell in musky folds onto the pillow. He blinked and focused on the bare bedroom wall, trying to ignore the voice, partially deadened by carpet and cinder blocks, as it floated to his one exposed ear from next door.

"It is said that Hera, moved by the death of a young woman who had slipped from the promontory during a storm as she waited for her husband to return, created the divine tree on the spot where the woman's last living step fell. When the storm abated, the fully-grown nascent tree was discovered. A temple was built within the embrace of its limbs. Sacrifices were made each year to thank the gods for the tree's sweet fruit and to memorialize the

young woman's death. Eventually the temple was transformed into a chapel, and on holy days flowers were cast into the egg-plant-colored sea."

The channel changed with a dry snap.

"But I never thought anything like this would happen. Never," a child said.

"That's always the way. We never know. And let that be a lesson to you."

Another static-filled burst reached Ransom.

"Isn't this shit supposed to be on another station?" his neighbor exclaimed. "I mean, come on."

"Two thousand years after the young woman fell to her death, the fishermen still remember. Of her husband nothing is known. He never reached the harbor. Romantics say that he met fate at the same moment as his young bride. Local cynics, fingering their wooden beads, remark that he never intended to return, that the husband's wanderlust was stronger than his love. Others claim that he loved another and lived to an old age on a distant island near Crete. A few swear that he was seen—"

Click!

Ransom rolled on his side; his form, dictated to by gravity, rearranged itself. The bedroom's double window chattered as the rising wind gathered strength. It had been snowing all day and with each snow-filled burst of air, the polyester curtains rustled.

"Bunch of bullshit. Did you ever—" his neighbor said dramatically, as he stomped from his living room.

Another voice, a woman's this time, echoed from a more distant room, somehow threading its way through the apartment's maze of doorways and halls.

"What?"

"Where's the game? I said."

Ransom drew the musty sheet to his creased neck as the bed squeaked, vainly resisting his weight. His feet were cold.

"Plenty more this—" the woman's voice reasoned.

"But the damn TV page said that there would be a replay at eleven-thirty. It's supposed to be a great fucking game. A classic!"

The voices evaporated. Ransom didn't want to hear them, didn't care. The wind gusted again, bringing with it the faint tap of ice particles on the glass. Ransom was thankful that his neighbor, a nameless man who walked with a slight limp and who had never introduced himself or his occasional companion, might not watch television tonight. His box of circuits, oblivious to anything but its own electronic impulses, might not be permitted to bellow into the early morning. But nothing was certain, especially when it concerned his neighbor's habits. Ransom needed sleep but hadn't been able to get more than an hour or two each night for several weeks. He had tried staying awake, waiting for sleep to overtake him, but discovered that the faint beginnings of another day arrived before drowsiness. Then he tried, without much success, to reestablish some type of pattern, hoping that within this he would resolve his dilemma. But his insomnia resisted any attempt at regulation. Finally he acquiesced and admitted to himself that a solution, beyond the sleeping pills he took, wasn't possible. And his neighbor's late-night habit only added to his problems. Ransom closed his eyes, his lids unfolding like crepe paper globes.

Lorraine waited for him on the small square porch that was always trimmed with sweet peas during the summer months. She held her hands in front of her waist, nervously twisting a blue cotton handkerchief between her fingers with an air of determined impatience, wondering why he had taken so long to arrive. Twenty-eight miles stood between her sagging, unpainted porch and the county seat, twenty-eight miles of potholes and gravel roads. It was late in the afternoon, and Ransom thought he saw a cold white vapor rise from her thin lips and pause before her horn-rimmed glasses before it vanished into the tight weave of her hair net. But it wasn't winter. She wore the same dress (one of only three she owned, if Ransom had guessed correctly) that she had had on a few years before when he first arrived to inform her of her sister's death. Even as a young woman Lorraine had been frugal, obstinately refusing to purchase an article of clothing unless it was absolutely necessary. She had always claimed that fashion didn't mean a thing to her. During the winter months she held on to her belief, layering her summer garments until they supplied enough warmth. Her twin sister, Eleanor, seemed to fall under the same spell, her sister's conviction reverberating in her own mind with a parallel intensity. Then Eleanor was found frozen to death early one winter morning with three cotton dresses on under her raincoat.

"Sam," she said as Ransom emerged from his car. When he reached the porch, Lorraine's face was directly opposite his as she remained on the top step. "Been waiting all day. Thought you forgot about us."

"It's been terrible busy Lorraine. Just terrible." He slipped his hands in his pockets and glanced up at the sky. "I suspect it'll rain soon."

She held the door open for him as he climbed the steps that shifted under his weight. Suddenly, he was nearly two feet taller and looked down on the top of her head as if she had knelt before him.

He sat in the same threadbare chair, the one nearest the door and the fireplace, which reminded him of a vigilant eye peering into the rectangular room. He had been out to see her over a dozen times since her sister had died. As she stood before him, her heavy black shoes on the brick hearth, he knew what she would say. She looked like an unruly school girl waiting to be berated, although he realized that beneath her old polite femininity touched with anticipation, there lurked something else: dread.

"Well Lorraine. How are you? Have you heard from your sister since you called?" he asked calmly, stretching his legs for a moment then returning the heels of his brown boots to the front of the chair.

"She's gone," she said abruptly in her high cracking voice, joining his courtesy with her proclamation.

"Eleanor?"

"Yes." Her voice, filled with helpless resignation, wavered as she strained to maintain her composure. She leaned forward, bending slightly at the waist, and looked at him over the rims of her glasses. "She left this morning and said she was going over to Lock's place to get fresh eggs."

"Eleanor told you this?"

Lorraine nodded, opening her mouth without speaking, then closing it.

"Said she'd be back by lunch?"

"Yes," she exclaimed as she sat next to Ransom. "And you know about Eleanor and her spells. When she gets distracted, look out!"

He hesitated, not wanting to show his impatience. He stretched his legs again until his feet rested in front of the fireplace grate.

"This morning you said?"

"My alarm went off at six as always. Not that I need one after all these years. I came out here and lit the stove, then put the kettle on. When the water was hot, I went to wake her. We ate breakfast and used the last of the eggs." Lorraine began to tremble, her arms moving with a nearly imperceptible shiver. "Eleanor said that she wanted to walk over to Lock's farm. I thought that it was too cold but she laughed. 'Lorraine,' she said, 'that is why God made clothing.' She put her raincoat on, grabbed the basket, and said she'd be back before lunch, that she'd probably stop off to see how old Mrs. Petroff was before coming home." Lorraine clenched her hands together, her handkerchief still entwined in her wrinkled fingers. "I'm worried, Sam."

"Now, now, Lorraine." He reached for her shoulder, feeling the sharp bone covered with old, pungent flesh. "Everything will be fine." He knew that by the next morning she would forget about his visit. "I'll drive over to Lock's farm. I'm sure there's nothing wrong. Eleanor probably forgot about the time. Or maybe she got caught up at Mrs. Petroff's place. You know she's a great one for gossip. And I heard in town that Lock's aunt is staying out there this week. Could be she decided to stay for lunch and forgot to call." He looked reassuringly at her. "I'll be back with her before you're asleep." He would call her in less than an hour, once he reached the courthouse, and tell her that Eleanor was fine. The Locks would drive her home, and her sister didn't want Lorraine to wait up for her, he would add. Then he would return to the business at hand.

When he backed his car from the driveway, Lorraine waved confidently, appearing relieved as she let her cloth hanky react to the movement of her arm. She didn't seem to be as worried this time, he thought. He hoped that she wouldn't call him again but knew, after so many visits, that more would come and that his unrelenting conscience would force him to go.

The fishermen still remember.

"And that's my final offer," George Raft grumbled from his neighbor's apartment. "Take it or leave it."

"I don't think so."

"It's your funeral."

He opened his eyes. The snow continued to blow against the frozen window. He searched for the dial of the alarm clock, his eyes trying to distinguish the numbers which glowed feebly in an orange ring. Two o'clock or was it three o'clock? Ransom ran his fingers along the edge of the mattress, feeling the exposed material which was embroidered with inexplicable stitching. Hot water clanked through the radiator pipes, sounding more like solid matter rattling against steel than heated fluid under pressure.

He waited for drowsiness, a return to sleep.

"I wouldn't do that if I were you," a voice said sternly.

"Watch me," Raft snapped.

Tires screeched and a woman screamed. Staccato gunplay erupted.

"I'm hit. The rats got me."

"Hold on kid. You're going to make it," Raft said.

"Will you turn that off and come to bed?" a woman's voice pleaded from several rooms away.

"In a minute. It'll be over in just a few minutes," his neighbor barked.

Outside, a solitary streetlight defied the heavy snow and sent a small amount of light through the curtains. Without wanting to keep his eyes open, he found himself staring at the stray light which fell past the iced glass and sagging curtains, creating a faint streaming shadow across the bed and his bloated body. He covered his head with a pillow.

A few minutes passed. His eyes, although slightly dry and burning, still wanted sleep. But it was his burning eyes, whether closed or open, that defeated their own desire. He slid his tired legs from the bed, leaving the warmth of blanket and sheets for the cold room. He groped for his flannel bathrobe, first on the foot of the bed, then on the floor.

The bathroom light froze his face in the mirror: unshaven, red, swollen with years of overeating. His hair, now a parody of its former glory, looked like an old rooster's comb. He looked once at his face, then reached for the faucet and a glass. He fumbled with a pill bottle, dropping it once, then retrieving it from under the sink and removing its lid.

"Howard!" the woman's voice yelled.

"You'll never make it," someone cried. "Don't go!"

"I don't have any choice," Raft replied. "I owe them."

"But would they do it for you?"

"That's not important. A man's gotta live with—"

Click!

Ransom sat in a chair before his bedroom window. Snow had covered everything below except for the lone streetlight and its glow at the edge of the parking lot. The world was somnambulant beneath the frozen cover. Small pitch pines bowed under their newly acquired weight. He plopped his feet on a small footstool and pulled a blanket that was draped over the back of the chair around his shoulders and onto his lap. He watched the snow, trying to follow separate flakes as they descended from the black indifferent sky. His eyes stopped burning and his eyelids began to feel heavy. Then, as if the interruption had been only a second long, sleep returned. His head slowly dropped to his chest, the fat of his chin rising and engulfing his lower face.

Forgetting about the snow, he only wanted the quiet cold peace of its enchantment.

"Carol," he mumbled, drawing images of his wife from his memory.

Flowers were cast into the eggplant-colored sea.

His wife had died suddenly in bed, late one evening, an evening very like the one that surrounded his sleeping form, while he was out trying to locate someone for questioning, or at least that is what he had told Carol when he had called. His hand unconsciously gripped his arm, his fingernails embedding themselves in the blotchy skin. He had spent the last seventeen years wondering if he could have saved her, could have been at her side during the moment of her failure. The doctor told him her heart gave out. Nothing could have helped the woman, nothing except immediate attention. But Ransom hadn't returned that morning until four-thirty, quietly slipping into the shower at the far end of the upstairs hallway to remove the scent of another woman before he got into bed next to his dead wife. It wasn't until seven o'clock that he realized she had died. And from that moment he speculated about the possibility of having resuscitated her if he hadn't been so late. So late. His wife sat, her eyes opened slightly, and she spoke.

But Ransom fought to stay asleep, managing to fend off any subconscious pressure to wake. The snow slowed, bringing with it a slight lightening of the sky. His body hunched forward and to one side. His hand, shifting with the involuntary movement, dropped from one of his swollen knees.

"Now don't be late," Carol said as he left that morning. "Don't be late. I'm making your favorite for supper," she added as she glanced away from the sink with an awareness that alarmed him. She knows, he thought, as he hurried from the kitchen, down the creaking steps to his car. But by the afternoon that alarm was dulled by the lethargy of the workday. By late afternoon, another woman's voice called to him over the phone lines—called once, then again. With this he telephoned Carol, telling her he wouldn't be home for supper, saying that he was sorry but there was little he could do.

The stillness of early morning and quiet snow gave way. The muffled scraping of a snowplow could be heard somewhere in the distance. Beyond the cleared perimeter surrounding the apartments, ducks broke from the freezing surface of a flooded cranberry bog. A truck door groaned as it was opened. Within an instant it was resolutely slammed shut by an unseen driver.

"Good morning out there. It's going to be a cold one today," a voice from the adjoining apartment said. "Highs in the teens. Yep, that's right. The teens. And that's nothing compared to tonight when the temperature will plummet way on down to three degrees. Yep, you heard me. Threeeee degrees."

Ransom snapped his head back as the voice pirouetted on the number three. Morning had almost arrived, but the single streetlight was still shining. He squinted, rubbing his eyes. Without thought his hand mechanically reached for the corner of his blanket. He could see a single set of footprints leaving the building from beneath his window; they meandered across the parking lot, getting lost between the cars for a moment then breaking free of the covered asphalt, heading in one graceful arc across an overgrown field toward a cluster of cedar trees not far from the apartments. He closed his eyes. His jaw slackened.

The tire chains clanked with an odd muffled brightness as he steered the car along the snowy road that passed Lock's farm. He asked the woman tight against him to lower her head while they passed, not wanting anyone to see her. She moved instinctively toward his lap as he held the car on the slippery road.

"Christ, it must be zero out there."

"Hmm," the woman said. "Two below somebody said earlier."

"At least the damn snow has stopped."

"Yeah." She grinned, her teeth stained with red lipstick.

His gaze left the passing farmhouse and he said, "We're almost safe now. Can't have you ruining my reputation."

"Heaven forbid. You might need it sometime."

"Things get around, you know."

"Can't have that." She touched his leg, her nails pulling on the material of his pants.

Then Ransom saw the tracks. Only a minute before he had convinced himself that his car was the first on the road after the snow, that they were the first to travel in this section of the county. He hadn't imagined that someone would be walking in the worst weather the state had seen in a decade. He studied the tracks, noting their depth and gait, thinking the stride too short for a man. The footsteps stayed along the shoulder of the road, then drifted up the low berm toward the tree line. The scrub pines and sweet gums formed a wall of snow and ice a few feet beyond, and the tracks disappeared in the green-brown tangle for several yards.

The woman started to raise her head, brushing loose wisps of hair from her face. Her cheek was flushed from the warmth of his thigh.

Ransom still followed the tracks. They stopped for a minute; a larger patch of snow was trampled. Then they continued, erratically shadowing the road for a mile.

"Who'd be out here in this?" the woman said, glancing at her reflection in the rearview mirror. She brushed her bluntly cut bangs into place with her hand. "I sure wouldn't."

"Hell if I know."

"But you're the law. Aren't you supposed—"

"Get your head down," Ransom said brusquely, his fingers reaching for the back of her head. A dark figure appeared in the distance.

As the car got closer, he could see who it was. The woman stood, silent and without expression, her startled eyes focused on the passing car. Her arms were wrapped around her waist, holding her black raincoat and egg basket against her body.

"Eleanor Blake," he said softly, looking to his left and away from the woman as they passed. "Eleanor Blake."

"Aren't you going to stop?"

"For what?"

"To see if anything's wrong."

"She'll be all right," he said, stroking the woman's auburn hair. "She lives up the road here."

They make the sign of the cross.

"And let's go to our early bird's early-bird traffic report with the one and only Jimboooo Mitchell."

"Thanks Ray. If you're traveling on any of the major highways today, use extreme caution, please. We'll probably have a lot of fender benders this morning, and we don't want you to be one of them—"

Although his body still leaned toward sleep, Ransom opened his eyes. The morning sky, now bereft of snow, was streaked with rose light. The lone streetlight had ceased to illuminate the far end of the parking lot. Someone laughed. At first he thought it was the woman next door, but realized within the same instant that the laughter came from the snow-swept parking lot. Waiting for another outburst, he searched beyond the glass, his tired eyes darting from car to car, but it never came.

Whitman's Tomb

Whenever Dr. Gathers turns his car onto Mickle Street, he shifts into a lower gear so that he can take a long look. Whitman's grey two-story house stands mid-block across the street from a modern, antiseptic prison. It's a tired street with worn and sometimes derelict houses, ragged vacant lots—no place to be at night. When Whitman bought the house in the spring of 1884 his brother George, angry that the poet wouldn't move to a Burlington farmhouse with his family, called the neighborhood a slum, comparing it unfairly with his former home on Stevens Street where Whitman had lived with his brother's family. Working-class would have been a better word to describe the neighborhood over a hundred years ago. Mickle Street was a place of factories and ferry terminals and trains, the kind of place Whitman relished and wrote about, even though in his old age he preferred to close his windows when the objects and sounds of his earlier praise got too loud.

As Gathers passes the house, he gazes up at the second story and imagines Whitman sitting in his bedroom with its three windows and wood stove. He is surrounded by piles of books, boxes, and bundles of never-discarded papers, his flowing white hair and beard somehow embellishing the disorder. It's his ship's cabin, cluttered with the paraphernalia of his profession, Whitman claims when Mary Davis, the sailor's widow who lived in the rear of the poet's house during the last seven years of his life, tries to organize it on different occasions. Because of his health, Whitman keeps a tin bathtub under his bed which Mary pulls out into a cleared space and fills for him when he needs to bathe, despite the gossip which follows her wherever she goes. Gathers knows that in the same room where the poet slept and wrote and bathed, he died, with his friends and admirers and even his brother George around him. Afterwards Mary Davis, who had lovingly devoted herself to making Whitman's final years comfortable, sued his estate to gain more than the thousand dollars left her by him, claiming that her investment there had been far greater.

It was a noisy street then, with fife-and-drum brigades, a church choir, yelling boys and crying children, and close, hard-working neighbors. When Whitman reminisced with his friends about the day Oscar Wilde visited him and Whitman served him elderberry wine, the noise outside the house continued unabated. When, on the day after the poet's death, Thomas Eakins and a student cast Whitman's death mask, the din was still there, rumbling on without interruption, passersby unaware that the old poet was dead. On the day of his funeral, when mourners and the curious waited in line outside his house to view the oak casket which rested in the first-floor parlor, the engineers of the Camden and Amboy Railroad casually sounded their shrill whistles and the noise rattled up Mickle Street, past the Methodist Church and into the poet's home.

Gathers accelerates once past the house, leaving Mickle Street behind. When he passes the periphery of the campus he thinks he sees his colleague, the fallen Dr. Ehrlich, get into his girlfriend's old black Cadillac where, at one time, they had spent countless nights in its roomy backseat, hidden in the dark parking lot near the building where the department offices are. That was when Val Weaver was a grad student; now she is a temporary faculty member. Next year she will no longer be employed by the college, a victim of Ehrlich's jealousy and ambition and of her own sweet willingness.

Without an explanation of Dr. Ehrlich's fall, Gathers' rise cannot be understood. It's true that Ehrlich hasn't dropped off the face of the earth. He's no longer the chair of the department and his leadership of the Whitman Society has been challenged. His wife, who should have dropped the bastard years ago, has finally left him, but he got a twenty-eight-year-old one-time graduate student in return, which I imagine Ehrlich feels is a fair trade. His credibility as a Whitman scholar has been damaged, but that probably can be partially restored with the production of a few esoteric papers and dogged persistence.

But Gathers' successes have shown him to be the favorite of Dame Fortune. Gathers' star is ascending. Gathers' plays on the first string. The dreaded Dr. Ehrlich, who at one time held Gathers' fate in his clenched hand, now finds Gathers, the man who will replace Ehrlich as the department's Whitman scholar when Ehrlich leaves or retires, in a position of power. Gathers is the name most heard during conversations that take place in faculty offices. Gathers has written a book, *Whitman's Camden Years*, which will soon be on the shelves of bookstores and libraries. Gathers is the man who officially uncovered something about Whitman on which Ehrlich, with his boundless ambition and arrogance, thought worth risking his reputation. And Ehrlich never knew what hit him, but I did because I walked Gathers through the entire process and tempted Ehrlich's curiosity. Craig Gathers just happened to be in a position to benefit. The results of what I thought would be a slight to Ehrlich, a personal affront at best, turned into something delectably more significant and lasting.

I've been told that there is something wrong with holding a grudge for too long. But I've never understood what that's supposed to mean. A year doesn't seem that long to me or my girlfriend, Julia Brown. Five years isn't a lot of time. Ten years is probably too long for anyone to hang on to the hurt and anger which originally created the grudge, I suppose. But my grudge, or vendetta as Julia describes it, against Dr. Ehrlich has been with me on and off for nearly fifteen years. I have thought about the day he humiliated me in front of an undergraduate English class. I just haven't let my desire for revenge become an obsession, until I discovered something that made me remember Ehrlich and the embarrassment he caused me, an insult directed at me that involved my first love and, in a coincidental way, Ehrlich's first love: Walt Whitman.

My studies in English, which ended the same semester as my confrontation with Ehrlich, soon developed into an interest in local history and the women who helped make it. Now Julia and I scour local archives and search through forgotten boxes of papers in cobweb-filled attics and dank basements, looking for clues of how women in the region lived fifty or a hundred or two hundred years ago, and what these women thought and felt. Our other consuming interest, which is an offshoot of the first, is in old tombstones and genealogy, which causes us to spend some of our weekends in overgrown cemeteries, doing rubbings and recording names and dates. Frequently we trudge deep into the Pines, searching for family cemeteries that have been lost or forgotten. When we're lucky, which isn't often, we uncover a marker that is unusual, and it forces us to pause and think about who is buried there and the life that the person led.

Over two years ago, I sent a letter to Craig Gathers. I knew that Ehrlich was away, attending a conference of like-minded individuals who had gathered in partitioned rooms to discuss unusual things like Whitman's use of the comma in his poetry and how many times the word *red* appears in *Leaves of Grass* and code words for the male genitalia. Two years ago Gathers was new on campus and considered by many to be Ehrlich's protégé, a budding Whitman scholar who might stay on and eventually become a cornerstone of the department. Back then Gathers was teaching at the college on a one-year appointment with the possibility of a tenure-track job the following fall. In my letter I told Gathers that I am the great-granddaughter of Harry

Stafford—*the* Harry Stafford. Just the mention of that fact was enough to catch Gathers' eye. When he saw the name, his mind immediately began considering the possibilities.

My great-grandfather had met Whitman in a Camden print shop when my great-grandfather was eighteen. Their relationship developed quickly, challenging Whitman's memories and loyalties to his other friends, Peter Doyle included. Within a few months Harry brought the poet to his parents' tenant farm in what was called White Horse. There Whitman was adopted by my family and it is there that he composed much of *Specimen Days*. Not too far from the family house, back in the thick pinewoods, there was a pond which was bordered by a marl pit. Whitman loved to roll naked in the pit, which was intersected by a running spring, lolling there for hours next to the lake at Timber Creek. He scrubbed his naked body with a brush, his blood rising in red patches just under the surface of his skin. He flouted his form and flesh, proclaiming himself one with all that surrounded him. There Whitman was consecrated by the natural world and felt rejuvenated. Whitman's life around the pond at the edge of the Pines was his answer to Thoreau and his Walden. He found great peace there. But eventually my great-grandfather married Eva Westcott and Whitman's thoughts of his adopted family and the friendship they had shared dimmed.

In my letter to Gathers, I didn't say exactly what I had that might interest him. As I said, the mention of my family name was plenty, along with a comment about the significance of my information and how I wanted to give it to a responsible scholar who would know what to do with it. That, I felt, was enough to pique his scholarly interest. This bait, a dream come true, dangled before Craig Gathers' sensitive nose, enticed him to call me the day he received the letter.

"What exactly do you have?" he casually asked after introducing himself, obviously excited about the unknown possibilities, but not wanting to appear too anxious.

"I think you should meet us and we can talk about it. After all, I'm willing to share it with you. And to get the complete picture, we need to meet," I said, wondering if Gathers would be the kind of person we could trust, even though I had heard through a friend that he was.

"All right," he said. "Where?"

"Berlin Diner. Do you know where that is?"

"Yes."

"Around one tomorrow, then. And come alone," I added.

He agreed, probably thinking that my request was slightly irregular but willing to accept my demand as long as there was something of value waiting for him.

I'll bet Gathers spent that night tossing in bed, his mind ripe with ideas. He knew that my information might help his career. He knew that his own position was tenuous at that point and that any boost would help him secure his job in Camden or at another institution if he had to relocate. I admit, his behavior has been very predictable. He is a dedicated scholar. But the one thing that has surprised both Julia and me is his honesty. Ever since my encounter with Ehrlich, I've been hesitant about academic types and the games they seem so fond of playing. But Gathers is an exception.

When Gathers appeared in front of the cash register at the diner, Julia and I knew who he was even though we had never seen him. He had a quizzical look about him. His unruly hair needed trimming. He looked comfortable but out of place, or maybe it was out of step. Berlin isn't the kind of place he would normally find himself. It's a place where yuppies and Pineys mix, usually not so well. When his eyes scanned the counter and then the booths, I motioned to him.

"Ms. Stafford," he said, looking at me, then Julia.

"Julia Brown," I said, introducing my girlfriend. He shook my hand, then Julia's, looking directly into our eyes. A good sign, I thought.

He ordered a cup of coffee after glancing at our empty plates. We fell into a few minutes of small talk; then, when a noticeable pause arrived, I removed an envelope from my bag. I never told him that I had attended the college where he taught. I don't think he suspected it until I mentioned the conditions attached to the information I was about to give him. But once he knew what could be gained, the topic never seemed very significant.

"The first condition, before we talk about anything, is that I don't want Ehrlich in on this. At least not now."

"But he's the president of the Whitman—"

"I know about that. But you're interested in Whitman, right?"

"Subject of my dissertation."

"Well?"

"All right," Gathers said, suspecting something was wrong but not knowing what it was.

"He'll find out in time. But I'm going to give you this information so that you can use it, not Ehrlich."

"Fine," he said, squirming in his seat.

"The second condition has to do with the location of this." I pulled a photograph from my bag and placed it next to Gathers' cup of coffee.

"What's this?" he said as his eyes fell to the photograph.

"What's it look like?" Julia said impatiently.

"A grave."

"A soul house," Julia quickly added with a melodramatic flair. "To protect the dead from evil."

"All right. It has a roof, like a mausoleum. The walls are only about two feet high. I'll buy that. Whitman did have a preoccupation with death. He was even interested in Egyptology. Spirits." Gathers looked at us. "So?"

"Whitman's buried in it," I said, dropping the bomb.

"Impossible," Gathers said as his eyes returned to the picture. "He's buried in Harleigh Cemetery in Camden with most of his family. That's a well-documented fact. Unpolished Quincy granite, built by Reinhalter and Company of Philadelphia. It cost four thousand dollars to build, which was outrageous for the time."

"I told you, Susan," Julia said to me, her eyes narrowing as she looked in my direction. "Didn't I? Blah, blah, blah."

I pulled a small leather-bound book kept together with string from my bag and placed it on top of the picture.

"What's this?"

"Eva Westcott Stafford's diary."

"Harry Stafford's wife?"

"Yes."

Gathers untied the string and let the limp pages fall open on the table. The yellow pages appeared almost pink under the diner's lights. Eva's delicate script, turned brown by the years, was finer than the silk of a spiderweb.

"In it she talks about my great-grandfather's relationship with Whitman and Whitman's death and his tomb—the one in Camden, the one for the world to see, and the real one, the one you have a picture of. Actually, part of that four thousand you mentioned was for the grave in the picture. Not even his friends knew. Remember how upset Traubel and Harned were. Harned paid twenty-five hundred out of his own pocket to settle the bill. And the other fellow—"

"Bucke." Gathers looked at me, his face bewildered.

"It's always been a joke in the family. You know, that Whitman wasn't in Camden; he's in the Pines, put there by my great-grandfather and his family. I never believed it until I came across this diary one afternoon last year when Julia and I were sorting through boxes in my dead aunt's house. My family wanted to hire someone to come in and cart the stuff off without bothering to look through it. They thought it was worthless. Moldy boxes filled with documents and keepsakes of what was her life. She was just an old woman who had never married and lived alone for most of her life, without much money or love."

Gathers listened intently then said, "What if this is Whitman's real grave site? You say it is. But obviously you want me to use this information. When can I see it?"

"That's part of the second condition. It took us six hard months to find it. And we had a pretty good idea where to look. It was covered with dead leaves and other debris when we found it, and after you see it, it will be recovered completely. We'll take you there once. You can see it, touch it, photograph it, but that's it. You'll never disturb it again. You'll never be able to find it. I don't want the location revealed. Whitman wasn't a modest man and thought that in death he might be revered. His Camden tomb is for the worshippers like you and Ehrlich. His tomb in the Pines was a spiritual decision. He wanted what he experienced at Timber Creek. He wanted to be absorbed into the natural world. I respect that, and you have to as well. But I think we can agree on your using a phrase like the greater Pine Barrens or somewhere in South Jersey."

"What if I don't agree?"

"I told you," Julia said sharply. "Fucking bloodsucker. The man's dead, you know? This is what Whitman wanted. He was the poet; you academics only wipe his—"

I touched her freckled arm, and to Gathers I said, "Fine. I'll take the diary and the photo and what we know and go home. You can write about it and everyone will think you're a nut case. You can call for an exhumation. The Whitman Society members will ride you out of the organization on a rail. If you get a court order to look for his body in Camden and find it there, you're washed up as a Whitman scholar. If you find an empty vault, well you still won't have the diary, and think about all those hungry scholars who will be on to it then. Ehrlich will lead the charge. With us, you can break it on your own; without us you don't have much of a chance to make a mark. And after all, isn't that what academics like you are all about?"

Gathers glanced at the photo and the diary for a minute, thinking about what I had said. He blinked as if he were trying to block out the commotion in the noisy diner.

"It's your decision."

"All right," he finally said. "I get to see the tomb and get access to the diary."

"With the page that discusses the general location of the tomb removed, of course," I said.

"Yes," Gathers agreed. "When?" he said, holding the photograph close to his face.

"Soon," I said, hoping that Gathers would live up to what I had managed to learn about him before I sent him my note.

Our trip to the site was arranged for the day Ehrlich was due to return to the college from his conference. Val would be at his side, his most promising student and teaching assistant in years. Everyone knew that Ehrlich was sleeping with her, that he was a leech, but no one cared, except for Mrs. Ehrlich. His return would be met with the congratulations of his colleagues and the anger of his wife. News of another successful presentation had preceded his arrival and so had news of his openly affectionate ways. But my news, something far greater in his mind than anything that had happened at his conference, would greet him as soon as he opened the cryptic little message I had sent to the president of the Whitman Society during his absence in Chicago.

"Craig," Ehrlich said, walking down the hallway from his office toward the suite where Gathers' office was with my letter still in his hand. Talking loudly in the hall was his way of announcing his arrival before he appeared. "Craig," he repeated as he spun through the open doorway of the suite to find Gathers' door closed.

"He's gone for the day," Dr. Sands said from her office. "He said that he was finished for the day. He'll be back at 8:00 tomorrow morning, I suspect."

Ehrlich peered around the corner at the slender middle-aged woman in the office next to Gathers'. Her long fingers were poised above her keyboard as she looked over her shoulder.

"Did you need him for anything important?"

"No," Ehrlich said. "No. I simply wanted to—" Ehrlich stopped when he noticed Sands had returned to her computer, her short blond hair framed by the green glow of the screen. He gazed at the publicity poster announcing the publication of her latest book tacked to the wall above her desk.

"I'm sorry," she said, glancing back to him for a moment. "I thought you were leaving."

"Yes," Ehrlich replied as he turned on his heels and fled the suite. He didn't speak to Sands often because he felt she was a threat to his position as chair. He had reached this unwarranted conclusion based on the fact that Sands was the one person in the department, a Victorian scholar, who had published more than Ehrlich. Recently, she had started to write novels. Ehrlich tried to ignore her, but reviews of her work, along with an occasional essay she had written, kept appearing in journals and magazines that he read.

My unsigned note to Ehrlich didn't say much. I wrote that Gathers was on to something and it could add a significant chapter to Whitman studies. Nothing more. I wanted Ehrlich to sweat a little. I knew that his petulance would make him think it might look bad if one of his own department members managed to uncover something of importance in his field without Ehrlich's knowledge or even his help. I suspected my duplicitous message would get the ball rolling. I had hoped that Ehrlich's tiny piece of information would be a splinter in his ass. But my hopes were far exceeded by Ehrlich's ego and his vanity.

The trip to the Whitman site took nearly two hours. We met at the Berlin Diner. Julia rode in the backseat with Gathers, who for the first hour was on his back, staring at the head liner of the car. Not until we were off the highway and deep into the Pines and riding on wavy sand roads did we permit him to sit. When he looked outside the only things he saw were scrub pines, blackjacks, and undergrowth. The monotony was broken by a rare stand of cedar or a trickling branch or an abandoned bog. We caught sight of a doe browsing in the deep shade. But nothing Gathers saw during that ride could be recalled by him with any discerning detail. His description of the area would match thousands of other descriptions of like areas. If we had abandoned him along one of the sand roads, he would have been lost for days.

"You know that Whitman believed in phrenology," he said, breaking the quiet that was punctuated by my car's nonexistent suspension.

"Head bumps?" Julia asked, unimpressed.

"It's not quite that simple. Physical traits, especially those of the skull, were thought to be an indication of character, ability, talent, and the rest."

"Hmm. Big heads make big men, or is it big men have big heads?" Julia said, glancing outside.

"When he died the doctors who performed his autopsy removed his brain so that it could be measured and weighed at a society—"

"The American Anthropometric Society," I interrupted.

Gathers looked at my eyes in the rearview mirror.

"And a laboratory assistant dropped it on the floor," I concluded.

"That's right," Gathers said. "You know Whitman well."

"That's not all she knows," Julia mumbled.

"I know that he wasn't always the good grey poet, the nation's sage and all of that. Most of that was created by his admirers and academics."

"True," Gathers responded. "He had his flaws. The money he used to pay for his grave, or graves, came from a summer cottage fund that was started for him by his followers. They wanted to get him out of the city during the hot months, to buy him a place on the shore or in the woods."

"Not a bad idea," I said. "It must have been ungodly hot in that house in the summer. There was a fertilizer plant on the Delaware, not far from where his house is. I've read that when the wind was right, the smell was unbelievable."

"Do you know that when John Townsend Trowbridge found out that Whitman had spent four thousand dollars on his grave after he had spent years living off the generosity of others, he thought it was heart-sickening."

"What would he say now?" Julia said. "I'd say that this is an extravagant ruse for a poor man to pull off, but maybe a necessary one. There are a lot of shits around these days."

Finally, I stopped the car along a sand embankment. The faint sound of running water could be heard. To our right the close trunks of scrub pines stretched as far as we could see. The white sand formed soft ridges that were marked with defining lines of black soil. We left the car and walked along the sand road for thirty or forty yards, then crossed the low embankment that gave way to a slope. Cedar trees broke the green ceiling formed by the pines. Patches of blue sky highlighted where the cedars stood. We descended to a small stream made larger by recent rain. We followed it for a hundred feet then crossed it and walked up onto higher ground for almost a mile. Our shoes filled with sand from the uneven forest floor. As we approached Whitman's tomb, which was nestled in a stand of blackjacks, the disturbed ground cover added to the well-measured rhythm of our steps.

"There it is," I said, pointing to my left. "In that depression over there."

Gathers scurried away from us, his notebook and camera clutched in his hands. He slipped and fell once but recovered without breaking his camera or hurting himself, his guarded enthusiasm diminishing with every stride. Julia and I took our time as we followed him. We had been there twice already.

"Jesus," Gathers said as he walked around the granite roof which was covered with lichens.

Julia and I watched as he read the epitaph which was carved into one of the gable walls.

"'W. W. 1819-1892. Sweet, peaceful, welcome Death.' That's from 'Death's Valley,'" he said. Then he took several pictures and a few notes. He paced around the depression in one direction, and after his lap was complete he changed direction and completed another swing around the tomb.

"What do you think—really think?" I asked him once we had turned away and started back to the car.

"I'm speechless. What can I say?" He slipped his notebook into his shirt pocket. "I can't put it into words."

"Thank you would be nice," Julia piped from behind us. Once Gathers was safely in our car, Julia would return with a shovel and recover the tomb.

When we parted that afternoon, I felt good about finding Gathers and about helping his career. Julia wasn't as certain, feeling that Gathers hadn't proved himself yet. Before we had met Gathers that morning, she had convinced me to let him only take notes from my aunt's diary. I could give him access to it whenever he needed it. Julia reasoned that with the notes, Gathers could still do his work. But without the actual diary or a photocopy of it, we still had some insurance. If we felt that he had involved Ehrlich or would attempt to pinpoint Whitman's grave, we could pull out and deny any knowledge of it or the diary. Gathers wouldn't have a documented source.

Over a month passed before I heard from him again. I had started to think that my earlier hopes of causing Ehrlich pain had failed and that Gathers had decided not to pursue our discovery. Julia was convinced that Gathers had welshed on our agreement and that he had discussed everything with Ehrlich. But I wasn't so sure.

"I have good news and bad news," Gathers announced when he called.

I have to admit that I was a little suspicious when I heard the mention of bad news. Julia's earlier comments returned to my mind and I waited for the weight to drop.

"Within two weeks of our trip, I finished a proposal for a book on Whitman's Camden years that I had been working on—with the new information added. And a publisher I've worked with in the past is interested. Of course I have to write the book now, but—"

"That's the good news."

"Yeah." He paused. "The bad news is that someone broke into my office over the weekend and rummaged through my disks."

"Did they take anything?"

"Not that I can tell."

"So, what's wrong?"

Gathers' voice dropped to a whisper. "I think it was Ehrlich."

"You're kidding?" I said, my mind filling with pleasure. Could I be so lucky? I thought to myself, then asked, "How do you know?"

"I just spoke with Detective Caudra. Camden Police Department. He was looking for Ehrlich. Wanted to know if I had seen him over the weekend. Caudra knew about the break-in. And he wanted to know if anyone around campus owns a black Cadillac."

"What does that have to do with your office?"

"Well, somehow Ehrlich found out about my book. He's been bothering me about it. I told him that I planned to write about Whitman's Camden years, that I would be using Traubel's work, *With Walt Whitman in Camden*. But he wanted to know what my angle was. For some reason he suspected that I had latched onto something very important, something that he said would add a new chapter to Whitman studies."

"And what did you tell him?" My face and hands started to tingle. This was pure delight.

"Well, I said I did have something significant. But that I wasn't permitted to discuss it at this point."

"I'm sure he didn't like that."

"That's putting it mildly. He was furious. He said he'd have my head, basically, that I wouldn't be getting a tenure-track slot. Then he stormed out of my office."

"God. He's on the hysterical side, isn't he?" I commented, thinking that my plan and the seed I planted had grown like a cancer in Ehrlich's brain.

"That's only half of it. I'm sure that whoever broke into my office read my proposal. It was in a folder on my desk and it's on one of my disks. When Caudra stopped by he mentioned that someone had tried to break into Whitman's tomb over in Harleigh Cemetery last night. A watchman saw a black Cadillac there. Ehrlich's girlfriend owns that car or one just like it."

I could see Ehrlich and his beautiful Val stumbling over the stones in the dark, as they tried to take the shortest route to Whitman's tomb from the road. Only a minute before, they had awkwardly climbed the black wrought iron fence, trying to avoid the cemetery's offices and maintenance building. They rounded the small oval pond that is bordered by mausoleums and approached the low rise of dirt and trees where Whitman's official tomb is. They could see the dim lights of Our Lady of Lourdes Hospital to their left, just beyond the boundary of the cemetery. When they reached the granite tomb, large cuts of stone forming a simple box with others forming a simple peaked roof, they stopped. To the left of the tomb's entrance they saw the stone wall, to the right a memorial stone with an image of Whitman etched in the stone. A large tree covered with carved initials stood directly in front of them. It was too good to be true, I thought.

"Let's get at it," Ehrlich probably ordered, carrying a pair of cutters and a crowbar and hammer.

Val followed her man silently, obediently holding a flashlight and the other tools that they might need.

When they reached the entrance, they found the stone slab was swung away from the portal. Someone had left flowers on the path next to the entrance. Only a gate fastened shut with a chain and padlock prevented them from entering. Ehrlich made short work of the lock and within a minute they stood in front of the six stone squares that marked the location of Whitman and most of his family. The recently placed beige tiles, which cover the side walls, reflected the battery-powered light. Ehrlich knelt before Whitman's stone marker, bottom row, center, and positioned his chisel.

"How far did they get?" I finally asked, trying not to betray my excitement.

"They almost made it. That's what Caudra said. Then someone heard them and walked over from the maintenance building, thinking it was kids. When the guy got there the people fled. There were two of them. The guy chased them, but they beat him to the fence. He saw a man and a woman get into an old Cadillac and speed away. Caudra said they left a maul and something else behind. In another minute, they would have been inside."

"Really. What's going to happen now?"

"I told Caudra that the car might belong to Val Weaver and that Ehrlich was living with her. I told him she lived in Moorestown. I didn't know the address. Caudra said that wasn't a problem."

The rest of it unfolded fantastically. The police went to Val's apartment and found other tools in the trunk of her car. From what Gathers said, Ehrlich tried to deny that he had anything to do with it. He said that Val and another man acted on their own. His interest in Whitman, he claimed, was scholarly, purely academic. But the police didn't believe him. And poor, heartsick Val didn't believe him, either.

Why Ehrlich thought it prudent to check on Whitman's body himself is still open for discussion. I'm sure that Ehrlich, once he read my note and Gathers' proposal, realized what he could gain by beating Gathers in breaking the news and what he could lose if he sat back and let Gathers uncover it. I guess he thought he could get away with it. I know that Ehrlich is an egotistical jackass and that he'll always be one. He probably thought he was doing the academic world a service or that the discovery was rightfully his or that there was much-needed money to be made. The soon-to-be-former Mrs. Ehrlich and her lawyer had already mentioned a sizable settlement figure. But I don't believe being a martyr ever entered into his selfish delusions.

Now Ehrlich is on the mend and Val is still with him, but I hope she is a little wiser. Evidently Ehrlich has mentioned around the department that he and Val might take jobs at another college in a different state, leaving Mickle Street and Harleigh Cemetery and the Pines behind. His crest has been tarnished, but I heard from Gathers that Ehrlich is doing work on Poe, someone who would be more sympathetic to his occasional dark flights. But wherever Ehrlich goes, he will always remember the night when he and his beautiful Val tried to discover where Whitman's heart truly lies, forgetting for a moment that his heart and his spirit, too, are in his poetry. Only his body is in the Pines.